If you crave it, eat it. Trust your instincts.

This person obviously knew me and knew where I lived, but it wasn't the stalker aspect of it that had me freaked out right now.

It was that they had to know what I'd been craving.

"Freak" is right.

No, that was insane. How the hell could anyone know that I'd been fighting the urge to chow down on . . . brains?

Yet what else could the letter possible be referring to? Usually if I craved something, I ate it. Simple. I didn't need anyone else to tell me it was okay and that I should go for it.

But I'd been craving *brains*. The smell was like chocolate and cookies and biscuits and gravy and everything else that was delicious. It damn near drove me crazy every time I had to touch one. I'd been fighting the cravings the way I'd never fought the urge to take drugs or get drunk.

No. It didn't make sense. It had to be referring to something else. A dull anger began to form in my gut. Why the hell couldn't Anonymous Letter Guy simply tell me what the hell was going on?

DIANA ROWLAND

MY LIFE AS A
WHITE TRASH ZOMBIE

DAW BOOKS, INC.
DONALD A. WOLLHEIM, FOUNDER
375 Hudson Street, New York, NY 10014

ELIZABETH R. WOLLHEIM
SHEILA E. GILBERT
PUBLISHERS
http://www.dawbooks.com

First Printing, July 2011

4   5   6   7   8   9

For Anna Marie Catoir

ACKNOWLEDGMENTS

I'm eternally grateful that I have so many friends, associates, and loved ones who are always willing to lend me their time or expertise. This book would not exist if not for them.

I owe very special thanks to:

St. Tammany Parish Coroner Dr. Peter Galvan and forensic pathologist Dr. Michal DeFatta for the heaping scads of inspiration and education they've provided.

Angel Galloway for telling so many hysterical stories about her life. There's a lot of Angel in Angel!

Nina Lourie and Sandra Wickham for being kick-ass beta readers who were willing to brave the many (many!) rough spots of the early drafts.

Nicole Peeler for continuing to be the best critique partner a writer could ever hope to have.

Roman White for being a terrific friend and pillar of support.

The members of the Rio Hondo 2011 workshop—Walter Jon Williams, Maureen McHugh, Daniel Abraham, Ty Franck, Karen Joy Fowler, David D. Levine, Ben Parzybok, James Patrick Kelly, Alex Jablokov, Karen Livdahl, and Jen Volant—for wanting to know what the story was about.

Matt Bialer, my incredible agent, for being, well, so darn incredible!

Lindsay Ribar for helping me avoid the pigeon poop. (This will make sense to her. I hope!)

Dan Dos Santos for creating the cover for this book.

This amazing, fantastic, trashy and gorgeous cover! Seriously, go look at it. I'm the luckiest author *ever.*

My wonderful editor, Betsy Wollheim, for completely appreciating the concept of a white trash zombie.

And finally, for Jack and Anna, for cheerfully accepting and loving my (many . . . MANY) quirks.

Chapter 1

"You should be dead," the ER nurse stated as she adjusted something on my IV. She was more husky than fat, with too much eye makeup, and hair that had been dyed a nasty shade of reddish orange. When I didn't immediately respond she glanced my way, as if to assure herself that I really was awake and aware. "You realize that, right?" she demanded. "You're pretty damn lucky to be alive."

"Um . . . okay," I muttered. Beneath the sheet I ran a hand over my stomach, frowned. "Have I been in a coma or something?" I asked.

Her thin lips pinched together. "A coma? No. You were brought in a few hours ago." She paused, set her hands on her hips. "You *overdosed*."

I scrubbed a hand over my face, shook my head. "No, I was in a car accident," I insisted. "I remember being injured." Didn't I? "I was bleeding," I added, less certain as I ran my hand over the unbroken skin of my stomach again.

She gave a dismissive snort. "There's not a scratch on you. You must have hallucinated it." Her eyes narrowed with contempt and disapproval. I didn't care. I was used to seeing that when people looked at me.

Glass and blood and metal. A broken body beside me. Teeth and hunger. Gobbets of flesh ripped away....

Cold sweat broke out on the back of my neck. How could that have been a hallucination? Hallucinations were strange and hazy and jumbled. I knew. I'd had a few.

Making an annoyed noise in the back of her throat, she snagged the chart from the end of the bed. "Unknown white female. Hmmm. Do you remember your name, sweetheart?" She flicked her eyes back up to me and gave me a sugary-bitchy smile that didn't have an ounce of true concern in it.

"Yeah, I know my damn name," I snarled. "It's Angel Crawford." I wanted to add, *And you can write it down with the pencil that's stuck up your ass,* but I managed to hold it back. I knew that nurses had the power to make your life suck worse than it already did, and it was clear that this bitch considered me to be one step away from starring in my own loser reality show. Screw her. I was at least *two* steps away.

The nurse gave a sniff as if she didn't truly believe I was smart or sober enough to know who I was. "Let's see what all was in your system—THC, hydrocodone, alprazolam, oxycodone...." She rattled off a couple of other drug names that sounded long and scary while I scowled blackly at her. After she finished she gave me a look full of smug satisfaction, hung the chart back up and left the room in a pompous waddle before I could respond. Good thing too, because what I wanted to say to her would have been too much even for a Jerry Springer special.

My anger withered as soon as she was gone, overwhelmed by my confusion and sick fear. I lifted the sheet up to see for myself—again—that I was uninjured.

I struggled to make sense of it. I remembered the

blood. Lots of it. There'd been some sort of long gash across my stomach, and I had a nauseating memory of seeing the jagged end of white bone poking from my thigh, blood pumping out and all over. But now there was nothing out of place. No scrapes, no bruises. Just perfectly normal flesh all over. A coma could explain that, right? A couple of months or so, enough time for me to heal up.

Except that I didn't have any scars, either.

Sighing, I dropped my head back to the pillow. I hadn't been in a coma. The nurse wasn't lying or messing with my head.

No, I was simply a loser.

Overdose. Great. Well, this was a new low for me, and it didn't help that it was totally believable. The only possibly shocking aspect was that it hadn't happened sooner. I didn't remember taking as many drugs as the bitch nurse had said, but the fact that I was in the ER was proof enough that I obviously had. The nurse hadn't gone and altered my lab results either. I did that all by myself, the old-fashioned way.

Weary depression rolled over me as I stared at the speckled tile of the ceiling. Beyond the door I could hear the frenzy of a stretcher being wheeled by and voices raised in brief concern. I knew what would happen next. Some social worker or psychologist would come in and tell me I needed rehab or counseling or some crap like that, which was a stupid suggestion since I didn't have money or insurance. Or worse, I'd get a seventy-two-hour commitment for "psychiatric evaluation," since I was clearly a danger to myself, and I'd probably end up in some nasty charity ward. There was no way I was gonna put up with that. I felt perfectly fine now and more than ready to get the hell out of here.

I kicked the sheet away and slid off the bed. The tile was smooth and cold against my bare feet. I needed shoes and clothes. I was wearing the stupid hospital gown, and my own clothes were so covered with blood that I'd draw all sorts of attention if I tried to walk out in them.

I shook my head. No, the blood had been a hallucination.

There was no sign of my clothes in the room. No closets—only one cabinet and an intimidating variety of medical equipment. I started to move toward the cabinet, remembering the IV a step before I accidentally yanked it out of my arm, then spent a couple of seconds trying to decide if I could carry the bag out with me instead of pulling the needle out. Needles freaked me out, but leaving it in would probably be worse than removing it myself. Hell, that was the only reason I'd never gone for the harder drugs like heroin or meth. Too chickenshit to stick a needle into me to get that kind of high. Pills were easy. Plus I could tell myself that I wasn't a real druggie.

Except that now I'd almost killed myself just as dead as if I'd ODed on heroin.

Pushing that unpleasant thought out of my mind, I peeled off the tape on my arm then clenched my teeth and pulled the needle out. I braced myself against the wave of nausea that always hit me whenever I saw blood—especially my own—but to my relief it didn't hurt at all, and I didn't feel sick. A tiny bead of blood welled up from the puncture site, and I wiped it away with the hem of my gown before I even remembered that I was supposed to be nauseated by it.

Maybe that's why I'd hallucinated about being covered in blood? There wasn't much that would freak me out more than that.

The door to the room opened again, startling me, and I dropped the IV line with a guilty flush as a different nurse walked in. She was a lot younger than the other one—maybe in her early twenties or so, with sleek blonde hair pulled back in a ponytail and the sort of fresh no-makeup look I wished I could pull off. I looked like death without makeup, and while my hair was blonde as well, it was that way because I dyed it myself, which meant it was a frizzy, damaged mess.

Her eyes flicked to the discarded IV, but she didn't seem to be upset that I'd removed it. "I wanted to make sure you were awake and decent," she said with a smile that was kinder than I expected. "There are a couple of detectives here who want to talk to you."

A frisson of terror shot through me. "Wh-why?" I asked, though I was pretty sure I knew. They were here to take me to jail. My probation officer had found out about the drug use and my probation was being revoked. Or they wanted me to squeal about where I got my drugs.

I must have gone pale because she closed the door and gave me a reassuring smile. "They only want to talk to you. You're going to be fine. Here," she said, gently but firmly pushing me back to sit on the bed. She didn't make me lie back down—simply pulled the bed sheet around so that my lower body and bare feet were covered. "That's better. I know I can't talk to anyone with any sort of authority if I'm half-naked," she said with a wink.

Her unexpected niceness had me a little off-balance, especially after the open hostility of the previous nurse. "Where are my other clothes?"

"You, uh, weren't wearing any when you were brought in."

Oh, shit. I swallowed hard. "Did they take them off in the ambulance?" Surely it wouldn't be as bad as if I'd—

"The cops found you on the side of the road ... naked." Her face twisted in embarrassed sympathy.

My throat tightened. "Was I—I mean, had I been . . . ?" I couldn't say the word.

Her eyes widened. "No!" She shook her head emphatically. "No, the doctor, um, checked. You weren't assaulted."

I scrubbed at my face and fought the urge to cry. Overdose *and* naked on the side of the road. This kept getting better and better. And not even the victim of a crime, just a stupid drugged-out skank.

The nurse made a concerned noise in her throat, reached out and gave my upper arms a firm rub. "Relax now. Everything's going to be fine. These detectives want to have a word with you, then you'll be ready to get out of here." She turned and left before I could form any sort of coherent response.

Right. Everything's going to be fine, I thought with a sour laugh. She didn't know. She couldn't possibly understand why I was freaking.

I didn't have to stew in my panic for long. No sooner had the door swung shut behind the blonde nurse than it opened again and two detectives walked in. But they weren't probation officers or narcotics detectives. That threw me. At least I was pretty sure they weren't narcs. Those guys usually went around in jeans and T-shirts, but these two were in dress shirts and ties. The first one in was a burly guy—at least six feet tall and stocky with a bit of a pudge working around his middle, blondish brown hair, and a scruffy-looking mustache. The second detective wasn't as tall, but he was big in a muscled way. No pudge on him. I could tell he worked out, and hard. He had dark hair, dark eyes, and an equally dark expression on his face. Both had guns, badges, and handcuffs on their belts.

In other words, they intimidated the ever-living shit out of me simply by walking into the room.

"Ms. Crawford," the burly one began, "I'm Detective

Ben Roth and this is Detective Mike Abadie." He cocked his head toward the dark-haired detective. "We're with the Saint Edwards Parish Sheriff's Office, and we'd appreciate it if you could take a couple of minutes to answer some questions for us."

"Do I need a lawyer?" I blurted. The two men exchanged a quick glance. Oh, great. Nice way to start. Now I sounded guilty as all hell.

"That's completely up to you, Ms. Crawford," Detective Roth said. "But we're only here to see if you might have witnessed anything that could help us solve a crime. You're not under any sort of suspicion at this time." His expression remained serious but his eyes were kind. At least, I wanted to believe that. The other detective looked like he had a permanent scowl on his face. Maybe they were about to play good cop bad cop on me. It would probably work, too. I always fell for that psychological shit. Especially when I was confused and stressed. Like right now.

I gripped the sheet in my hands. "Uh, sure. What . . . um, what crime?"

Detective Abadie cleared his throat. "You were found on Sweet Bayou Road right off Highway 180." His lips pressed together and I could see the same derision in his eyes that I'd seen in the red-haired nurse's. Maybe he didn't know why I was in here, 'cause of privacy laws or whatever, but he sure as hell had his suspicions.

"Okay," I said, doing my damnedest to not hunch under his gaze. "If you say so."

"At about the same time," he continued, eyes hard and flat, "a body was found a few miles further down Sweet Bayou Road. It had been decapitated."

"Wh-what?" I said, staring at him in horror.

"Decapitated. It means that his head was chopped off," he explained, tone thoroughly patronizing.

A sudden burst of anger managed to burn away a good portion of the panic and fear that had been controlling me up until then. "I know what 'decapitated' means," I replied with a scowl. "But I don't know anything about this. *I* sure as hell didn't do it!" The two men exchanged another quick glance and a sliver of the fear came back. "You don't think I did it, do you?"

Detective Roth shook his head firmly. "You're not a suspect at this time, Ms. Crawford. However, right now you're the only possible witness we have. Anything you can remember might be useful."

I swallowed. *At this time.* He kept saying that. In other words I sure as shit hadn't been ruled out, even though I knew there was no way I would have chopped some guy's head off—no matter how high I might have been.

So why did I remember blood . . . ?

I took a shaking breath. No. There was no way. I wasn't a killer. "Sweet Bayou Road?" I asked, stalling for time to get my thoughts into something other then a jumbled mess.

"That's where you were found," Detective Roth said patiently. "What do you remember?"

"I . . . don't know." Sweet Bayou Road was only about five minutes down the highway from where I lived, but there wasn't a whole lot on it. A few fishing camps near the end, and the rest of it was several miles of desolate and twisty road through the marsh. "I mean, I was at Pillar's Bar with my boyfriend. We had a fight and . . ." I rubbed my eyes, odd flashes of the hallucination swimming through my head.

Blood and pain . . . I thought I was dying. No, I died. But then I was hungry. Starving-to-death hungry. . . .

I took an unsteady breath. "Then I was out on the road, and there was an ambulance."

I was arguing with the paramedics after they got me

*into the ambulance, begging for something to eat because
I was so damn hungry. Maybe that's why I didn't walk
into the stupid white light. Maybe I knew they wouldn't
have anything to eat down that way.*

"I must have passed out." I looked up at the two men.
"Then I woke up here. Sorry."

No pain. No hunger. No clue.

Detective Abadie let out an exasperated snort. "Why
were you out there?"

"I don't know," I said. "I guess I was trying to walk
home." Walking home from the bar would definitely
rank as one of the more boneheaded things I'd done in
my life. In other words, totally believable. And somewhere along the way I'd decided to strip naked. That
must have been one helluva high.

Detective Roth tugged a hand through his hair,
clearly frustrated. "I need you to think real hard, Angel.
Did you see anyone? Any cars? Someone walking along
the road?"

"I'm sorry," I mumbled, hunching my shoulders. "I
didn't see anyone."

Fatigue and disappointment etched itself across Detective Roth's face. "All right, Miss Crawford. If you
think of anything else—anything at all—please give
me a call." He pulled out a business card and handed it
to me.

"Yeah, sure thing," I said, obediently taking the card.

A sour expression twisted Detective Abadie's mouth.
"C'mon, Ben," he muttered. "We're wasting our time."
He turned and stalked out. I couldn't even get annoyed
at his reaction. I *had* been a waste of their time.

Detective Roth let out a low sigh but gave me a tired
smile. "I appreciate your talking to us, Miss Crawford,"
he said. "I hope you get to feeling better." Then he too
was out the door, and I was alone in the room once
again.

Wrung out and depressed, I dropped the card into the wastebasket. This day couldn't get much worse.

The blonde nurse entered again, this time carrying a cooler and a large paper grocery bag which she set on the bed beside me. "This was left at the nurse's station for you," she said, smiling brightly. "Looks like you won't have to go home in a hospital gown after all! I'll go get your paperwork ready, and as soon as you're dressed you should be able to get out of here."

She was out of the room with the door closing behind her before I had a chance to respond.

I stared at the closed door in confusion then looked over at the stuff on the bed. The cooler was one of those mini plastic things, big enough to hold a six-pack of beer. I opened it to find six bottles of Frappuccino. At least that's what I thought it was at first. It was the same type of bottle as those kind of coffee drinks, and the contents were brown and opaque, but there were no labels on the bottles, and there was also some sort of pinkish lumpy sediment at the bottom.

What the hell?

I checked the bag with the clothes next. A pair of exercise-type pants, a sports bra, underwear, a plain blue T-shirt and some flip-flops—all stuff that could be bought if you weren't sure of someone's size. I was skinny with no tits and no muscle tone. As long as the pants had a drawstring at the waist, I was probably good to go. At the bottom of the bag was an envelope and a twenty dollar bill with a little sticky note that had "cab fare" neatly printed on it.

Again, what the hell? My first reaction was to get pissed. I didn't need anyone else's help. I took care of myself because, frankly, depending on someone else meant standing outside an empty, locked elementary school at six P.M. and telling Mrs. Robichaux that no, really, my mom would be here any minute and I didn't need a ride while a) Kerrie Robichaux, who gets 100s on her spelling tests is looking out the car window at me in a way that I'm pretty sure says, *Don't you even think about getting your trashy ass in the back seat of this nice car,* and b) Mom is again conveniently forgetting I exist because her life was so much fucking better before she got saddled with a kid and had to do boring things like pick me up from school and make sure I had clean clothes and socks that matched. I took care of myself because I figured out that it was better when she didn't remember I was around. And even after she was gone I took care of myself, because Dad couldn't handle being a dad, and instead sat on a bar stool at Kaster's remembering when his life was simple and his wife was fun and he had his job on the oil rig.

Except right now I was naked—well, not counting the hospital gown. And I couldn't take care of that without help, though I was damned if I could figure out who'd bother getting clothes and cab fare for me. The only person who came to mind was my sort of boyfriend, Randy, but I couldn't see him giving me money for a cab when he could come and get me. Plus, he knew my size.

I ripped open the envelope and read the letter. Then I read it again, because it didn't make any sense the first time through.

Angel—
    Take good care of the contents of the cooler because it should get you through the next couple of weeks. It's very important that you drink one bottle every other day, starting tomorrow, or you'll start to feel very sick. Be sure to shake it up well before you drink it.
    There's a job waiting for you at the Coroner's

Office. They have an opening for a van driver, and the arrangements have already been made. Go to the office at 9 A.M. tomorrow to fill out the paperwork and start work.

Now, here's the deal: You <u>will</u> take this job, and you <u>will</u> hold it for at least one month. If you quit, or are fired before one month is out, your probation officer will be informed that there were drugs in your system when you were brought to the ER, and you'll go to jail for violating your probation. And if you go to jail, you'll probably die there within a few weeks. This isn't a threat. It's a warning. I'd explain, but there's no way you'd believe me. You'll understand eventually.

Good luck.

Hey, look, I thought with a miserable laugh, *this day just got worse.*

I stared down at the letter in confusion and disbelief. My mom had gone to prison when I was twelve and died while still incarcerated, on the day I turned sixteen. That was a little over five years ago. Then last year I'd been more of a moron than usual and had bought a nearly new Toyota Prius for five hundred dollars from some guy Randy knew. A week later I was pulled over and arrested for possession of stolen property. Yeah, my "bargain" of a car had been jacked a couple of weeks earlier in New Orleans. But the seriously sucky part was that I'd kinda suspected that it hadn't been legit but went ahead and gave the guy the money for it anyway, too excited about what a great deal I was getting, and convinced that I wouldn't get caught. Moron. I'd spent two days scared shitless in a holding cell before I could find someone to bail me out, and had been lucky as hell to get a three-year suspended sentence and probation.

I read the letter again, hand shaking. I thought I'd dodged a bullet with that visit from the two detectives, but here was another one right behind it, ready to flatten me. I didn't want to go back to jail, and I didn't want to end up like my mom and die there. But why would I die within weeks? What was that all about? Maybe someone who had a grudge against me was in jail already? I'd pissed off plenty of people in my life, but as far as I knew there wasn't anyone who hated me enough to want to kill me.

I turned the letter over, searching for any clue as to who had sent it. It was printed on plain white paper and the envelope was an ordinary white envelope. No signature. No postmark. None of this made any sense. I couldn't think of a single person who'd bother finding me a job, much less threaten me with jail to make sure I kept it.

Why jail? Why not rehab?

Because jail's a bigger threat, I realized. Rehab would suck, but jail. . . . Whoever sent this stuff had to know that jail scared the shit out of me.

I read the letter one more time, then took a deep breath and started getting dressed while my thoughts continued to tumble. It wasn't as if I'd set out to be a loser. I didn't wake up every morning and say, "Hey, how can I screw my life up today?" But the universe sure seemed to be rigged against me, and most of the time it didn't seem to matter how hard I tried since I was obviously never going to catch a break.

Except. Except this letter wasn't a couple of hardass cops questioning me about something I didn't know shit about. This was someone holding a big whopping threat over my head, who also seemed to be crazy enough to give the slightest crap about me—and give me that break I kept saying I wanted. Me. Loser girl. If this job was for real and I didn't at least give it a shot I'd be right back at being a Grade A Screwup. But who the hell would do this for me?

I had a feeling the only way I was going to find out would be to take the stupid job.

Drive a van for a month. How hard could that be?

Chapter 2

I made it home from the hospital and obediently set my alarm for 7:30 A.M. This was my chance to turn things around, to not be a complete screwup.

My alarm went off at 7:30. I slapped the snooze and rolled over.

I woke up again at 9:15.

Crap!

I took the fastest shower of my life, yanked on jeans that I hoped were clean, grabbed the first T-shirt I could find that didn't show my navel or have something obnoxious printed on it. Great. I had a job handed to me, and I screwed it up the first day. That I didn't understand why I supposedly had this job was beside the point. If it paid real money and didn't involve me getting naked, I was willing to give it a shot. Besides, I'd been doing some thinking. I was a huge fan of all those crime scene shows on TV, so I knew that coroners did forensics and that kind of stuff, and carried all their equipment around in big vans or Hummers—which most likely needed drivers, right? In other words, there was a really good chance that this job could be exceedingly cool.

But hell, anything's better than working a minimum wage job at Bayou Burger, I thought as I pulled the shirt over my head and raked my fingers through the frizzy mess of my hair.

I lost several precious minutes in a frantic search for my purse. I had a vague memory of having it when I went to the bar the other night, which meant I had zero idea where it had ended up. Hell, I didn't even know where *I* had ended up, other than the ER. Oh yeah, and naked on the side of the highway.

I finally dug the spare keys to my battered little Honda out of the bowl on top of my dresser, then ran for the front door. At least my dad wasn't up yet. Not that I expected him to be any time before noon. That was fine with me because it meant I didn't have to try to explain to him where I'd been or what had happened. He probably had no idea I'd even been in the hospital. Again, I had no problem with that.

I hit the door at a run, then turned around and ran right back to snag one of the stupid drinks from the little fridge in my room. It usually only held beer, but I hadn't wanted to put the drink-stuff in the kitchen fridge and risk my dad drinking one or throwing them out by mistake. I knew he wouldn't believe me if I told him they were medicine. At least that's what I assumed they were. In fact he'd probably be more likely to throw them out if I said that. He got drunk damn near every night, but he acted as if I was a serial killer if he found a joint or pills in my room.

I remembered to shake the bottle, then opened it and gave it a dubious sniff. There was a faint coffee-chocolate smell, but beneath that there was a tang of something I couldn't quite place—nutty or meaty, with a faintly metallic edge. "Whatever," I muttered. I'd consumed disgusting crap before.

It was thick, with a texture that reminded me of tapioca. I had a split-second desire to gag and spew it all out, then it suddenly shifted to a craving for *more*. I didn't think I'd be able to drink the whole thing, but before I realized it I was shaking the bottle to get the last few strange tapioca-like chunks out.

I lowered the bottle slowly as an energizing warmth spread through me—kinda like a shot of Everclear, but without the getting drunk part. I felt awake, alive. The only thing that kept me from slugging down another was the fear that I might overdose on it, and I sure as shit didn't want to end up back in the hospital.

I dropped the empty bottle in the trash can and glanced at the clock: 9:30.

"Crap!"

I ran for the door.

The St. Edwards Parish Coroner's Office was in Tucker Point—about twenty minutes from my house. Despite a couple of wrong turns, I managed to make it there before ten and by some miracle still managed to get the job. I didn't have to interview or anything, which was a relief since I was a pro at tanking interviews. The human resources lady had apparently been expecting me because she pulled out a folder with my name on it and plopped down a big stack of paperwork for me to fill out. That I could handle. I was pretty darn good at filling out employment forms. It was the whole bit about *keeping* a job that I wasn't so great at.

Unfortunately, the human resources lady didn't know anything about how I'd managed to get hired and gave me a funny look when I asked her about it. I finally shut my mouth and concentrated on filling out the million forms in front of me. The last thing I wanted was for her to realize I didn't deserve this job.

Once I finished with the paperwork the lady turned me over to a guy named Nick Galatas who was supposedly going to train me as a van driver. Nick was a couple of inches taller than me, though that didn't mean much since I was only five foot three if I really stretched. He had dark brown hair and green eyes, and would have probably been kinda good-looking except for the fact that he seemed to have a permanent smirk on his face.

"You're going to be partnered with a death investigator," he informed me over his shoulder as he led the way through the building that housed the Coroner's Office. It was a new building and everyone seemed to be really proud of it, but to my disappointment it didn't look anything like the forensics shows I watched on TV. Instead it seemed like any other government office—over air-conditioned, low-key colors, boring posters, generic office furniture. There were a few doors that required a key card to enter, with impressive names like "Toxicology" and "DNA." But I was again disappointed on discovering that the labs weren't full of nifty chrome and cool blue and pink lighting. Total letdown.

"Twice a week you'll be on call for a twenty-four-hour period," Nick continued. "Otherwise you'll be working mostly the morning shift. That's when I have *class*," he said, making it sound like he had an appointment to see the frickin' pope.

"Okay," I said with a shrug. I didn't really care what shift I worked. They all sucked equally as far as I was concerned.

"I'm pre-med," he added smugly.

"Okay." I said again. I didn't shrug this time, but his jaw tightened a bit as if he was annoyed that I wasn't displaying the proper amazement at his accomplishment.

"And I'm next in line to be promoted to death investigator." The look he gave me was nothing short of a challenge, and I had to fight to not roll my eyes. What, he expected me to start crowing about my own accomplishments so he could top them? He'd be waiting a long time for that.

"Cool," I replied, forcing my face into a smile. I didn't even know what a death investigator was, though I assumed it had something to do with investigating death. But Nick sure as hell didn't need to worry about me horning in on his position. I only had to get through a month of this.

We came to the end of a long hall, stopping in front of another locked door. Nick glanced at me as he pulled out his key card. "Here we are," he announced. "You're going to be spending a lot of time here."

I registered the word on the door. *Morgue.* A sick, sinking feeling began tugging at my insides. "I will?" I said, hoping my voice didn't betray my sudden unease.

The smug smile returned. "Well, yeah. Your job is to pick up bodies and bring them here to the morgue."

Van driver. *Oh, Angel, you moron. What the hell did you think the coroner needed a van for?*

One month. I took a slow deep breath. That's all I had to do. "Oh. Okay," I said as calmly as I could manage. I was totally *not* okay, but damn, I didn't want Nick to see it.

He swiped the card and pulled the door open, stepped through and gestured for me to follow. I hesitated half a second but forced myself forward.

The smell hit me first. I'd expected a putrid and nasty rotting-flesh smell, but instead the air held a confusing mix of antiseptic cleanser, blood, and another odor that I couldn't immediately place. A second later recognition smacked into me, and I realized it was the stench of the stuff used to preserve dead things, like the frog I had to dissect when I took Biology in high school.

Except, I never did dissect the frog. I was so grossed out and freaked at the smell and the mere *thought* of cutting into the thing and seeing its insides and guts and

organs and everything, that I threw up all over the floor
of the Biology lab. The teacher yelled at me, the other
kids laughed, I started crying, then I threw my books
down into that puddle of puke and marched out of the
classroom and out a side door of the school. About a
week later a social worker came to the house because,
even though I was sixteen and old enough to drop out of
school if I wanted, there were still procedures and shit. I
don't think Dad even knew I'd stopped going to school
until the social worker showed up, disgust in her eyes
and a fake-caring smile on her pinched face as she
minced across the flattened beer cans in our driveway.
But Dad didn't make me go back to school, just told the
lady I was going through a lot 'cause my mom had killed
herself a couple of months ago, even though I wasn't
"going through" anything and was totally fine. He was
the one being all grieving and stuff, and I think he simply
didn't have the energy to get into it with me. So I told the
lady Biology and high school were useless crap, I was
going to get a job, and I was never coming back to school.

And I didn't.

Yeah, I sure showed them.

I stopped in the doorway of the morgue and clenched
my jaw shut in preparation for the heave of nausea that
I knew would hit me any second now. All I could think
about was that frog and me throwing up all over the tile.

"You okay?" Nick asked, except I could tell he didn't
really want me to be okay. He wasn't even bothering to
hide his smirk, and it was obvious he wanted me to lose
it because then he'd be able to feel even more superior.
Like all the kids who pointed and laughed when I lost it
in Biology.

Jerk. I took a cautious breath, surprised and relieved
to discover that my stomach was apparently on my side
and was going to behave, at least for the moment. I
slowly unclenched my jaw and returned his smirk with

one of my own. "I'm fine," I replied as I stepped in and allowed the door to close behind me.

Disappointment flickered briefly in his eyes which only strengthened my desire to not wimp out in front of him.

The morgue was mostly what I'd expected—cold and vaguely creepy, like I'd seen in the movies. The walls and floor were off-white, but in a shade that made me wonder if it was the original color or if they'd somehow been stained by the strange and gross smells—kinda like the way the nicotine-yellow walls in my dad's bedroom had once been beige.

The tour continued as Nick showed me the procedure for logging bodies in and out and took me into the cooler where the bodies were stored. I'd expected a wall full of little doors with the slide-out tables that held the bodies, but instead it was simply a giant walk-in cooler—like you'd find in a restaurant or liquor store—with some big shelves on the wall and about half a dozen stretchers lined up beside them. The shelves were empty, but three of the stretchers had black body bags on them. *Dead people.* I backed out of the room as quickly as I could without looking like a total weenie. I was sweating from the stress of waiting for my stomach to wake up and realize what was going on. Any second now I was going to heave and puke all over the floor—or perhaps all over Nick. That would be fine with me.

The next room he took me to held hundreds of plastic containers full of tissue samples, floating in a sickly, brown soup—formalin, as he informed me rather pompously. But still not a whisper of nausea. I could hardly believe it. I even got queasy if I saw someone spit on the sidewalk, and don't *ever* ask me to change a diaper.

Finally, Nick brought me into the room where the autopsies were performed—the cutting room, he called it. I tried to avoid looking directly at anything in there.

Metal tables. Drains in the floor. Lots of really scary tools and equipment. Yeah, I had the basic gist of it. I didn't need to see it up close and personal.

Nick started pointing things out in the cutting room, blathering on about the duties and the responsibilities and the procedures, with this cocky air about him as if he was the damn coroner. I'd almost tuned him out when I heard him say, "When you're assisting the pathologist during autopsies, you'll need to—"

"Whoa!" I jerked my hand up to stop him. "Wait, what?" I asked as sick horror shot through me. "You mean, like when the bodies get cut open?"

Delight lit his face. "Yes, you'll be helping with the autopsies. You didn't *know* that?"

I couldn't speak for several seconds. There was no way I'd be able to do this. I couldn't even handle the thought of a frog getting cut. How the hell was I supposed to be all right when it was *people?* What kind of vicious joke was it to put me in a job like this? Maybe that's all this was—a big whopping practical joke. Take the loser girl with the weak stomach and no nerves and put her where she's guaranteed to make an ass of herself. And threaten her with jail and death to make sure she plays along.

Except, why would anyone go through all that trouble just to play a trick on *me?*

"It's cool. I'll be fine," I somehow managed to say. I wouldn't be, but I wasn't going to let him see it. He'd enjoy it far too much if I walked out right now. I didn't have a whole lot of self-respect going for me, but this was as good a time as any to pretend that I did.

Besides, I wasn't going to go to jail just because Nick was a prick.

"Good to know," he said, smirk stretching to a grin. "Because we have one scheduled to begin in about twenty minutes. Might as well get you suited up so you can start learning the ropes!"

Chapter 3

Three hours ago I was in bed, I thought miserably. I should have stayed there.

I was decked out in a blue plastic smock, a paper apron over that, latex gloves that made my hands sweat, and little paper bootie-things over my shoes.

Lying on the metal table in front of me was a middle-aged man decked out in absolutely nothing at all. A *dead* man. Buck-ass naked with his little shriveled junk right there for everyone to see.

Standing on the other side of the table was another middle-aged man, but thankfully he was quite alive and fully dressed. Dr. Leblanc was the parish's forensic pathologist and performed all of the autopsies. I'd always assumed that the coroner was the one who did them, and was even dumb enough to tell Nick that it would be cool to meet the coroner. Of course he then took way too much pleasure in telling me that the coroner was an elected official who hired people to do the investigations and the autopsies and stuff like that. It made sense once it was explained to me—kinda like the way the sheriff hired deputies to do police work. Still, it annoyed me that I'd given Nick such an easy shot at showing how much smarter he was than me.

Dr. Leblanc was probably in his early fifties or so—average height and weight with a bit of flab at his waist, hair a thinning mix of blond and grey, and eyes a light blue. My first impression was that he looked more like a high school history teacher than someone who cut open dead bodies. Not that I had a lot of experience to draw on since, as far as I knew, I'd never met a pathologist before. For that matter I'd only ever known two high school history teachers. My freshman year I'd had Mrs. Pruitt, a nasty old hag who gave tests full of essay questions and who'd marked off points for misspelled words. I'd failed her class since I couldn't spell for crap—even though I knew the answers. I had to repeat it the next year and got Mr. Landry who looked a little bit like Dr. Leblanc in that they were both middle-aged white males. Mr. Landry was a whole lot cooler than Mrs. Pruitt, and I actually did really well in his class, getting A's and B's on the tests.

But then the whole thing with the frog in Biology happened, and I dropped out before finishing the semester. Yet another shining moment in the life of Angel Crawford.

"This your first time seeing an autopsy?" Dr. Leblanc asked, jerking me out of my brief pity party as he peered down at the body and made notes on a clipboard.

"First time seeing a dead body at all," I admitted sheepishly. I heard Nick give a low snort of derision, and I could feel my face beginning to heat.

"Really?" Dr. Leblanc said, and to my surprise his expression was one of approval. "I'm impressed that you're handling all of this so calmly." His eyes crinkled in a smile. "Nick here lost his breakfast his first day in the morgue."

I had to resist the urge to grin as Nick went white

then sullen. "I had a stomach virus," he muttered. Dr. Leblanc gave me a little wink that Nick couldn't see, then quickly returned to his examination of the body.

My tension faded to a more reasonable level. At least if I did end up puking, it wouldn't be the end of the world.

"So, uh, how do most people get jobs doing this?" I asked, trying to make it sound oh-so-casual and *not* full of my maddening curiosity as to how the hell I'd landed this bizarre gig.

Dr. Leblanc shrugged. "Usually people simply come in and apply. It's a good start for someone interested in forensics or pathology." He gave a nod toward Nick who gave a proud smile. "But sometimes, the coroner tells me, he's hired someone—usually as a favor for one of his political cronies or supporters." His eyes flicked back to me briefly before dropping back to his clipboard. "You came pretty highly recommended."

I struggled to control the *are-you-kidding-me?* look I knew was on my face. Highly recommended? Me? How the hell would any of the coroner's political buddies even know who I was?

I could feel Nick's eyes on me, no doubt trying to figure out what special connections I had.

Dude, if you figure it out, let me know, I thought. *I'm as baffled as you are.*

Dr. Leblanc finally put his clipboard aside and picked up a scalpel. He gave me an encouraging smile. "It helps if you try to look at this as 'interesting' instead of 'disgusting.' And if you do have to pass out, please do so out of the way. Also, all puke goes in the garbage can, please." His eyes flashed with humor, and I found myself grinning.

"Deal," I said.

I did my best to keep Dr. Leblanc's advice of "interesting versus disgusting" in mind as I watched the procedure, but there were some parts that *were* disgusting, no matter how much I attempted to convince myself otherwise. In particular, the search through the stomach contents was unspeakably nasty, but I was a bit encouraged to see that Dr. Leblanc's face was twisted in a grimace as well. Apparently some things were always gross.

Yet, shockingly, I still hadn't barfed. Not even the slightest desire to gag. It was almost surreal. I was the chick with the weakest stomach in the whole damn world, but here I was looking inside a damn body with the organs and guts and blood, and I was . . . hungry? I blinked in surprise as my stomach gave a little nudge that clearly wasn't nausea. What the hell? Okay, so I hadn't eaten any breakfast other than that coffee-drink thingy, but this was still a bizarre time to have a healthy appetite.

"Angel, come look at this," Dr. Leblanc abruptly said, holding the dead guy's heart in one hand and gesturing me over with the scalpel in his other. I obediently moved to his side, absurdly reminded of a movie where an evil priest ripped people's hearts out with his bare hands. "That's how he died," he continued, using the tip of the scalpel to point to a slice he'd made in a small blood vessel on the outside of the heart. "See the blockage?"

I stared at the tiny yellow glob of what I assumed was fat or cholesterol or whatever the heck it was that blocked blood vessels. "That? But, it's so small!"

He nodded then set the heart down on the white plastic cutting board in front of him. "I know. A bit humbling to think that something that looks so minor could have dropped this guy like a stone. He never had a chance."

I stepped back as Dr. Leblanc finished his examination of the heart. And if I'd died from that overdose they'd be doing all of this to me. For the first time today I could taste bile, though it had nothing to do with anything I was seeing or smelling. If I'd died it would be me naked on the cold metal table, sliced open from throat to crotch. . . .

I straightened, eyes narrowing. I knew what was going on. Highly recommended, my ass. This whole job had obviously been arranged so that I could get a little more appreciation for the life I'd managed to screw up so well. Work in a morgue instead of going through stupid rehab. Now *that* was a scenario that made sense. I found myself smiling smugly, stupidly pleased that I'd figured it out. *That's cool. I can play this game.* Hell, so far this was still a thousand times less annoying than rehab. A month of this and then I'd be home free. And this was even a paying job.

I watched as Dr. Leblanc removed the organs to weigh and examine them. *Is he in on it?* I wondered idly. Did he know I was really a pill-head loser? *He probably doesn't*, I decided. *There's no way he'd be so nice to me if he knew.*

Dr. Leblanc dropped a fist-sized kidney-shaped thing into a large plastic bag between the dead guy's legs then picked up a towel and wiped his gloved hands. "Almost done," he said to me with a smile. He turned and gave a nod to Nick. "You can do the head now."

Nick stepped up to the table. "At least this body has one. We cut two yesterday and neither had a head. First one was that murder that was all over the news." He flicked a glance at me. "You heard about that one?"

I responded with only a nod. I wasn't about to let him know that I'd been questioned about it.

"And then we had one come in who'd been in an MVA—motor vehicle accident. The victim was so mangled it took our guys half an hour to find the head, and when they did, it had apparently been squished by a passing car. They ended up bringing the pieces of skull back in a plastic bag." He gave a snort of amusement, and I simply stared at him. How could he be so casual about describing something so awful?

"Now pay attention," he ordered me. "You'll be doing this pretty soon."

Resisting the urge to flip him off, I watched in sickly fascinated horror as he took a scalpel and made a cut from ear to ear over the top of the corpse's head. Once the cut was made he set the scalpel aside, then dug his fingers between scalp and skull to peel the scalp back on top and bottom, exposing the entire top of the skull.

And I *still* didn't have even a whisper of nausea.

Unbelievable.

Next he pulled a mask and a face shield on. "You probably want to put a mask on," he said as he plugged in what I suddenly realized was a bone saw. "This kicks up a lot of bone dust, and you don't want to breathe it in."

I hurriedly yanked a mask on as he started the saw, quickly realizing that Nick hadn't been exaggerating. By the time he finished making a cut around the top of the head there was a fine film of pinkish-white dust covering the area around him. I tried not to think about the fact that I probably had bone dust in my hair. I planned on taking an *epic* shower after this day was done.

He set the saw aside and picked up a T-shaped tool with a chiseled bottom. "These are called skullcrackers," he said with a grin that was almost genuine. "Swear to god, that's their official name in the catalog." He jammed the chiseled end into the cut made by the saw and gave the skullcracker a sharp twist to pry the cut wider. I cringed involuntarily at the sound of breaking bone as the tool lived up to its name.

Nick stuck his fingers in the widened gap and pulled. The top of the skull came off with a tearing, sucking sound, and suddenly there before me were the grey and pink convolutions of a brain.

"There ya go," he said with a silly little flourish as he

pulled his mask and face shield off. "Your first time seeing a real live brain." Then he sniggered. "Real dead brain, that is."

I followed his lead and pulled my mask off, then froze. All of a sudden it seemed as if I could smell the brain, and not in a *oh-how-gross* way, but as if someone had taken the lid off a pot of gumbo to let the aroma fill the room. And I *knew* it was the brain that smelled so utterly enticing—knew it with every single cell of my being.

What the *hell* was wrong with me?

To my shock and horror my mouth began to water and my stomach gave a loud growl—loud enough for the others to hear. Both of them turned to look at me and Dr. Leblanc gave a laugh. "Okay, you're officially the toughest morgue tech who's ever worked here if you can still be hungry during an autopsy!"

I gave a weak laugh in answer as I struggled to hide my confusion. Yeah, that's all it was. I was just starving.

So why did I have the horrifying urge to grab a handful of that pink and grey mass and shove it into my mouth like movie popcorn?

A shiver crawled down my back. I was being stupid. I'd skipped breakfast, that's all, and was probably still recovering from my dumb overdose. There was no possible way that I really wanted to eat the brain. It had to be some sort of flashback to that whole crazy hallucination.

Fortunately, Nick seemed to be oblivious to my anxiety. He picked up a scalpel. "The rest is easy. Slice the spinal cord where it connects to the base of the brain—" he said, somehow shoving the brain aside and sticking the scalpel in and around. "—and you're good to go." He set the scalpel aside and tipped the brain out into his hands, cradling it carefully.

He turned to me with naked challenge in his eyes. "Want to hold it?"

I froze for several seconds. I did *not* want to hold it, but there was no way I could admit it was because I was afraid I'd start hallucinating and crave it again.

I saw the smirk begin to form on his face. *Oh, hell no.* I was *not* going to let him win this one. Even Dr. Leblanc was watching to see what I was going to do. *It's a stupid little initiation, that's all. I can do this.*

I stepped forward and stuck my hands out, meeting the challenge in Nick's eyes with my own. He grinned, placed the thing in my hands. It was slippery and a little mushy—a bit heavier than I expected it to be. *I'm holding a brain in my hands. Holy shit.* An unfamiliar sense of pride began to trickle through me. I'd risen to the challenge. It was a stupid and gross challenge, but I'd done it.

"You can go ahead and put it in the scale," he said.

I set it carefully in the scale and stepped back. Dr. Leblanc gave me another sly wink, then peered at the numbers on the scale and wrote them on his clipboard. I smiled, absurdly pleased with myself.

Then I quickly grabbed a towel and wiped my hands off before I could give in to the insane urge to lick my fingers.

Chapter 4

It was after five P.M. by the time I finally left the morgue and climbed into my Honda. I turned up the volume on my cheap-ass car stereo, slapping the steering wheel in time to the beat as I drove, my mood a lot brighter than I'd expected it would be after my first day on the job.

Okay, so the job was weird, gross, and nothing I'd have ever signed up for on my own. But it was also kinda cool, in a freaky way.

Plus, I hadn't screwed up. In fact, I'd done all right. I wasn't used to feeling proud of myself. It was definitely something I could get used to.

After Dr. Leblanc had finished the autopsy I got a crash course in how to sew a body back up—nasty! And, even nastier, I learned that the organs taken out during autopsy didn't get put back in before the body was sewn up. Instead they went into a big plastic bag and were sent to the funeral home in the body bag, where they'd then be put into the casket between the legs of the dead guy, all covered up with a pretty blanket so that no one at the funeral would know the bag was there. At least that's what Nick told me. I wasn't completely sure if he was fucking with me or not.

Once that was all done and we finished cleaning the morgue—which was more scrubbing and mopping than I'd ever done in my *life*—Nick took me to meet the coroner, Dr. Duplessis, and the Chief Investigator, Allen Prejean. The coroner seemed pleasant enough as we went through the "Glad to have you on board" crap that bosses always say, but there was a weird tightness to his smile that made the neurotic part of me wonder if he'd been pressured into hiring me and resented it. Then again, maybe he was always like that.

Allen was a different story, though. I had no doubt he knew about me and my history. That wasn't me being neurotic either. It was stamped all over his face when we were introduced. He didn't say anything about being glad to have me on board. Instead it was, "Your background makes you an interesting choice for this position," delivered in a scowly, gruff voice, and which made Nick give me a funny look. I could only hope that Nick would take that to mean I used to be a secret agent or some shit like that.

But other than the awkwardness of meeting my bosses, pretty much the only ding against me the whole day was the fact that I didn't have my driver's license and the human resources lady needed a copy of it, since I was supposed to be a van driver and all.

I made a face as I took the turn onto the highway that led toward my house. I still had no idea what had happened to my purse, which meant I was probably destined to spend my morning at the DMV in Tucker Point. Joy.

I'd lived in this area my entire life. The farthest away I'd ever been was Talladega, Alabama, when I was ten. I lived in Nice, Louisiana, which was probably supposed to sound like the town in France—pronounced "neese"—but everyone around here called it Nice, as in, "Ain't that nice." There really wasn't much about the town that *was* all that nice. It was a teensy little town in the southeast corner of St. Edwards Parish, which wasn't much more than a big stretch of swamp and marsh in the southeast corner of Louisiana. Nice had a couple of groceries and some hardware stores, a few strip malls with consignment clothing shops and hairdressers, and a scattering of diners, bars, and gas stations. Most people drove the twenty minutes to Tucker Point if they wanted to do any kind of real shopping. We didn't even have our own police force—the St. Edwards Parish Sheriff's Office patrolled and answered 911 calls.

The sign for Pillar's Bar came up on the left, and I slowed, memory abruptly flickering. That's where I was the other night. I'd gone there with Randy, right? Maybe I left my purse there. I'd just quit my job at Bayou Burger 'cause some lady tried to tell me we'd made her stupid burger wrong and that we had to give her another one. Except she'd already eaten most of the first one so I told her No, and then my boss jumped my ass because the "customer is always right" or some bullshit like that. I'd been in a shit mood after quitting, so I downed a Lortab before going to the bar, and after we got there I went out back and smoked some pot with Terry, the bartender. Randy was doing something to piss me off, so I traded Terry a couple of joints for a couple of Percocet. After that the memory was a lot foggier. . . .

My mood dimmed. I sure as shit didn't get this job as a van driver because I deserved it. I got it because I nearly overdosed and now someone was trying to teach me a lesson.

Yeah, yeah, the value of life. Just Say No. *Whatever.*

I didn't really know what had happened between going to the bar with Randy and ending up naked on the side of the highway, but I had a feeling it hadn't been pretty. *Probably a good thing I don't remember it*, I thought with a sour grimace.

There were only a couple of cars in the parking lot. Another hour or so and it would start filling up with all the people who had shit lives and shit jobs—or no jobs— and who wanted to forget about all that before heading to whatever passed for home. Still, even a couple of cars was too many people for me to face without knowing just how much of an ass I'd made of myself the other night. I kept driving past and simply called the bar instead to see if anyone had seen my purse. No one had turned it in, so either I hadn't left it there or someone had walked off with it.

I hung up, annoyed, then called Randy. I didn't really want to go home. Home was where I slept and showered. I didn't want to hang out there. But Randy wasn't picking up, and I couldn't think of anywhere else to go.

I need a life, I sighed.

As I turned into my driveway the crunch of aluminum greeted me—a few hundred beer cans that had been tossed into the driveway over the past several years and which now served as the paving material. Dad used to make the crack that it was cheaper than gravel. His truck was here—a piece of shit Ford that was more bondo than paint—but I didn't see any fresh empties in the driveway.

However, as I walked up to the house I did see my purse, right in the middle of the porch steps.

I picked it up, mystified. I was certain it hadn't been here earlier. There was no way I could have missed it, even in my panicked rush this morning. Rifling through quickly, I saw that everything was still there—driver's license, debit card, and even the thirty-three dollars in cash that I'd stuffed into my wallet before going to the bar.

"Ain't that some shit," I murmured. My address was

on my license so there wasn't much mystery of how it had ended up here. I still didn't know where I'd managed to lose my purse, but at least it had been found by someone honest. More honest than me, I had to admit. I might have made an effort to return the purse, but I would have totally taken the thirty-three dollars.

I guess I was lucky there were people better than me in this world. Not that it took a whole lot to accomplish that.

I swept my gaze around, on the off chance our closest neighbor was outside and had maybe seen something. We lived right off the highway on a mile-long dead end street that had less than a dozen houses along its pothole ridden length. Most of the neighbors couldn't be seen through the pines from our front porch, but the house across the street was in plain sight. And excellent hearing distance too, to judge by the number of times they'd called the cops on us over the years. Complaints about everything from loud music to the trash in our yard to the occasional yelling matches that my dad and I got into.

Assholes. Then again, maybe I didn't give that much of a fuck who'd returned my purse.

Dad wasn't in what passed for our living room. It held a couch and a TV—both of which were almost as old as I was—but it stank of stale beer and cigarettes. I didn't spend any time in there if I could help it, though that was probably more due to the fact that my dad spent most of his time there than because of the way it smelled.

I cautiously peeked through the open door to his bedroom, relieved to see that he was asleep. Passed out, more likely, to judge by the empty beer cans on the nightstand and the bottle of Jack Daniels out in the kitchen. I stood there for a few seconds to make sure his chest was actually going up and down and decided against going in and tugging the blanket over him. More chance that he'd wake up from the movement of the blanket than from being cold. And we got along a lot better when he was like this.

I turned away, headed to the kitchen, found a package of macaroni and cheese and a clean bowl. I thought briefly about watching some TV while I ate, maybe smoke a joint, but decided I didn't want to risk waking my dad up with either. Instead I scarfed down the mac and cheese, dumped the bowl into the sink with the other dirty dishes and headed to the bathroom to take the epic shower I'd promised myself earlier. It ended up only being a few minutes of "epic-ness" thanks to our ancient water heater, but it was enough to get me feeling less gross.

Toweling my hair dry, I headed to my room and glanced at the clock. It wasn't even six P.M. yet, but I wanted to get to bed nice and early. I sure as shit didn't want to oversleep again. I got down on my hands and knees and reached up under my bed, feeling for the pill bottle wedged between the springs. I pulled it out, pried the top off, shook a bunch of pills out into my hand. There were six or seven different kinds, but I knew them well enough that I didn't need them to be in separate, labeled prescription bottles. Good thing, since I didn't have prescriptions for any of them.

Resisting the urge to snag the Vicodin out, I settled for a Xanax instead. I only had the one Vicodin, and there was no sense wasting it when all I really wanted was some help getting to sleep. I returned the other pills back to the bottle, replaced it in its hiding spot, and washed the Xanax down with a beer from the mini-fridge in my room.

Flipping off the lights, I crawled under my blankets and waited for the lovely wave of relaxation to wash over me.

Twenty minutes later I was still wide awake.

By six-thirty I was forced to admit that whatever I'd taken must not have been Xanax.

I scowled into the darkness. Well, this sucked. Since I didn't know what the hell I *had* taken, I didn't dare try to see if something else would do the trick. I'd hit my OD quota for the month already, thank you.

I stubbornly stayed in bed. At some point after eight I finally fell asleep, still waiting for the Xanax to kick in.

Chapter 5

Despite the failure of Xanax, I managed to get a good night's sleep, and actually got out of bed when my alarm went off. As soon as I made it in to work, my training began in earnest. Nick was an obsessive-compulsive, anal-retentive jerk with no social skills, but he took his job damn seriously and was hell bent on making sure I was totally prepared for anything. For the rest of the week I was drilled, instructed, trained, and learned to fucking death, but I gritted my teeth, managed to keep from bitch-slapping Nick, and actually got the hang of the whole thing faster than I ever expected. It helped that there wasn't much about the job that was particularly difficult or complicated. The van drivers were also called bodysnatchers, and that's basically what our job was: Go to the death scene, grab the dead person, stuff 'em into a body bag. And if there were ever any doubts or questions, the investigator was there to clear things up.

I'd braced myself for all sorts of gross or weird stuff when it came to the dead people. Rotten bodies, bizarre suicides, that sort of thing. I was ready for it. I was determined not to freak out, no matter what.

What I wasn't prepared for was the cops.

Cops everywhere, and me trying to keep from looking all guilty and spastic every time one happened to glance my way. I kept having to remind myself I wasn't in trouble, wasn't being hassled—I had no reason to instantly get all defensive. And for the most part the cops and detectives ignored me, or at least didn't give me anything more than the grunt and nod that they gave various other non-cop types who happened to be on the scene.

I'd been on the job for a whole four days before I managed to run into the two detectives who knew exactly what kind of loser I was.

It was Detective Abadie who recognized me first. We were in the front yard of a two-story house in a nice-as-hell gated subdivision. The overweight and out of shape guy who owned the house had apparently decided that having a half-million dollar house meant that he couldn't afford to hire someone to clean out his gutters. Now he was dead with what looked to me like a broken neck after the ladder had slipped. He'd taken the plunge into his fancy landscaping—complete with rock garden. But hey, his fucking gutters were clean.

Abadie's dark eyes scanned the area, skimmed across me and then came back, narrowing. He took in the insignia on my shirt—his mouth pursing as if he'd eaten something bitter. Meanwhile I pretended to be focusing on something intensely interesting near the body so that I didn't have to meet his gaze. But I could still see him nudge Detective Roth and whisper something. It wasn't too difficult to figure out the general gist of what he was saying. The burly detective turned around, but to my surprise a smile spread across his face, and he lifted his hand in a wave. I couldn't really pretend I didn't see it, and it would've probably been horrible and rude to ignore it, so I gave him an awkward and hesitant wave back, hoping that it wasn't one of those cases where he was actually smiling and waving to someone behind me.

Abadie shook his head and stalked off toward his car with the same expression on his face that Allen Prejean had worn—contempt mixed with a healthy dollop of disgust, and a side of disbelief for good measure.

Roth watched him walk off, then looked back to me and gave me a shrug and a smile before returning to his work. I let out a breath I hadn't realized I was holding, tugged a hand through my hair to cover the fact that I was shaking a little. *Okay, so Abadie thinks I'm lower than dirt, but Roth seems all right. And the other cops are all pretty much ignoring me.*

Sounded like a tie game to me—and that was an improvement over "loser" any way you looked at it, right? Still, I wasn't in the best frame of mind for what happened that afternoon.

I'd been through another three autopsies since my first day on the job and each time the damn weird-as-hell craving for brains hit me as soon as the skull was opened up. Each time I gritted my teeth and got through it by not looking directly at the brain and by pretending I was somewhere else.

It worked great until we started the autopsy of the guy we'd just picked up, and Nick handed me the scalpel and bone saw and told me to give it a try. I couldn't pretend to be somewhere else when I was trying to slice through the nasty rubbery thickness of scalp and keep my teeth from rattling out of my head while maintaining something resembling a straight line around the top of the guy's head. And I had to admit that it was weirdly satisfying to give that skullcracker a twist and feel the crack of bone all the way up my arms. Of course by the time I dug my fingers into the crack and pulled the top of the skull off, my damn mouth was watering like a dog who hadn't been fed for a week, looking at a steak.

But that wasn't the worst part. No, the really bad part was that I froze—stood there with half the guy's skull in my hands and stared at the pinkish-grey flesh. Didn't snap out of it until Nick smacked me on the arm.

"Angel? You're not done," he said, eyes narrowing. "Are you about to puke or something?"

I took an unsteady breath and tore my eyes away from the brain. "Don't be stupid," I snapped, a hell of a lot more sharply than I meant.

It didn't seem to faze Nick though. He simply gave a snort and jerked a thumb toward the brain. "Then keep going. Did you forget what to do?"

I scowled behind the mask I'd put on to keep from breathing in bone dust. "It's not fucking rocket science. I was only looking for a second. Gimme a damn break." With that I set the top of the skull on the table and fiercely set about removing the brain from its former home—and a teensy bit grateful to Nick for pissing me off enough that I could get through this.

Maybe that's what I need to do, I thought as I grimly set the brain on the scale and wiped my hands. *Distract myself. Do whatever it is guys do to keep from coming too soon. Baseball scores or some shit like that.* Not that I'd ever known a baseball score.

Still the fact that I'd frozen like that had me more than a little freaked out.

I made it through the rest of the day, but when I finally climbed into my car I knew without any doubt at all that I didn't want to go home just yet. I tried calling Randy again, but when it rolled to voice mail I didn't bother leaving a message and simply headed to his house. I was used to him not answering the phone since he was usually out working in his garage.

Randy lived at the end of several miles of long and narrow rural road. There were only a few houses on the entire road, and the rest of it was dense pine forest. At night it was creepy as all hell, though during the day it was practically scenic—until you made it to the end.

Randy lived in a trailer—which really wasn't so bad since it was actually a pretty decent trailer, as far as trailers went—but the part that really killed the "scenic" aspect was the ramshackle garage. Made of corrugated sheet metal and god-only-knew what else, it was over fifty years old and looked it. Randy's daddy had worked out of it as an auto mechanic until he'd met a lady and moved to Houston with her a couple of years ago. Now Randy was the mechanic, though sometimes I suspected he had a side business going on when it came to cars. After all, the guy who'd sold me the stolen Prius had been a buddy of his. It hadn't been worth the trouble, though, to accuse Randy of knowing it had been stolen. It wouldn't have made any difference at that point.

Randy was out front when I pulled up, his tall, lanky body under the hood of an El Camino. He lifted his head as I got out of my car, a puzzled look crossing his face before it was replaced by his usual lazy smile.

"Hey, babe," he said, wiping his hands on a rag. "Didn't think I'd see you around here anytime soon."

I paused and frowned. "Why?" I asked, right before another memory flickered into place. We'd had some sort of fight that night I'd ODed, though I hadn't the faintest idea what it had been about. It couldn't have been too serious, since he didn't act like he was still mad or anything. But we never had fights about anything major. Sure, we argued, but it was always stupid crap like me getting pissed because he was paying too much attention to how short Ida Miller's skirt was or him thinking I was banging every guy who looked sideways at me.

He lifted a shoulder in a mild shrug. "After that scene at Pillar's the other night," he said, confirming my memory of some sort of argument. "I been worried about you."

I bit back the urge to ask him why the hell he hadn't called in the past few days if he was worried about me. I was feeling good. I sure as hell didn't want to get over one fight just to get into another.

"Busy. Got a job," I said instead. "Been at it almost a week now."

"Cool," he said as he gave me a hug. He smelled of tobacco and grease. A faint whiff of pot clung to him as well, and I could feel myself mentally focusing on that scent. A faint spark of annoyance passed through me that he didn't ask about the job. Then again, I was the queen of minimum wage. He probably assumed I was working another convenience store gig.

"I'm working at the Coroner's Office as a van driver," I told him.

He pulled back and gave a sharp bark of laughter. "You? Touching dead people?"

"Yeah, well, I haven't puked yet." Suddenly I didn't want to talk about my job. If I started thinking about that, then I'd start thinking about why I was working there. "You wanna go get a drink or something?"

"I need to finish this up." He gestured in the direction of the El Camino. "But there's beer in the fridge if you want to hang around. This won't take more than about ten minutes."

Well, that was the best offer I was likely to get today. I headed into the trailer and snagged two beers out of his fridge. A frying pan on the stove held congealing bacon fat, and the kitchen table was covered with old newspapers and engine parts—both combining to give a faint bacon/engine grease tang to the air. It didn't bother me. I was pretty used to it since I usually slept over here as often as I could. Randy's furniture was old and battered, and the carpet had more stains on it than a bum's underwear, but the trailer didn't have roaches, rats, or my dad.

I plopped down on the couch and put my feet up on the coffee table, shoving aside a stack of old *Car and Driver* magazines and about six remotes. Even though Randy didn't seem to give much of a shit about his living arrangements, he took his entertainment pretty seriously: wide screen HDTV, Blu-Ray/DVD player, Xbox, and a kick-ass stereo system. Yet another reason why I preferred spending my time over here.

I didn't turn the TV on. After the day I'd had, I was more in the mood for quiet. No fights. No insults. Nothing weird or disturbing.

I'd finished the first beer and was well into the second by the time Randy came in. He headed straight to the kitchen, returning after a moment with a beer in one hand and baggie in the other. He cracked the beer open and took a long swig, then snagged an already-rolled joint out of the baggie and lit it. After several puffs he passed it to me.

I took a long hit, then tipped my head back and waited for it to take effect.

"You been to Pillar's since the other night?" he asked.

"Nope," I said, without moving. The mellow hadn't hit yet, and I felt that if I shook my head it would kill it.

"Me neither." He paused. "Gotta admit, I was kinda surprised to see you come by here after all that."

Damn. Must have been more of a fight than I thought. I took another hit off the joint as a missing fragment of memory abruptly slid into place. Oh yeah, he'd gone off with some chick, so I'd tried to get back by flirting with a guy I didn't even know. Then the guy had offered to drive me home, because I was way too drunk to drive. Or too stoned. I didn't remember drinking all that much. No, wait, the guy had been buying me drinks. But I didn't leave with him. I was sure of that. There was no way I'd go off with someone I didn't know. I could be stupid as all hell sometimes, but I knew better than to do that. *So instead I tried to walk home. Yeah, that was so much smarter.*

"Guess that's why I haven't called you." Randy was still talking.

I took another pull on the joint, a hard one, as if I could get it to take effect faster. Why the hell wasn't I high yet? "Umm, okay."

He frowned down into his beer. "You know I didn't fuck her, right?"

I blinked at him. "Hunh?"

"Alison," he said. "The chick I left with? You came after me, asked where the fuck I was going. Acting all jealous and shit—"

"I remember," I interrupted. "And you laughed and said you were gonna go bang her in the parking lot."

A grimace flickered over his face. "I was just fucking with you," he muttered. "I didn't think you'd believe me. I was going out to take a look at her car. She was having trouble with her battery. Then I came back in and you were all over some asshole. Pissed me off."

Yeah, I'd believed him. It wasn't as if he'd never cheated on me before, though now I could see that doing so in the middle of our night out together would have been a stretch, even for him. And I'd overreacted like a moron, trying to make him jealous. I remembered that much, though I couldn't for the life of me remember who the other guy was. Hopefully I hadn't made too much of an ass of myself.

"Well, it was a dick thing to say," I told him.

"I know," he said with a wince. "Sorry. So how'd you get the job?" It was pretty obvious he wanted to change the subject, but that was fine with me. If we kept hashing over what had happened at the bar we'd probably end up in another fight.

"Umm, through my probation officer," I said after a second of mental scrambling for an answer. I wasn't totally sure why, but I didn't want to tell him the truth about the whole thing. Maybe 'cause he'd want me to explain, and I didn't know how to? "It's a weird gig, but kinda cool, too. And it even has benefits."

"Oh yeah?"

I nodded. "After three months I get health insurance, and if I stay ten years I get vested in their pension plan."

He laughed out loud. "The day you keep a job for ten years is the day I grow a twelve-inch dick."

"Fuck you," I shot back. "That doesn't even make sense. Besides, you're one to talk."

He grinned and gave me a light punch on the arm. "I know, that's why I said it. You and me, we're too alike. Hell, I'll be shocked if you can keep this job long enough to get the health insurance."

I scowled. "Gee, thanks for having so much faith in me."

"Aw, c'mon, Angel, lighten up. It's not that. You like to do your own thing too much to stick with the same job for so long."

And what the hell *was* my own thing? Whatever it was, so far it sucked.

"This is shit pot," I announced after a moment, stubbing out the half inch of joint that was left. Normally I'd smoke it down as far as possible, but I still wasn't feeling any buzz. Didn't seem to be any point to smoking the rest of it.

He shrugged without looking at me as he picked up a remote and turned on the TV. "So get your own."

"Seriously," I said. "I don't think that's pot. I'm not feeling a damn thing from it."

He flicked a glance my way. "It's the same goddamn bag we started the other night. You liked it enough back then."

I grimaced, then stood.

"Where y'going?" he asked.

"Dunno." I rubbed my arms. Everything felt weird and faded, like the world was turning into a black and white movie. And the dialogue and music on the TV seemed flat and tuneless. But I wasn't feeling the beer or pot at all. I was still cold sober and I didn't want to be. "Home, I guess."

"Nice." His mouth curled into a mild scowl. "You come over and drink my beer and smoke my shit and then leave? What's up with that?" He grabbed my hand and gave it a small tug, then offered a sly smile. "C'mon . . . stay."

I hesitated. I liked sex with Randy, even though we were so on-again off-again that I'd pretty much lost track of whether we were dating or not. After almost four years, we were so damned used to each other that whenever we were together we ended up in the same comfortable patterns.

And I knew what part of that pattern would be. I'd stay, we'd screw, then we'd get high on whatever he had around, and I'd probably oversleep.

"I can't." I tugged free of his grasp. "Sorry. I gotta go. I have work tomorrow. Y'know? That job I won't last at?"

"Are you actually pissed at me about that?" he asked, a frown forming between his eyes.

"No! I'm not," I insisted. "I just need to get home. I can't screw this up."

"Sure. Whatever," he muttered. He didn't reach for my hand again and shifted his attention to the TV. For a brief instant I wanted to go ahead and pick a fight, simply to see if that would snap everything back into focus. Get him and me all riled up and see if that could somehow get him to act like he gave a shit if I was around. We'd yell and scream, then we'd make up and get high and fuck.

And I'd oversleep and lose my job, I thought. I knew myself too well. *But it's only a job, right? Whoever wrote that letter can't have been serious about the whole go-to-jail thing. . . .*

I shook my head, scowling. God, I was weak. How could I even be considering risking it?

The same way I've risked everything else in my life. By not giving a shit. Or getting so fucked up I couldn't give a shit, even if I wanted to.

Yeah, well, I needed to give a shit about going back to jail.

"I'll, um, see you later, babe. Okay?" I said.

He grunted something that might have been a yes. I left to the sound of him changing channels.

Chapter 6

The ringing of my phone jerked me out of a nightmare—*rotting flesh and crawling maggots, reaching hands and flesh dripping off bones.* I struggled to shake off the lingering horror as I groped for my cell phone, almost grateful to be woken up even though it had to be obscenely early, since I could see through my crooked blinds that it was still dark outside.

I finally found the answer button. "Yeah?" I croaked.

"Good morning!" my partner, Derrel, said in an insanely cheerful voice. "I need my Angel to come out and play."

The display on my nightstand clock showed 5:10. Ugh. Being on call sucked the big one. My usual shift didn't start until eight A.M., but twice a week I was on call, which meant that if anyone died in the middle of the night, my ass got to go pick them up and bring them back to the morgue. On the other hand, it also meant that I took the van home after my regular shift was over on those nights, which saved me a few bucks in gas money.

Still, waking up this early was just wrong. "Why can't

people be reasonable and only die after eleven A.M.?" I whined.

"You're cute when you're cranky. I'm texting you the address. See you there!"

I'd been on the job two weeks, and I still hadn't thrown up. I had no idea where my iron stomach had suddenly come from—because I sure as hell never had one before—but considering some of the gross stuff I'd seen and smelled, I wasn't about to complain. One of the bodies we'd brought in the day before had been a decomp— the decomposing body of an old man who'd died in his trailer about a week and a half earlier. I seriously thought I was going to pass out from the smell, and I damn near ran screaming when I saw there were maggots crawling in his mouth and nose. The only reason I didn't was because Nick the Prick was also there, and I knew he'd tell everyone I'd wimped out. And, once again, I wasn't going to go to jail because of his smarmy little ass.

I'd been partnered with an investigator named Derrel Cusimano—a big, bald, black dude who'd been a linebacker at LSU a decade ago and looked like he was still perfectly capable of stopping the rush. He'd been a death investigator with the Coroner's Office for about five years and was as friendly and nice as Nick wasn't. He didn't seem to give a rat fuck that I hadn't finished high school or that I was on probation or that I was twenty-one years old and didn't have a clue what to do with my life. He simply did his job and cracked inappropriate jokes when the general public wasn't around and teased me about my bleached-blonde hair. Somehow when he gave me crap about being redneck trailer trash it was funny instead of mean, perhaps because he gave everyone equal amounts of crap. Plus, he consistently referred to Nick as an "over-privileged cocky asstard" which pretty much made him my hero, despite the fact that he was disgustingly cheerful at five in the morning.

I put my phone back on the nightstand, then ran my fingers through the tangled mess of my hair. The desire to lie back down was damn near overpowering, but I knew if I did I'd be asleep within seconds. And fired within hours. I'd been warned several times that "failure to respond in a timely manner to a call-out" was grounds for immediate termination.

"Only two more weeks to go," I muttered with a scowl as I forced myself to get up from the bed. Then again, so far this job sure beat the hell out of working as a clerk at a convenience store. Though the convenience stores had fewer maggots. Usually.

The faint stench of rot wafted by me as I shambled down the hall to the bathroom. Great. Another rat died in the wall. The house I shared with my dad was . . . well, "piece of shit" was a pretty accurate description. Single-story with a tin roof and rotting front steps. Half the windows were cracked and had been repaired with duct tape, and the other half were so dirty you could barely see anything through them. I kept telling myself that one of these days I'd bust my butt and at least get the kitchen and bathrooms properly cleaned but somehow never quite found the motivation to do so. I kept things wiped down enough so that it wasn't completely toxic, but there was no way I'd ever be comfortable having anyone over.

I did my business in the bathroom, squinting in the mirror after I washed my hands and face. The light above the sink was on but my reflection looked washed out and grey. Not too surprising considering the obscenely early hour, but the flowered wallpaper looked faded as well. To add to the joy, my toothpaste's usual minty freshness wasn't terribly minty, and I even double-checked to make sure I wasn't trying to brush my teeth with something nasty like anti-itch cream.

Maybe I was coming down with something. I'd felt

like this after leaving Randy's last week—so faded and low-energy that after I made it home I'd cheated and downed one of the energy drinks, even though I was only supposed to drink them every other day. But I hadn't overdosed, and in fact had felt fine the next morning. *Or maybe I'm simply allergic to being awake at five A.M.* That was more likely.

I swiped some deodorant into my pits, then wrinkled my nose. The stench was in here as well. I couldn't seem to smell anything else, but I could sure as hell smell whatever it was that had died. I sniffed around in an attempt to trace the source of it, then on an absurd whim took a deep whiff of the back of my hand.

Oh, gross. It was me! I'd showered before going to bed, but apparently the funk from yesterday's decomp had clung to me more than I'd realized. Derrel wouldn't be pleased if I took too long to get out to the scene, but I figured he also wouldn't be thrilled if I smelled like roadkill.

I took a quick shower and toweled off, then sniffed my arm again. It wasn't nearly as bad, yet there was still a lingering aroma of *something dead* that clung to me. No time for another shower, though. I spritzed on a flowery body mist, but I might as well have been spraying water on my bod for all that I could smell it. I scowled and resisted the urge to give myself a second spritzing. If my sense of smell was off, I'd be running the risk of knocking Derrel over with the lovely combo of *something dead* plus *way too many flowers*.

My stomach rumbled as I returned to my bedroom to pull on cargo pants and a Coroner's Office shirt. I yanked open the door of the little fridge to pull out a bottle of the coffee-drink stuff before remembering that I'd downed the last one two days ago. Or was it three? *Damn.* That bump of feel-terrific energy would've been pretty nice right now. Closing the fridge, I got down on my hands and knees and reached up under my bed, feeling for the pill bottle wedged between the springs. I pulled it out, pried the top off, snagged out two white, oblong pills. The rest went back into the bottle and the bottle to its hiding place. Coffee-drinks weren't the only things that could give me a boost. I pulled a beer out of the fridge, washed the pills down, and stuck the open beer back in the fridge. It'd be flat when I got home, but it was better than wasting it.

Holding my shoes in my hand, I walked as silently as I could to the front door.

"Where the fuck you sneakin' off to at this hour?"

Shit. I turned to see my dad sitting in the stained recliner, an open beer in his hand. More empties were piled haphazardly beside the chair. He was probably at the bar last night, got kicked out when they closed at four A.M., then kept going when he got home.

"I'm not sneaking out," I replied. "I got called out to work, and I was trying to keep from waking you up."

His mouth curled down into a scowl. He was only in his late forties, but a couple of decades of booze combined with a ten-year-old back injury from his time on an offshore oil rig, had him looking a lot older. A scraggly beard tried to cover his sagging jowls, and his light brown eyes seemed perpetually glazed. He had on the same battered jeans he'd been wearing the day before, wedged above his bony hips and under his slight pot belly. No shirt. Just pale, flabby chest and spindly arms.

"Between your phone and the shower, no way to sleep around here."

"Yeah, well, sorry." I dropped my shoes on the floor and shoved my feet into them. "Next time I won't even bother trying to be quiet since I obviously suck at it." What the hell did he need to be rested and alert for anyway?

"That sicko job of yours paid you yet?" He peered at

me as he lit a cigarette. "Or you already spent it on pills?"

Crouching, I yanked my laces tight. "I haven't been paid yet," I lied. "Maybe later this week." I really didn't want to get into it with him right now. He expected me to give him half of any money I made to cover my "rent" and expenses, which was a load of bull because this stupid old house had been paid for over a decade ago, since it had actually belonged to his parents, and he got it when they died. Plus, he got his disability check every month—also a load of bull—which covered utilities and food and stuff like that. He only wanted my money so he could go get drunk.

It was beside the point that I usually spent my money on getting drunk—or high. It was my damn money, so it should be my damn buzz. Right?

"So, how much do necro-freaks like you get paid?" He asked, still watching me intently.

"Dunno, Dad," I replied, keeping my attention on the laces of my sneakers. "It's a special program ... part of my probation." More lies. Yesterday I'd been handed a check for my first week's pay, and I'd about died when I saw the amount. More than double anything I'd ever made anywhere else. I had no intention of ever letting him know what I was making.

"Sounds fucked up to me," he said. He took a long pull on the beer and chased it with a drag on his cigarette. Ash dribbled onto his hollowed chest, but he made no move to brush it away. "Why the fuck didja sign on for this? Why can't you keep a real fuckin' job? Or is that the only place that'd take a pillhead?" He scowled. "Only a freak would wanna touch dead bodies."

"Well I guess your daughter's a freak," I shot back as I stood up. "What does that make you, huh?" It wasn't the first time he'd called me names. "Freak" was pretty tame by his standards.

I stalked away from him and yanked open the pantry in the kitchen, muttering a curse as a couple of empty pickle jars tumbled out and rolled across the kitchen floor. One of Mom's "things" had been saving and washing out jars in case she ever wanted to make jelly or pickled who-the-hell-knew-what. I'd never seen her do anything of the sort, which meant we had a couple hundred empty jars stuffed under every cabinet in the damn house. One of these days I was going to actually get around to throwing them all out. Probably about the same time that I cleaned the rest of the kitchen. Yeah, any day now.

I'd eaten pizza last night, but my stomach was acting as if I hadn't eaten in days. There wasn't much food in the house, but I managed to find a packet of Pop-Tarts that didn't look too old. That would have to hold me until I finished at the scene. I was already running late.

My dad muttered something obnoxious under his breath as I headed to the door but I managed to make it out of the house without getting sucked into any more father-daughter bonding. I started to climb into the van, then paused at the sight of an envelope stuck under the windshield wiper. Frowning, I snagged it from beneath the wiper. It was a simple plain white envelope, sealed shut, with nothing written on the outside. I hesitated a few seconds as an unpleasant sense of foreboding shimmered through me, then I ripped it open and unfolded the piece of paper within.

Angel,

If you crave it, eat it. Trust your instincts. It's cool.
Good luck.

What the fuck? My entire body went cold and my

hand shook as I stared down at the note. I had absolutely no doubt that it was from the same person who'd sent me the letter in the hospital. This person obviously knew me and knew where I lived, but it wasn't the stalker aspect of it that had me freaked out right now.

It was that they had to know what I'd been craving.

"Freak" is right.

I crumpled the note into a tight ball and shoved it deep into a pocket. My heart pounded in a combination of terror and anxiety as I started the van and headed out. No, that was insane. How the hell could anyone know that I'd been fighting the urge to chow down on . . . brains?

Yet what else could the letter possibly be referring to? Usually if I craved something, I ate it. Simple. I didn't need anyone else to tell me it was okay and that I should go for it.

But I'd been craving *brains*. The smell was like chocolate and cookies and biscuits and gravy and everything else that was delicious. It damn near drove me crazy every time I had to touch one. I'd been fighting the cravings the way I'd never fought the urge to take drugs or get drunk.

As if to taunt me, my stomach chose that moment to snarl again. *Stop it!* I silently wailed. I ripped the packet of Pop-Tarts open with my teeth and ate them as quickly as I could, even though they were so stale and tasteless it was like eating cardboard. Maybe the uppers I'd taken would help. They'd always done a good job of killing my appetite in the past, so hopefully they'd help kill this screwed up hunger.

Or maybe I just needed crazy-meds instead.

If you crave it, eat it. I shook my head. I'd gotten comfy with the thought that this job was a substitute for rehab, but this letter threw that completely out of whack. Why on earth would it ever be all right to give in to that?

No. It didn't make sense. It had to be referring to something else. A dull anger began to form in my gut. Why the hell couldn't Anonymous Letter Guy simply tell me what the hell was going on?

I struggled to put the whole craziness out of my head as I focused on getting to the scene in a timely manner. Fortunately the van had a GPS which efficiently guided me to the address Derrel had texted—a one-story brick house in the sort of upper middle-class neighborhood I'd once hoped to live in. An ambulance and a police car occupied the driveway, and a black Dodge Durango with the Coroner's Office logo on the side was parked at the curb behind a maroon Ford Taurus with so many lights in the windows and antennas on the back that it was screamingly obvious it belonged to a detective. Why the hell did they call them "unmarked" cars when it was obvious to anyone with eyes that it was a police car?

I pulled in behind the Durango, but paused before getting out and surreptitiously slathered more deodorant into my pits. I could *still* smell myself. It wasn't overpowering or anything, but I couldn't seem to shake the faint whiff of *yuck*—the same kinda sickly, almost sweet, rotting flesh smell of a decomposing body. I was also so hungry I was ready to eat the damn steering wheel, and the Pop-Tarts hadn't made the slightest difference. It didn't feel as if the pills had kicked in at all, which was really strange since I could usually count on feeling the effect within about ten minutes, and it had easily been half an hour.

I hurried up to the house, kicking myself for not bringing more pills with me. *Though, with my luck, I'd take more and then overdose again,* I thought with a sigh.

The stupid clawing hunger had me so distracted I didn't even see the low step in front of the house. I tripped and only a sudden strong grip on my arm saved me from a humiliating sprawl.

"Careful there," a deep voice murmured

I clutched at the hand on my arm as I struggled for enough balance to stand on my own. "Thanks, man," I said with an embarrassed grimace. I got my feet under me, looked up. And froze. *A cop. Shit, it's a cop*.

He released me and stepped back while I fought down the stupid instinctive flare of alarm that shot through me. After two weeks on the job and a few dozen death scenes I should've been used to running into cops all the time, but this was the first time I'd been up close and personal with one. Besides, this cop was kinda hot. I didn't usually go for the men-in-uniform type, but he rocked it. There was no spare fat on this guy. His hair and eyes were both dark, but he didn't look Italian or Arabic or anything like that. I took a quick glance at his nametag. *M. Ivanov*. Was that Russian? That would explain—

My thoughts came to a screeching halt. Ivanov. *Shit*. Marcus Ivanov. This was the cop who'd arrested me for that stolen Prius.

I could feel my face heating. "I, um, need to get inside," I quickly muttered, avoiding eye contact.

"Of course," Deputy Ivanov replied. He gave me a neutral smile, then continued on past me and headed toward his car. He hadn't recognized me. I gave a small sigh of relief, even as a wistful little twinge shot through me. What the hell had I been so worried about? I wasn't the sort of chick guys like that remembered, and certainly never in a good way.

I pushed aside my stupid disappointment and continued on in, stepping out of the way of the paramedics as they carried gear back to the ambulance. Their presence was routine. Unless a body had very obviously been dead for a while, it was standard to have them run an EKG strip to make absolutely certain the person was solidly dead. I was starting to get the hang of all the various procedures involved when someone died. It wasn't something I'd ever thought about before. I mean, who really wants to, other than maybe deciding whether you wanted to be buried or cremated?

I waited patiently inside near the front door and tried to ignore my churning gut while I did my best to stay out of the way. Detective Roth stood near the entrance to the kitchen while he talked on his phone. A curvy blonde woman wearing fatigue pants and a shirt with *SEPSO Crime Scene* printed across the back was crouched by the wall as she carefully packed a camera into a bag. More procedure. Unless someone was under hospice care or in a hospital or nursing home, a detective and a crime scene tech were dispatched to investigate and process the scene. Though I'd already learned that, unless it was clearly foul play, "investigate" meant that the detective took down the decedent's information and then referred to the coroner's report; and "process" meant that the crime scene tech took pictures of the scene and the body.

But I guess that makes sense, I thought. *Going all out on every dead body would get to be a pain in the butt and a waste of time pretty fast.*

I snorted. Look at me, being all understanding about cops. Who'd have thought that would ever happen?

I leaned against the wall, watched as Derrel spoke in soft and comforting tones to the dead man's wife. For all his imposing size and looks, Derrel had a way of dealing with family and loved ones that was nothing short of a gift. I could hear him gently inquiring about her husband's medical history and what medications he was on. From what I could overhear it sounded as if the guy had a history of heart disease and had died in his sleep.

I slid further in and peeked down the hall. The bedroom door was open, and I could see the dead man lying on his back in the bed, the sticky pads from the paramedics' equipment still stuck to him in various spots on his body. He didn't look very old, maybe in his fifties or so, which meant that he'd be brought in for autopsy— which was why I was here. A geezer in his eighties with a bad heart probably wouldn't be autopsied unless he had a few bullet holes in him or a knife sticking out of his chest.

I stepped back as one of the paramedics returned. "Forgot my stethoscope," he explained with a smile as he continued on in to the bedroom. He came back out with it in his hand, then paused in front of me, a slight frown creasing his brow. He looked faintly familiar but the "Quinn" on his nametag didn't help me out. He was tall and slender, with reddish brown hair and a faint scattering of freckles across his nose and cheeks. Not bad-looking at all. I'd probably met him on a different scene sometime in the past two weeks.

He continued to frown down at me. "Something wrong?" I asked, oddly nervous that I'd screwed up somehow.

His expression abruptly cleared, and he gave me a broad smile. "I knew I'd seen you before. You're looking a lot better now."

My expression must have echoed the *What the hell?* going through my head because he chuckled and shook his head. "I'm sorry," he said. "I'm Ed Quinn. I . . . uh," he lowered his voice. "I worked on you a couple of weeks ago when you were found out on Sweet Bayou Road."

I could feel my face heating in embarrassment. *Found dying of an overdose.* "Oh. Great." Then I grimaced. "I mean, thanks, y'know."

His smile abruptly shifted to a look of chagrin. "Sorry," he said. "I guess I shouldn't have brought that up."

I shrugged, trying to appear casual. "It's cool. That's behind me now."

"Good to hear." His gaze swept over me, pausing briefly on the Coroner's Office logo on my shirt. I could see the question forming in his eyes: How the hell had I managed to land this job? I struggled to think of something plausible but to my relief he seemed to sense my discomfort and left the question unasked. "Well, I gotta run," he said, glancing toward the door. "Take care of yourself."

I gave him a nod and a forced smile as he headed out. As soon as he was gone I blew my breath out and leaned back against the wall. *Awkward.* First the cop who'd arrested me, then the paramedic who'd kept me from accidentally killing myself. I didn't even want to think what a third thing might be.

I groaned under my breath as a wisp of a too familiar odor reached my nose. Oh yeah, how about stinking like a week-old corpse?

Derrel came over to me with a paper bag in one hand and his keys in the other. I could see his nose twitch but thankfully he didn't seem to associate the stink with me. "Okay, we'll be taking him in," he said. "Would you mind sticking this in the lockbox in the back of the Durango on your way out to get the stretcher and body bag?"

"Sure thing," I said, taking the bag and keys from him. "What is it?"

"All of his meds. The Coroner's Office collects them and disposes of them."

I blinked. It felt like about a dozen bottles in the bag. "They throw it all out?"

Derrel nodded. "I have to count all the pills and log everything first, but yeah, they get incinerated. It's not like they can be given to anyone else."

"Gotcha." I flashed him what I hoped was a nonchalant smile. "Okay, be right back." I hurried out to the Durango and popped the latch for the back. A metal lockbox was there and a quick search through the keys revealed one that opened it. I paused with the bag in my hand. *They can't be given to anyone else, huh?* My pulse thudded as I quickly looked through the pill bottles in the bag. I didn't recognize most of the drug names. Heart medicines of some sort, I assumed. But there were also some anxiety meds, and even a prescription for my little uppers. And Xanax. A whole damn bottle—and I knew this stuff would be the real thing.

Hunger clawed at me again. Maybe Xanax would make the crazy cravings go away, or at least dull them a bit? It wasn't as if I was going to take the pills to sell them or anything. That would be stupid. I'd be looking at serious jail time for something like that.

My mouth felt dry as I stood there with the bag in my hand. Taking a deep breath, I pulled the bottle of Xanax out, crumpled the bag shut and shoved it into the box. I started to put the bottle into the pocket of my cargo pants, then paused. What if Derrel had already written down the names of the drugs? Even if he hadn't actually counted the pills yet, he'd be sure to notice a whole bottle missing.

I'm being a moron, I thought with a scowl. *And now I've taken too long. He's going to know something's up. I'll be busted for sure.*

I quickly crammed the bottle of Xanax back into the bag and shut the lockbox. A strange relief settled over me and I let out a slow sigh. It had been stupid of me to even consider taking the drugs. So far I'd managed to go a whole two weeks without doing something bone-headed. I only had two more weeks to go and then I could be out of this job and away from brains and bodies and all that craziness.

I locked the box and closed the back of the Durango. I turned to get the body bag and stretcher from the van, but stopped dead at the sight of Ivanov leaning against his car and looking straight at me.

My heart gave a guilty leap until I realized that he was talking on his cell phone. And that he wasn't looking directly at me at all, merely in my general direction. *Cripes, Angel. Guilty conscience much?*

But I couldn't shake the feeling that if I'd taken those pills, he'd have been on me like white on rice.

Chapter 7

More than ready to get the hell out of there, I had the dead guy bagged, on the stretcher, and shoved into the back of the van in record time. Derrel gave me a funny look, but thankfully didn't say anything about the fact that I was probably looking as guilty as I wasn't. At least the cop and the paramedics were gone by the time I was ready to load up the body. If Ivanov had still been there, I'd have probably done something stupid like drop the body, finally proving to everyone that I couldn't be trusted with anything.

As soon as I was on the road and headed to the morgue my tension eased slightly—only to be replaced by a knifing stab of hunger. My hands tightened on the steering wheel, and it didn't help that I kept thinking I could smell the body in the back of the van. My stomach gave an encouraging growl, and I clenched my teeth as my mouth started to water. Within that skull was such a lovely brain. Maybe I could pull over and use the tire iron to break the skull open, kinda like a coconut. I could scoop out handfuls of that sweet, luscious—

I sucked my breath in, absolutely horrified at the direction of my thoughts. I'd get fired for sure if I showed up at the morgue with a body with a caved-in head. And if I got fired, I'd go to jail for sure, and then—

"Oh, god," I groaned. I wasn't horrified at the thought of eating brains. I was worried about how to explain a hole in the corpse's head.

If you crave it, eat it.

"This is so fucked up," I muttered. Maybe I was suffering from some weird post-accident trauma. Some lingering hallucination from my overdose? That made as much sense as anything else.

The morgue was empty when I arrived. No surprise, since it was a Sunday. I yanked the stretcher out of the van, wheeled it into the cooler. No, I was *not* going to bash in this guy's head. I wasn't that crazy.

But my stomach screamed at me the second I entered the cooler. I didn't even have to look at the other body bag already in there. That guy had been autopsied on Friday and was waiting to be picked up by the funeral home. His organs were in a bag between his legs, and there was brain in there. I could smell it—through the plastic bag, through the body bag, through all the other stenches and odors of the morgue. The scent of that brain cut through them all.

I looked down at the organs swimming in the clear plastic bag. I didn't even fully remember walking to the other stretcher and unzipping the body bag. A weird calm descended on me. I was really going to do this. I was probably completely crazy and hallucinating, but I couldn't fight it anymore. I wasn't that tough. Hell, that was the reason I was in this situation—I had no damn willpower. Get clean? Yeah, right. Too much work and too much of a bummer. Your life sucks and the only thing you're good at is fucking up? So much easier not to think about it—wipe the worry away with a Percocet or a Xanax. Go numb.

I carefully untied the plastic bag and pulled it open. I didn't look at any of the other organs. I wasn't grossed out by them; they simply held no interest for me. It was the segments of brain that held my attention. Most of the brain had been sliced into neat half-inch slices during the autopsy. It looked like pieces of bread pudding that had been soaked in raspberry syrup.

Not that I needed the comparison. I didn't have to psych myself up to eat a piece. The hunger took over and the next thing I knew I was on the second slice—and I felt *good*. I closed my eyes in bliss. It was almost like the kinda good that some drugs could give you—and I *knew* drugs—except that it was somehow . . . cleaner.

So what if I was nuts? This was fantastic. The hunger was gone. More than gone. I felt sharp and clear and alive and completely sated. I felt awesome.

My eyes snapped open. I could feel the puzzle pieces fall into place as the last bite of brain slid down my throat. I knew this feeling. The coffee-drinks . . . those gooey chunks with the same consistency, given to me by the same mystery person who told me to give in to my cravings.

Holy shit. I'd been eating *brains* for two weeks. And loving it.

I couldn't make my mind figure out what that meant. I didn't want to know what it meant. It had to be some sort of disease, right? I mean, anything else would be crazy.

"Oh, man," I whispered. "I am way beyond crazy."

There was still nearly half a brain in the bag. I grabbed a towel, quickly wiped my face and hands, ducked out of the cooler and snagged a clean and empty plastic container from the room where the tissue samples were kept. My pulse hammered as I returned to the cooler and stuffed what was left of the brain into the container. Whether I was crazy or diseased, I obviously needed to keep eating brains unless I wanted to feel like I was dying of hunger. If my heart was beating, that meant I was alive, right? Couldn't possibly be anything else.

So what if I'd seen enough horror movies to know what kind of creature eats brains. That wasn't possible. There was no way I was ... that.

I shoved the container into a paper bag, then did my very best to clean everything up so that no one could possibly know what insanity I'd been up to.

Am I insane? Or am I a monster?

I had no idea which was the better option.

Chapter 8

My stress levels were so high that when my cell phone rang I let out a shriek and damned near threw the bag containing the tub of brains into the air. Yeah, that would have been an impressive mess.

I took a deep breath in an effort to settle my galloping heart, then yanked my phone out of my pocket. "Yeah?"

"Yo, Angel. It's Derrel. You okay? You sound out of breath."

Thank god I sounded out of breath and not ... *completely fucking insane*. I took another long breath. Insane maybe, but at least I wasn't hungry anymore. And I felt fantastic. Then again, the fact that I felt so good after what I'd just done was so fucked up I almost felt worse.

No, I felt fantastic. No denying it. This was wrong all over. "Um, yeah, sorry," I said. "My phone was in the other room, and I had to run from the cooler."

"Shit, girl, you could have called me back," he said with a smile in his voice. "Anyway, I was checking to see if you were finished up there, 'cause I'm going to grab some late breakfast, and I figured I'd see if you wanted to join me."

"Sure," I replied automatically, then felt a spasm of nerves. I just ate *brains,* and now I was supposed to sit down and eat normal ordinary food like a normal ordinary person?

"Great!" he replied before I could take it back. "Meet us at the Top Cow Café over on Ninth Street. We'll hold a spot for you."

"Okay," I said faintly and hung up, then realized he'd said "us." Who the hell else was going to be there?

I looked down at the bag I had cradled in my arms. I ate brains. Holy shit. I couldn't stop thinking about it. It was like an earworm running through my head. *I ate brains. I'm crazy. Completely batshit crazy.*

My gut clenched as a hideous thought occurred to me: If I was crazy enough to eat brains, what if I was crazy enough to kill someone? What if I *was* somehow involved in that murder out in the swamp?

My knees shook, and I had to grab for a chair. I sat, fingers tightening on the brown paper bag. I didn't remember much, if anything, from that night. Maybe I was some sort of schizo. Maybe I was just as much of a sick fuck as Jeffrey Dahmer. I needed to go turn myself in or something, right? I mean, I couldn't risk walking free. What if I killed someone else? The thought of going to jail gave me cold sweats, but being a murderer.... No, that was even worse.

I stood and dug my hand into my pocket to retrieve my keys, then frowned as my fingers touched a crumpled piece of paper. I pulled it out, uncrumpled it, let out a ragged breath.

The note from Anonymous Letter Dude. I wasn't hallucinating that. Which meant that I probably *wasn't* crazy.

Somehow that didn't make me any happier.

I hurried out of the morgue with the bag cradled to my chest, certain that at any second someone was going to jump out from behind one of the scrawny bushes surrounding the small lot and demand to know what I was doing. I reached my car without anything like that happening, though I managed to drop my keys twice while trying to get the trunk open. On the third try I got it unlocked, then took several deep breaths in an effort to calm down and chill a bit. *Just because I'm insane doesn't mean I have to act all crazy*, I thought with a harsh scowl.

I gave my head a sharp shake. No, not insane. It wasn't some sort of split personality of mine that sent me the stuff at the hospital. The drinks in the cooler had been some sort of brain concoction. I was *sure* of that. And I didn't start getting drop dead starving until about two days after I'd finished the last one.

But what did it all mean?

I stuffed the bag of brains into a corner of the trunk, stopped at the first drugstore I saw and bought an insulated lunchbox and a bag of ice. I drove to a remote corner of the parking lot then transferred the bag into the lunchbox and stuffed the space around the bag with ice. The paper bag tore as I went to close the lunchbox, and I paused, pulse thudding as I looked at the grotesque undulations of the brain visible through the plastic. What if I got caught with this? It was obvious what it was. I needed a better system.

I let out a shuddering laugh. Right. I needed a better system for this completely fucked up insane thing I was doing. I finally closed the lunchbox and slammed the trunk lid shut.

Unfortunately, my mind was so scattered that I slammed the trunk right down on my left hand.

I let out a scream of pain and tried to pull my hand free but the fucking trunk had somehow latched on my crushed fingers. Pain and panic swirled together as I struggled to get the trunk open. My keys had dropped onto the ground and in a burst of utter desperation I grabbed the lip of the trunk with my right hand and yanked as hard as I could, even though I knew there was no way I'd be able to force it open.

To my shock and relief I heard a sharp crack of metal, and the trunk swung open. I pulled my poor hand to my chest, cradled it while tears of pain streamed down my face. I was afraid to look at it. I'd caught a glimpse of the twisted fingers. I knew they were broken. This was fucking great. And I didn't have health insurance yet. How the hell would I do my job with a broken hand?

I leaned up against the back bumper while I hunched over my hand and cried in misery and pain. Though . . . the pain really wasn't as bad as it was at first, I realized after a few seconds. Maybe I was going into some sort of shock. I risked a peek at my hand, involuntarily sucking my breath in at the way the first three fingers bent backwards between the top two knuckles.

A sudden tug of appetite made me flinch in surprise. How the hell could I be hungry at a time like this? And why didn't this hurt more? I'd had broken bones before. I knew the pain involved a bit too well. This felt as if I'd already taken some kind of painkillers.

Hunger tightened my gut again, and my eyes fell to the lunchbox in my trunk. *Oh, come on*, I thought with a sudden weary despair. How often was I going to have to eat this shit to keep from being ravenous all the time? I quickly looked around to make sure there was no one anywhere nearby before unzipping the lunchbox one-handed. At the sight of the plastic container the hunger gave a little jump, as if to say, "Yes! That!"

I scowled. Fine. Whatever. I could chow this shit down and then go to the hospital for my hand. At least I wouldn't have to worry about being caught with brains in my trunk.

I nervously checked my surroundings again, tugged the top off the container and let the stupid, crazy hunger have its way. Less than a minute later I'd managed to finish off everything in the container, and my appetite had settled down again.

I'm gonna be screwed if I end up needing to eat brains every couple of hours, I thought, worried and depressed, as I walked over to a nearby dumpster and chucked the empty container into it. *There's no way enough people will die for me to—*

I stopped dead, staring down at my left hand.

The fingers were straight again. I slowly flexed them. No pain, not even a hint of it. The bones were most certainly in the right number of pieces. There was no swelling or blood—not even the slightest hint of a scrape.

Oh my god.

I swallowed hard then forced my legs to carry me back to my car. I hadn't imagined or hallucinated my hand getting slammed in the trunk. When I got back to my car I could definitely see flecks of blood on the edge of the trunk lid where my hand had been.

The brains . . . they healed me up. I couldn't think of any other possible explanation. A hysterical giggle escaped me. Guess I didn't need health insurance after all.

And maybe I wasn't crazy either. I wanted to be relieved, but. . . .

A chill crawled through me. What kind of monster was I?

Making sure I had my hands safely out of the way this time, I shoved the trunk closed, scowling as it popped right back up again. I peered at the latch—or rather, what was left of the latch. It was in pieces, and when I looked around I could see that the hook part had somehow cracked off and was lying in the bottom of the trunk.

Okay, so my car was an old piece of shit. The latch

was probably already cracked or something, and when I pulled on it I got lucky, that's all.

Right?

I went back into the drugstore and bought some duct tape. I taped my trunk shut and got in the car, but paused before cranking the engine.

Something else was different.

It took me several seconds to figure it out, but finally I realized it was something that was missing. *My stench.*

I didn't have to lift my arm and smell myself. I'd grown a bit used to it over the course of the day, but I knew that the aroma of rot that clung to me all day was now gone. I smelled as fresh as if I'd showered that morning—which I had, of course, but this was the first time all day I could believe it.

When I eat brains I don't smell like rotten meat. I heard a low whimpering noise, then realized it was me.

Starting the car, I turned the radio up, then drove to the café to meet Derrel, while I did my best to pretend the last ten minutes had never happened.

Chapter 9

The Top Cow Café, situated in a slightly crummy section of Tucker Point, was a cramped little hole-in-the-wall with a sign out front so weatherworn it was barely readable and waitresses who didn't waste their time with little things like courtesy and smiles. But the food was terrific, and the coffee kicked ass, and I'd never been there when half a dozen people weren't patiently waiting their turn to be scowled at.

I walked into the café, bypassing the waiting people as I scanned for the hulking figure of my partner. *It's official*, I thought with a sigh as I spied him at a table for four and realized who else was with him. *God hates me*.

Derrel gave me a broad smile and wave as I fixed my face into something other than the pained grimace I wanted to wear. Marcus Ivanov glanced my way and offered the most neutral of smiles. I couldn't tell if he was annoyed that I was there, but then I figured that surely Derrel would have told him I was coming, and if the deputy had a problem associating with my type, he could have shoved off before I got there. Not that I would have had a problem with that.

Screw it. I wasn't going to be chased off. Besides, my stomach was giving a very ordinary sort of hunger grumble at the smells of pancakes and waffles. *Well, that's one good thing*, I thought as I slid into the empty chair that wasn't right next to Ivanov. *I'm insane, but at least I don't have to give up syrupy carbs.*

"Angel, do you know Marcus?" Derrel asked with a smile. "Angel's our newest employee," he told Ivanov without waiting for me to reply. "She started as a van driver and morgue tech a couple of weeks ago."

"We met on the scene this morning," the deputy replied with an even smile, saving me from trying to figure out a way to explain how we'd actually met.

Well, that was cool of him. "Um, yeah, he saved me from doing a face-plant on the sidewalk," I said with a laugh that I was sure sounded forced and self-conscious.

Derrel grinned. "Marcus takes the whole 'serve and protect' thing pretty damn seriously. That or he simply wanted an excuse to put his hands on a cute chick."

I could feel myself flushing, and the only thing that saved me from total embarrassment was the fact that the deputy looked slightly flustered as well. Derrel simply laughed and shoved a menu my way.

"Here. Order food," he told me. "We've already ordered, but you're the one who's all skin and bones."

My stomach gave another soft little rumble, but I couldn't be sure what the hell it was rumbling for. "I, uh, kinda just ate," I mumbled.

Ivanov's mouth curved in a smile. "You'll need to keep your strength up if you'll be working with this beast here," he said with a nod toward Derrel. Then he looked back at me, smile still on his face. God-fucking-damn but he was seriously good-looking. "Have you ever had the stuffed pancakes here? They're evil. I highly recommend them."

"Heh. The cop is recommending evil," I said. "Too funny."

To my surprise, Ivanov chuckled. "You've discovered my dark side."

Derrel made a rude noise. "And you've also seen all there is to his 'dark side.' This is the squeaky cleanest fucker I've ever met. How he manages to not be a complete dick is beyond me."

Ivanov's smile stretched into an actual grin. "You've obviously never talked to any of the, uh, guys I work with."

He didn't even flick a glance my way, but I knew with an odd certainty that he'd been about to say "the people I've arrested" and then changed it because I was sitting there. Part of me wanted to be totally self-conscious but there was a bigger part of me that couldn't help but be really grateful that this cop wasn't saying anything about that time he arrested me, or even hinting at it. Or even saying anything that could make me feel uncomfortable. That was cool. And unexpected. Maybe he was just messing with me. Waiting to let loose with that info when it'd be really humiliating.

But even as I thought it, I had a hard time believing it was true.

A surly waitress came by and poured coffee for me, and I went ahead and ordered the stuffed pancakes. Marcus gave me a smile when I did so. I smiled back out of reflex then quickly busied myself with the cream and sugar, getting my coffee the way I liked it. Sheesh, I was starting to act like a high school kid with a crush. This was a cop. I was a convicted felon. He was simply being nice. That was all.

The waitress returned less than a minute later, slid plates of food in front of Marcus and Derrel, muttered something about refilling their coffee when she could get a damn free second and left. I told the two men to go ahead and eat, and they didn't need any more urging. I sipped my coffee while they ate and absently listened to the short order cook yell for a waitress to come pick up her damn order. Her retort was equally harsh but no one in the diner paid any attention to it. It was all part of the "ambience" of this place.

"So," Derrel said after a moment, eyeing the deputy, "have y'all come up with any leads in the headless hunter case?"

I'd just taken a sip of coffee and barely managed to keep from spraying it across the table in a scene that could have been right out of a sitcom. Of course, then I had to keep from breathing the coffee right back in, which would have resulted in the sort of coughing fit that would have looked even more suspicious. I grabbed my napkin and managed to pretend to sneeze which had the added effect of covering up most of my face which was surely completely beet red with embarrassment at this point. Yeah, I was classy and suave like that. *Jesus Christ, Angel, get a grip!*

Ivanov cast an uncertain look my way then, thankfully, returned his attention to Derrel. "Nothing so far. The victim's been identified, as you know, but that's about it."

Derrel dipped his head in a nod. "Adam Campbell."

"Right," Ivanov said. "The guy lived in a fishing camp not too far from where his body was found. Kept to himself, worked as a technical writer or some such thing." He shrugged. "The detectives questioned people in the area but haven't come up with squat."

Derrel huffed out a sigh. "Monica was working that night. I know she wasn't thrilled to be working two scenes back to back, but it sounds like that one was pretty interesting." He glanced my way, slight frown creasing his forehead. "Have you even met Monica yet?"

I nodded. "Met everyone in the staff meeting last

week." Although "met" was a strong word for what was more like: "Hey, everyone, this is Angel, our new body-snatcher. Angel, this is everyone!" There were three death investigators: Derrel, Monica Gaudreau, and Allen Prejean—the *Chief* Investigator. There were also three van driver/morgue techs: me, Nick, and a pasty-looking older guy named Jerry Powell. Supposedly the coroner, Dr. Duplessis, wanted to hire one more of each to make scheduling easier, but that was on hold for some sort of budget reasons. The only reason my position had been open was because the previous van driver had been caught stealing lab supplies. I almost never saw Monica or Jerry because of the way the shifts fell. If it wasn't for the fact that the office had a staff meeting every other week I probably wouldn't know anyone except Derrel. And Nick, but only because he'd trained me.

"I don't know about interesting, but it's definitely something different," Ivanov said to Derrel. "So far about all they can be sure of is that it was someone reasonably strong—and they only have that much because of Dr. Leblanc's findings in the autopsy."

"How can he know that?" I asked before I even realized I'd opened my mouth.

Derrel answered. "I haven't read the report, but often that sort of thing can be determined by the extent of the damage. Chopping off a head isn't an easy thing to do, so someone with spindly little arms like you would have a hard time of it." He chuckled and I joined in, more out of incredible relief than from the teasing.

Okay, so another vote against the "Angel is a psycho killer" option. Whew.

My food finally arrived along with a refill of my coffee. The stuffed pancakes were as good and evil as the deputy claimed, and I managed to survive the rest of the meal without looking like a total idiot or doing anything that would make the others realize that I had no business being in that line of work.

But, while I ate, one niggling thought occurred to me and refused to leave me alone.

If I really did break my trunk open, then I *would* be strong enough to chop off someone's head.

Chapter 10

All next week I was the goddamn model of a good worker. I arrived at the morgue early to get everything set up and cleaned up. I stayed late to get stuff cataloged or put away.

And whenever I was alone, I scooped the brains out of the bags and squirreled that shit away. I bought a bunch of ice packs, started saving plastic water bottles, and I washed out a bunch of the old pickle jars from underneath the cabinets at home. I also decorated the jars to make it a little less obvious what was in them. Back when I was a little girl my mom and I had done this craft thing where we'd take empty wine or liquor bottles—which we always had tons of—and cover every bit of glass with inch-long pieces of masking tape. Once the bottles were covered in tape we'd smear brown shoe polish all over and then wipe the excess off with a rag, and when we were done we had a bunch of bottles that looked cool and antique—kinda leathery, in a way. At least, they looked cool to seven-year-old me. Maybe I'd loved them because it was one of the few pleasant memories I had of my mother. Funny how it's so much easier to remember the bad shit.

Then again, there'd been a lot of the bad shit.

I couldn't decide if it looked dumb or not when I did the masking tape/shoe polish thing to the pickle jars, but it served its purpose. Someone would have to actually open the jars to see what I had inside them. I also went to the dollar store and bought a cheap little hand held, battery-powered blender. Once blended, the brains weren't really recognizable as brains at all, but to be on the super-safe side, I borrowed a trick from Anonymous Letter Dude and started blending brains up with soup or fruit juice or chocolate milk—stuff that looked normal so that no one would freak out if they happened to open the cooler. I could fit half a brain and about a cup of soup or chocolate milk into each jar or water bottle, and so far it seemed that a jar or bottle every other day kept me from getting smelly. I really wanted to see if brains could freeze and, after thawing, still retain whatever it was that I craved. But I didn't want to risk putting them in the freezer at home. Either my dad would eat them by mistake, or—worse—he'd throw them out.

Things were going as well as I could possibly expect, considering my circumstances. I had a seriously fucked up diet, but I still ate real food and was starting to get to where I could tell the difference between hunger and Hunger. Plus, the one month mark was coming up fast, and while I'd figured out that I probably wasn't in any sort of position to tell my boss to fuck off, still, finally getting the straight scoop from whoever'd set all of this up for me was the thought that kept me going. It also helped that I was actually starting to enjoy the job.

Drive a van. How hard could it be, right?

*   *   *

Three A.M. on a Tuesday night and the body in the back of the van was being nice and quiet. Not that I expected it to sit up and start talking or anything stupid like that. But sometimes bodies made weird noises—farts and belches and shit like that—and I was still new enough to this gig that it gave me a bit of a freakout whenever I heard it.

Yep, the freak who ate brains could still get freaked. I had the iron stomach thing going for me, but there was still plenty of other shit that had the ability to creep me right out.

I had the radio in the van on, but the left speaker was blown and Shania Twain sounded more like Axl Rose, so I had the volume pretty low. Still, it was better than silence, especially since it was dark as all hell, and I was in the middle of Swamp Bum-fuck-nowhere on Highway 1790. I hadn't passed another car in over ten minutes, and I had at least another twenty to go before I hit what passed for civilization in St. Edwards Parish.

So that was my excuse for screaming like a little bitch when I saw someone standing in the road in front of me.

I slammed on the brakes even as I realized that it was only a fallen tree with a branch sticking up that was kind of person-shaped. *Person woulda been better to hit,* flashed through my head as I yanked the wheel to the left in stupid panic. *Really* stupid panic, because I was already too close to the tree, and all I did was make sure the van went into a really spectacular flip and roll.

My head smacked hard against the doorframe as the van slammed down on the driver's side, and for several seconds all I could see were bright bursts of light. The van scraped along the highway with a horrible shriek of metal on pavement, then everything stopped, and all I could hear was the sound of my panicked breathing.

I was lying against the driver's side door, partially

suspended by the seatbelt. I'd only been wearing it be-cause I knew I couldn't risk getting written up for not wearing one in a Coroner's Office vehicle. *Score one for the rulebook*, I thought with a wheezing laugh. Half the windshield had pulled free like a banana peel, and I could see the crescent moon and about a million stars. Muggy air flowed in and a mosquito buzzed near my ear, probably drawn by the blood I could feel trickling across my forehead. Part of the doorframe had buckled and twisted inward, and it wasn't until I unpeeled my fingers from the wheel that I realized my left arm was badly broken, complete with a jagged end of white bone shoved through the skin of my forearm.

I stared at the end of the bone for several seconds, still trying to process what had happened. I wasn't ex-actly the go-to gal in an emergency. I was usually the one who freaked out enough to need a good hard slap. But there was no one here to slap me.

My phone. Yeah, I could do that. I could find my phone and call for help. And then I needed to find my lunchbox.

The end of the bone seemed to take on a surreal glow in the moonlight. "Damn," I murmured. It wasn't all that long ago that the sight of blood—anyone's blood, not just mine—would have had me puking and close to fainting, yet here I was staring at the end of my arm bone. "That is *seriously* disgusting."

Sudden worry clutched at me. How much trouble was I going to be in for wrecking the van? If I lost this job, I was dead meat.

I fumbled for the seat belt release. It sprang free, and I let out a strangled scream as I crumpled against the door and banged the broken arm hard. Curling my arm to my chest, I lay there and took several deep, gulping breaths. It hurt like a bitch, but I knew too damn well that it could have been a lot worse. I could already feel that bizarre fading of sensation creeping through me, and right now I was more than happy to have the edge taken off.

I winced as a sharp tug of hunger replaced the pain. First priority was to find my lunchbox. I peered uncertainly at the end of the bone again. Would the brains heal that up? Or did I need to set it or something first? I shivered despite the warmth of the night. I'd lost a lot of my squeamish fears, but I was pretty sure that setting my own broken arm was still one of those "Oh, hell no!" things.

One thing at a time. Find the lunchbox. Find my phone. Call for help. Whether I could heal myself up or not, I was still in a real mess.

The creak of the back doors cut through my flailing thoughts. Relief hit me like a wave as the door banged down against the pavement. *Someone saw the wreck. They'll help me.* I struggled to my feet, but the van-on-its-side thing had me all disoriented, and it took me a couple of seconds to find my balance. The whack on my head and the blood running into my eyes didn't help. But I was coherent enough to see the figure crouched on the open back door of the van.

"Hey, man. Can you call 911?" I said. "I need some. . . ."

I trailed off as the stench hit me.

Rot. Death.

I knew that smell.

Oh, god. It's true.

The figure shifted forward, its breathing a low, rasping growl. I could only make out the silhouette, but it was enough.

Terror shot through me and my eyes fell to the stretcher and body bag, now lying cockeyed against the wall of the van. That's what this . . . this thing wanted. I *knew* that. This creature had probably dragged the tree into the road to make me stop.

Panic jabbed through me. I could maybe explain away the accident, but there was no way I could explain losing the body.

"No!" I struggled to get up and around the damn seats. "Get away! You can't have it!"

It ignored me and grabbed the black plastic and pulled, but the bag was still belted to the stretcher and the whole thing was pretty well jammed into the corner. That bought me a few more seconds. I could see it better now. Male, probably white, though the face was too decomposed to be completely sure. One eye was clouded over and dark teeth were visible through a bloodless gash in one cheek. Its hands had ribbons of skin trailing from them and several fingernails were missing.

That . . . is a zombie, I silently shrieked to myself. *Holy fucking shit. That's a motherfucking zombie, and this shit is real.*

I didn't dare think about what that meant. I wanted to curl up and moan in horror, but I didn't have time for that shit. I couldn't let this thing—this *zombie*—get my body. Pain twinged somewhere deep in my chest as I clambered over the seat, but I barely noticed it. I lost my balance but somehow managed to fall on top of the bag and the stretcher without crushing my broken arm any further, though my vision went dark for a couple of seconds from the flash of new pain. I wanted to lie there for a minute and wait for the nausea and dizziness to fade, but the zombie growled and tugged harder.

"Let go!" I said, gasping the words out. "Get out of here. You can't have it!" I wrapped my good arm through the bars of the stretcher and did my best to pin the bag down with my skinny-ass weight. I didn't know how much good it would do. The zombie was still damn strong, even as rotted as it was. It was probably hungry as all hell too, I realized—which meant it wasn't about to give up.

Hungry.

I scanned frantically around the back of the van. Crap was everywhere—my purse, extra body bags, boxes of latex gloves, sheets and plastic for really messy bodies. . . . I finally saw my lunchbox, lying open and empty. *Oh, shit.*

The zombie gave the body bag another hard yank, and I let out a shriek as the stretcher and I slid forward. Then I saw what the movement had revealed—a plastic bottle wedged in the corner.

Releasing my death grip on the stretcher, I snatched it up. "Here! You can have this!"

The zombie merely snarled and tugged again, nearly dislodging me. My pulse slammed with barely controlled panic. One more tug and we'd all be out on the pavement and, as hurt as I was, I'd have no chance of fighting it off. I clamped my teeth around the cap of the bottle and twisted, performing the fastest one-handed bottle-opening I could manage.

I spat the cap out and I thrust the bottle forward again. "Take this!" I tried to wave it under the creature's nose but only managed to spill some of it onto the body bag.

It worked anyway. The zombie froze, nose twitching. Then its good eye locked onto the bottle. It let out a low growl, rotting lips pulling back from even nastier teeth.

"Take it!" I pleaded, still holding the bottle out. "Just don't take the body. Please. I'll lose my job!" Not that the zombie cared, I knew. It looked like it was too far gone right now to listen to any sort of reason.

The zombie snatched the bottle from my hand and tipped it back, draining the contents in a matter of seconds. Shuddering, it dropped the empty bottle, then crouched again and wrapped its arms around its legs. I watched, hope and terror doing the tango in my gut.

After about half a minute he lifted his head. Most of the rot had receded, and already I could tell he didn't smell anywhere near as bad. And now I knew who he was. Zeke Lyons, and he worked at Billings Funeral Home.

No. *Used* to work there. He'd been fired about two weeks ago when he was caught taking jewelry off the corpses—which explained why he was in his current state. I tasted bile on the back of my tongue. Two weeks without brains . . . and he was a rotted mess.

"More," he rasped.

I shook my head, frantic. "No. I can't give you any more." My voice sounded shrill and thin to my ears, and I knew I looked and smelled terrified. I'd stopped him for the moment, but I'd also made him stronger. I could only hope he was coherent enough to listen to reason now. "I can give you more tomorrow, okay?" I said, nearly stammering. "Come by the morgue tomorrow."

He flexed his hands, looking down at them. They were whole again. He looked almost normal. Disheveled and dirty, but now he simply looked like a bum, not the walking dead. "I'm hungry *now*," he said in a snarl, then his gaze snapped to me, both eyes whole and clear. And blue. He probably wasn't bad looking at all when he was whole.

"What are you?" I had to force the question out. I didn't want to hear the answer. I didn't want to know it was true.

His eyes narrowed. "Zombie," he said, then gave a dry laugh that sounded like tearing paper. "You're new."

I gave him a shaky nod, nausea roiling in my gut. I was still lying on top of the stretcher, clinging tightly with the one hand. I didn't trust him to not snatch for the bag again.

"I remember when I was new." His voice was so low I could barely hear him. "Starving all the time. Like this." Desperation glittered in his eyes. "You won't share."

"I will! I swear!" Panic surged as he reached for the bag again. "But not if you take the body." I was babbling, struggling to get the words out to make him understand. "If I lose my job I won't be able to help you." And I'd be screwed too, but I knew he didn't care about that.

A flicker of light in the distance seized my attention. "There's a car coming," I told him. "Please, go. Run! Come to the morgue and I swear, I'll give you more." I was crying now. "*Please.*" I didn't know what else to say.

He jerked his head around, lip curling at the sight of headlights far down the highway. He let out a low hiss, and I could see the two survival instincts battling within him—his current, desperate need versus the fear of discovery.

Fear won, and a second later he spun and loped off into the swamp.

I wanted to sag in relief and curl up into a ball, but I wasn't in the clear yet. I was a mess and I needed to do something about it. Being out of work because I was injured would be as bad as losing my job.

I pushed myself up to my knees and began frantically shoving body bags and other crap aside. My broken arm screamed in pain even through the dulling of my senses, but my panic was a lot louder. There'd been two bottles in the lunchbox. The other one had to be somewhere around here.

The approaching vehicle was close enough for me to hear the engine by the time I finally spied the second bottle wedged behind the driver's seat. I grabbed it and repeated the trick of opening it with my teeth, chugged it back as fast as I could, shaking it to get the thick chunks at the bottom.

I sagged against the wall of the van and closed my eyes. A lovely warmth spread through me, coupled with the eerie sensation of my bones sliding back into place and the skin of my arm and forehead knitting back together. Then the sensation faded and a jab of hunger spiked through me.

I opened my eyes and let out a low sigh of relief. The bone wasn't sticking out of my arm anymore, and I could sense that it was pretty much back together though not fully healed by a long stretch. And when I lifted my hand to my forehead, I could feel my skull through the break in the skin, but at least now it was only a gap of a few centimeters instead of several inches. I'd probably been hurt worse than I'd realized. One bottle wasn't enough to deal with it all.

Might be better this way, I tried to convince myself. It would be pretty damn weird to be covered in blood if there wasn't a scratch on me. I simply had to hope to god that I wouldn't be forced into taking time off for medical leave. If I still had a job at all.

My stomach twisted again as I crawled over the body bag toward the back door. I almost laughed as the scent of the body inside it hit me, and I pushed back the brief urge to rip open the bag and take care of the deep craving. Yeah, that would be my usual method, doing the right thing and then screwing it all up anyway.

I made it out of the van just as the approaching pickup screeched to a stop. Two middle-aged men leaped out and came toward me at a run—the driver already on his cell phone, calling for help. I tried to stand, but my legs weren't having any of it, and I ended up sitting on the ground by the van.

Glass and shards of broken mirror littered the pavement, echoing the night sky. I kept my eyes on the two men and didn't look down. If I saw my reflection right now, I knew I'd see the same hunger I'd seen in the zombie.

The *other* zombie.

Chapter 11

"Angel. Angel? How many fingers am I holding up?"

Blue and red lights flickered across my vision, bouncing off the broken glass littering the highway and casting bizarre shadows as highway workers pulled the tree out of the road. The crackle of radios mixed with the buzz of conversation in an excited white noise that made it tough to concentrate on any one thing. The metal of the van was warm on my back, and I found myself pressing against it in a vain attempt to keep the slight chill in the air from seeping into me. Mist was beginning to form in the swamp, slowly creeping out onto the road to give the entire scene a surreal and far-too-spooky feel. *I was just attacked by a zombie*, I thought sourly. *I don't need the horror movie special effects, thank you very much.*

I dragged my gaze away from the swamp and back to the paramedic crouched in front of me. "Three," I replied. I was tempted to make a smartass remark but managed to resist. Even if I'd had a concussion right after the accident, I was fairly positive I didn't have one now. And the last thing I needed was to be kept out of work for any longer than necessary.

The paramedic made a low noise in his throat and proceeded to shine an annoying light into my eyes. He looked familiar and a glance at his nametag confirmed it. *Quinn*. Oh, right. Ed Quinn. The paramedic who'd worked on me when I overdosed.

"We need to stop meeting like this," I said, making myself give him a wry smile. I didn't feel much like smiling, wryly or otherwise, but I figured I'd make as good a show as possible of being all right. "At least I have clothing on this time," I added. Yeah, much better to make a joke out of that last horrible time. Not that I remembered any of it. Then again, that made it easier to laugh it off.

His eyes crinkled as he smiled. "I could say something really inappropriate here, but I'll be good." He peered at my forehead. "That cut doesn't look very big, and it's not bleeding anymore. If you're worried about a scar they can probably throw a few stitches onto that in the ER."

I already knew I didn't need to worry about scars, but I gave him a small nod anyway.

He patted me lightly on the shoulder. "Looks like you got out of this one with only a couple of cuts. Good thing you were wearing your seatbelt."

"Damn straight," I said, and I didn't have to fake the note of fervor in my voice. Maybe I wouldn't have died, but I probably would have been too messed up to fight the zombie off.

Zombie. *Holy shit.* I managed to hold in the shudder of horror until Ed turned away. I didn't need him thinking I was going into shock or anything like that. Though in a way I kinda felt like I was. *Is that what I have to look forward to?*

There were advantages, though. Right? I mean, the whole "eat brains and heal up" thing could come in pretty handy. Plus there was that whole business about being strong and fast—as long as I was tanked up on brains.

So, yeah, this whole thing had its moments.

But, damn, I could do without the *hunger.* I had a bit of a stash at home right now—enough to get me through at least a week, I hoped. And if I was out of work for longer than that, then what? How long could I go without brains? Not two weeks, that was for sure. I'd already figured out that the more active I was, the faster I got hungry—which made sense in a way. But how much of my stash would I go through to get me back to normal?

A deputy crouched beside me, and I stiffened automatically when I saw that it was Marcus Ivanov. For a stupid instant I wondered if the guy was stalking me, then instantly dismissed the thought as completely retarded. I hadn't even seen him since that day we'd all gone to breakfast. St. Edwards Parish wasn't very big, which meant there weren't that many road deputies. It made sense that I'd see him more than every now and then.

He gave me a tight smile that didn't come anywhere near his eyes. "Angel, I need you to tell me as much as you can remember about the accident."

I let out a breath and forced myself to chill. I was the victim this time. So what if I felt like I was going into an interrogation? "Sure, though there's not much to tell," I said. "I was driving. I came around the curve and saw a tree in the road. I hit it."

His eyes narrowed. "Did you see anyone?"

I hesitated. "I thought the tree was a person at first. Then I realized it was only a branch sticking up. Why?"

He pursed his lips briefly and looked back toward the tree that was still partially in the road. "It looked like someone deliberately dragged that tree onto the highway. There are footprints and scuff marks." He paused and returned his gaze to me. "And dirt on the van door."

My pulse thudded as my mind raced. I hadn't said anything to anyone about the zombie trying to get the body bag, for obvious reasons. But if there was physical evidence that someone had caused the accident, would they get suspicious if I didn't say anything?

"That's fucked up," I finally managed. "I'm pretty positive that tree wasn't in the road when I was going the other way. I figured it fell or something." I shook my head, and I didn't have to fake the wince the motion caused. "Sorry. I was kinda rattled there right after it happened, y'know? Maybe the dirt was from someone checking to see if I was okay." I gave a helpless shrug. "I dunno. It had to be random, right? I mean, why would anyone want me to crash?" I made myself laugh. "Unless they wanted to steal the body so they could make a monster."

His expression grew tighter, if that was even possible. "It was probably some punks being stupid," he said. Then he took a deep breath as if forcing himself calm. "I know you're shaken now, but if you remember anything later on, that'll help us find out who did this."

"Fuckers," Ed muttered as he jotted notes on his pad. "You could have been killed."

"The whole situation is fucked," Ivanov said. My stomach knotted at the vehemence in his voice. I *thought* he was angry at the idea that someone else had done this, but the paranoid side of me wasn't sure if maybe part of it was directed at me. He knew me, knew my whole sordid history. Surely he thought I was somehow at fault. How could he not?

I looked away and blinked quickly at the flashing lights of the ambulance as stupid tears filled my eyes. Crap. Here I was getting all weepy because this deputy might think I was even more of an irresponsible piece of shit than I was. God, I was pathetic.

"Hey, dickhead, you're upsetting my girlfriend," Ed said with a not-so-gentle shove to Ivanov's shoulder. "Cut it out."

Ivanov leveled a scowl at Ed. "I'm sure Angel has higher standards than a jackass like you. Besides, the girlfriend you already have might have an issue with this."

Ed merely gave a snort. "Yeah, well you're doing your angry-scary-grouchy face. You keep doing that you're going to get unsightly wrinkles."

Ivanov blinked and gave me a sharp look, then his expression softened, much to my surprise. "I didn't mean to upset you. You're going to be fine. And we'll find those asshole punks who did this."

"I'm cool," I said as I fought to get my emotions under control and maintain something vaguely resembling dignity. "Sorry."

Ed smacked Ivanov on the back of the head. "Yeah, 'cause I'll kick his ass if he doesn't."

Ivanov lifted a fist with a threatening snarl, and I sucked in a breath. His gaze flicked briefly to me, registering my shock, and he grinned and lowered his fist. "Sorry," he said, and now I could see the laughter in his eyes. "Ed and I have known each other since we were kids. He thinks he can get away with battery on a police officer, and one of these days I'm gonna slap cuffs on his skinny ass."

Ed merely smiled serenely. "And the next time you get a boo-boo in the line of duty, I'll be sure to tell the ER folks that you're too much of a man to need painkillers."

The deputy snorted. "Speaking of, you need to stop dicking around and get her to the ER."

"Get the hell out of my way, and I'll do that," Ed said with a glare at the deputy. Ivanov gave a low laugh, then gave me a wink as he stood and walked off. I stared after him for several seconds as I struggled to make sense of this side of the gruff deputy.

"He can be Mr. Grouchy Pants," Ed said quietly, "but I think this time it was more worry than anything. We'll get you checked out, and then everyone will be happier."

"I'm not hurt that bad," I insisted, even as I wondered if the deputy had really been worried about me. "All I need is a Band-Aid for my head."

"You could be an extra in a slasher movie with all the blood you have on you," Ed said, "but I'll be damned if I can find any other cuts besides that one. You must have hit one hell of a bleeder."

I gave what I hoped was a neutral shrug. "I feel all right. I really can't afford to miss a bunch of work."

"I don't know if you'll be kept out of work, but since you were driving the Coroner van, I'm sure you're going to have to do a urinalysis—a piss test." He shrugged.

"Oh." Shit. It had been weeks since I'd smoked that pot with Randy, and it'd been over a week since I'd taken any pills, so surely I was clean now, right? "Oh, yeah. Okay." God, I hoped so. "But I really don't need to ride on the stretcher, okay?"

Ed gave me a reassuring pat on the shoulder. "If you can walk, that's fine."

I made it into the ambulance without falling over, then proceeded to worry about the piss test the entire way to the hospital. Would the drugs show up? Or worse, would the fact that I was a . . . a zombie? I had a feeling I was being stupid, but at least it managed to distract me from all of the other stuff on my mind. Maybe someday I wouldn't have anything to worry about. Wouldn't that be a shock.

When we got to the ER, Ed hopped out then gave me a hand to help me down. I gave him my left without thinking, then had to bite back a yell of pain when he took hold of my arm to assist me. The crap on my arm had closed up all the way, but obviously it wasn't totally healed.

"You gonna make it?" he asked, peering at my face with worry. "You just went pale. I can put you on the stretcher if you need it."

I took a deep breath. "I'm cool. Sorry. Probably straightened too fast." I pulled away from his grasp as gently as I could, trying to not be obnoxious about jerking my arm away or anything. I sure as shit didn't want anyone to know about the arm thing. If they x-rayed it and saw that it was still kinda broken, I'd definitely be out of work for a while. I simply had to make it until I got home, and then I could down a Percocet or....

I scowled to myself. No. No painkillers for me. None of that shit worked on me anymore. That sucked ass.

Brains instead. I sighed. *Too fucking weird.*

Ed somehow managed to cut through the usual procedures, and I was settled into an exam room within a few minutes. The nurse came in and I nearly flinched when I recognized her as the bitchy redhead from the last time I was here. I kept waiting for her to start in with the snide looks, but she merely took my vitals and left.

"Hate that fuckin' bitch," Ed muttered, and I had to stifle a bark of laughter. He gave me a sheepish grin. "Sorry. I got bit by a dog last year, and she was so nasty it was as if she thought I deserved to get bit."

I wanted to respond, but the door opened and half the Coroner's Office poured in. At least it seemed that way. In reality it was only Derrel and Allen Prejean, followed by—to my enormous shock—the coroner, Dr. Duplessis. But none of the men were small, and the already tiny room seemed suddenly overcrowded.

Ed gave my arm a squeeze—the unbroken one, thankfully. "Take care of yourself, Angel. And don't take this the wrong way, but I'd rather not meet you like this again."

I grinned. "I'm cool with that."

He gave me a parting smile, then left me to fend off a barrage of questions from the three remaining men.

Chapter 12

I gazed morosely at the contents of the little fridge in my room. Actually, gazing at the contents didn't take long since the damn thing was empty, but I crouched there with the door open for several minutes anyway, as if my stash would magically regenerate if I wished hard enough. The cold air flowed out onto my bare feet but I might as well have been wearing socks for all I felt it. I absently rubbed my fingertips together, dully annoyed at the faint lack of sensation. My stomach gave an unpleasant twist—like I needed the reminder that I was a few hours past my usual, every-other-day feeding schedule. Great. Everything else faded, but I could still feel the damn hunger.

Used to be that I *wanted* the edge taken off the world. Hell, that's why I'd turn to pills or pot or booze. But this was different. It was like the longer I went without brains, the more dead I became.

And that scared the living shit out of me.

After Ed had left me in the ER I'd been subjected to a barrage of questions that made Ivanov's "interrogation" look like a poetry reading. Derrel was clearly worried and distressed, Allen was annoyed and suspicious—and kept muttering under his breath about the loss of the van—and Dr. Duplessis was somewhere in between. I told my story as best I could, keeping it as close to the truth as possible while leaving out the bit about the zombie. To my relief the faint shadow of suspicion in the coroner's eyes faded as I finished up my version of what happened. And when my piss test came back clean—thank god—even Allen seemed to unbend enough to show actual concern.

Unfortunately, I still ended up with three days off from work. It wasn't even punishment either, which was the totally bizarre thing about it. It was *with pay*, and the coroner most likely thought he was being super nice, giving me extra time to make sure I was all right. Normally I'd have been thrilled to get time off with pay. I mean, the coroner was being incredibly cool to do that for me, especially since I was so new. Usually you had to be there for three months before you could get any type of paid leave. And what was I supposed to say? "Gee, thanks for giving me paid time off, but that's not why I need to come to work. I need to dig through dead bodies 'cause I'm starving, yo."

At least it was only three days. If I hadn't tanked up on some brains out at the accident scene, I'd have probably been forced to stay out for a couple of weeks to hide how fast I could heal up when properly fed. *And then I'd have been like that other zombie.* A chill went through me that had nothing to do with the open fridge.

I closed the fridge, stood. I was back on call tomorrow. One more day. I could last until then, right? I wasn't even smelly yet. Well, not too much. I counted the days: I'd slugged down my last brains day before yesterday, and I was supposed to go back to work tomorrow. Three days without brains. I'd never gone that long before.

Unfortunately, I'd burned through my stash faster

than I'd expected getting healed up. I'd been able to bullshit the ER doc, but my stupid body had let me know that it felt like shit. I wasn't tough enough to fight my appetite when it was clawing at me like I'd swallowed a wolverine.

But how long did I have? I needed a goddamn manual. And why the hell couldn't Anonymous Letter Dude give me some clues and pointers? *Okay, I ate the damn brains. I've figured out that I need to keep this job. Great. You win. Now, could I please get a clue?*

The "one month" mark was in a few days, and still no sign or word from whoever'd arranged the whole thing with the job. I'd really been hoping that at some point I'd get a "Way to go!" or "I knew you could do it!" or even a "Hi, my name is blank, and I've been your mentor." I scowled. Not a mentor, though. A mentor would have given me some actual advice and instruction on how to handle this whole brain thing. Not just a stupid "If you crave it, eat it" note.

I really hoped I wasn't expected to figure this crap out on my own.

I peered at myself in the mirror. What would I look like all rotted and gross like that guy had been? There were shadows under my eyes, and I looked as if I'd been awake for way too long, but I didn't have parts falling off. Yet. I shivered, then stuck a Band-Aid onto my forehead where the cut on my head had been. I didn't want people wondering how I could have healed up so fast. I still wasn't sure what I was going to do about the fact that there wasn't a scar. Maybe get my hair cut so I had bangs that covered my forehead? I made a face. Bangs. Ugh. I'd rather have parts falling off.

My dad wasn't home so I checked my money situation and then headed out. I had an attack of responsibility and used a good portion of my last paycheck to do stupid things like paying bills—even paid the cable bill, which had been cut off. Hopefully this would get around having to give money to my dad, especially since I wasn't so sure he'd actually pay bills with the money anyway.

My stomach grumbled at me after I dropped off a payment at the power company and I wavered badly on whether to try and sneak into the morgue to snag some brains. The big problem was the fact that I had to use a key card to get in—which meant that it would be logged in the system. Coming in once or twice off-shift wouldn't be a huge deal, but it would definitely be noticed if I made a habit of it. Especially since the previous van driver had been caught stealing. The last thing I wanted was any more attention.

It's only one more day, I reminded myself. *It's not worth the risk.*

I caught a scent of fried chicken as I passed a diner on the corner, and my stomach gave another lurch. I almost laughed in relief. This was hunger . . . not Hunger. I still needed to eat regular food—something I'd almost forgotten to do when I was healing up from the wreck. Hell, I tended to forget it a lot when I was low on brains, and forgetting had the unfortunate effect of making me even *more* ravenous for brains since I was basically starving myself. It didn't help that food tended to be kinda tasteless if I wasn't tanked up on brains.

Maybe I can start a new diet craze, I thought with a snicker as I turned in to the parking lot for the Piggly Wiggly. *Become a zombie. Cut your appetite in half.* For real food, at least.

Pausing my cart by the meat section, I peered down at the various selections of animal flesh. Did it have to be *human* brains? If I could get the same effect from animal brains, that would make this whole thing a helluva lot less fucked up and a helluva lot easier. Animal brains would be easier to get, right? Though I couldn't see myself actually killing an animal. Yeah, I was a bit of a redneck, but I got squeamish putting worms on hooks. *Would I still be?* I wondered suddenly. I used to throw up at the slightest gross thing, and now I was handling brains like a pro. *Yeah, but actually killing something is a whole 'nother thing entirely.*

"Can I help you?"

I jerked my gaze up to see the butcher giving me a bored and questioning look. "Um, yeah. Do y'all ever sell, um, brains? I mean, like, animal brains?"

He didn't look bored anymore. Now his expression was more along the lines of "are you fucking nuts?"

"I mean, not to eat or anything," I quickly added, tacking on a laugh for good measure, though it sounded strained and fake to my ears. "That would be pretty gross, right?"

He eyed me dubiously. "And dangerous, too. Mad cow disease. That sort of thing."

I blinked. Maybe that's what I had? Some sort of disease?

"But to answer your question," he continued, "No, we don't carry that sort of thing here. Does it have to be a cow brain?"

I shook my head, not trusting myself to speak in case I came across as a complete lunatic. Instead of the partial lunatic he probably already thought I was.

He pursed his lips and frowned. "Is this for some sort of school project or something?"

"Yeah!" I exclaimed, leaping on the excuse. "That's it. A project." Did I look young enough to be in high school? Or maybe he thought I was in college. Ha. Like that would ever happen.

A low snort escaped him. "My advice would be to find someone who hunts. Get them to give you the brain when they process the carcass."

Process the carcass. That sounded oddly hideous. I gave him a weak smile. "Gotcha. Thanks."

He gave me a stiff nod, then moved down the counter to help another customer—no doubt someone who actually wanted meat. I let out a breath. Wonderful. Getting animal brains was as hard, if not harder, than getting human brains. And I had no idea if they'd even work the same way.

"Hey, Angel!"

I swung around with a guilty start to see Monica Gaudreau, one of the other death investigators at the Coroner's Office. Monica was a short and chunky redhead with a bright personality and a voice raspy from too many cigarettes. Not that she let her raspy voice stop her from talking fast enough to make your head spin. *Oh, god, did she hear me asking about brains?*

But to my relief she merely flashed me a broad smile. "So the rumors that you're alive and well after doing somersaults in the van are true!"

I blinked. "Umm. Rumors?"

She laughed. "Rumors, fact, whatever. You know how it is around that office. I swear, I think the secretary moonlights as a gossip columnist. Hell, she'd make a killing. Maybe I'll suggest it to her! Anyway, good to see that you're doing all right. I saw the van in the wrecker yard. I can't believe you're up and around!" Then she surprised me by giving my arm a squeeze. "Damn glad, too. It would suck having to deal with one of our own. Besides, you keep Nick on his toes."

I managed a weak grin in the face of her machine-gun style of speech.

"Ew. Do you smell that?" she said, nose wrinkling. "I think the meat in the cooler's going bad. Anyway, good thing you were wearing your seatbelt, huh? Heck, the main reason I wear mine is because I don't want any of the schmucks we work with to see me naked on the table in the cutting room." She gave a mock shudder. "Pervs!"

"Yeah, no kidding," I finally got in, somehow keeping

the smile fixed on my face. It wasn't the meat in the cooler going bad.

"Well, good to see you doing so well. See you at work!" And then she was off down the aisle, pushing her cart at breakneck speed and snatching items off the shelves without a hitch in her stride.

I took a deep breath after she was out of sight, partly to regain my equilibrium after the less than a minute in her presence, but also to try and ground myself in the realization that the people I worked with had been worried about me and gave a shit.

How cool was that?

In odd parallel to my earlier fridge staring, Dad was staring bleakly into the fridge in the kitchen when I got home. He looked up and closed it when I entered, surprise lighting his eyes as I plopped several plastic grocery bags onto the counter. He had a beer in his hand and when I did a quick scan of the kitchen I saw only one empty. Good. That meant I was hitting the sweet spot in his sobriety. Just enough buzz to take the edge off and keep him being a cranky asshole, but not so much that he'd progress to being mean and ugly and compelled to detail my numerous failings as a person and a daughter. Defensive much?

"Hey, Dad, I got those burritos you like so much." I dug through the bags and pulled a couple out. A smile flickered across his mouth, and I felt a little bump of pleasure that I'd thought to get them. He could be a real shit sometimes, but he was still my dad. He'd been there for me when it had mattered the most, even though it had damn near killed him. Yeah, everything had gone to shit after that in other ways, but it taught me to keep my expectations real low.

"Thanks, Angelkins. I was about to go down to the corner and get some fried chicken."

I made a face. "That stuff'll give you the runs."

He snorted. "Like the burritos won't?" But he pulled a plate out of the cabinet and snagged one of the frozen burritos.

"Yeah, well, I got some decent food too." Glancing at my dad as I unloaded the bags, I pulled out a bag of apples. "You should eat some fruit after you eat that. You'll feel better."

He didn't look up as he unwrapped the burrito and stuck the plate into the microwave. "I'd feel better if my daughter had told me she'd been in an accident." He punched the start button, then turned to me, an odd expression of hurt shimmering in his face.

I sighed. Small towns and the gossip mill. *Yeah, well, you were passed out on the couch when I made it home from the ER the other night, and I was relieved since I didn't want to deal with questions about why I was covered in blood. I knew you'd either be an asshole or you'd pretend to be concerned and caring—depending on how drunk you were, and I didn't want to deal with either reaction.* The times that he was like this—almost normal and real—were so rare that they were damn near precious. And I'd learned to never count on them.

"I didn't want to worry you," I said instead. "I wasn't hurt other than a little cut on my head. It wasn't my fault, so I didn't get in any trouble or anything."

"You still coulda told me," he mumbled, though there wasn't much conviction behind it. It was as if he knew how unpredictable his reactions could be. Hell, I was sure he did know, though that made it tougher to deal with in a way. If he knew how much of an asshole he could be, why couldn't he stop being one?

"Sorry," I mumbled back. I busied myself with putting food away for a few minutes. "You going anywhere? I was gonna cook dinner tonight for the two of us."

He gave me a doubtful look, and I had to grin. "Okay, I bought some stuff I can heat up," I amended. "But it's still better than that gas station chicken, right?"

"That'd be nice, Angel. Did you buy more beer?"

I ignored the twinge of uneasiness in my gut and pointed to the bag at the end of the counter. "Just a six-pack. I paid all the bills today, and I was running out of money." That was a lie. I had a case in the trunk of my car, but I wasn't going to bring the whole thing in. Things were cool right now. If he drank a six-pack it probably wouldn't make much difference except to keep him mellow. But if I brought the case inside, he'd be drunk and vicious by the end of the night.

I'd learned how to dole it out to him. Sure, I was a shit daughter for giving him booze and enabling his alcoholism. If anyone wanted to call me out on it, they were welcome to spend a week with him and see what it was like.

He shuffled off to the living room with the six-pack while I finished putting things away. The instructions for the frozen lasagna said it would take thirty minutes to cook, so I stuck that in the oven and set about trying to clear out some of the dirty dishes in the sink. The dishwasher hadn't worked in years, and the usual routine was that one of us would break down and hand wash dishes about the time we ran out of either clean plates or counter space.

A soapy glass slipped out of my hand to burst into a million pieces on the kitchen tile.

"You okay?" my dad shouted from the living room.

"Yeah," I called back, crouching as I watched the larger pieces slowly spin to a stop in shallow pools of suds. A shudder swept over me, along with a memory from what had to be over ten years ago. I'd been carrying my plate from the kitchen to the table and had dropped it in this exact spot. The plate had broken into three perfect pieces, but the food—red beans and rice—had spattered all over the floor.

I couldn't remember what happened next, but I didn't really want or need to. The next piece of the memory was of me huddled in the corner by the refrigerator and bleeding from a cut on my arm, Dad wrestling a piece of the broken plate away from my mom, her screaming about me and how awful I was and her horrible life. . . .

My fingers brushed the scar on my tricep. After ten years I could barely feel it anymore. Taking a shaking breath, I began to gather up the larger pieces of glass. After dumping them into the trash bin I found the broom and swept up the rest of the glass, then went ahead and swept the whole kitchen. Yeah, Mom had been crazy, but at least the house hadn't been a shithole when she was around.

Bending to pull the mop bucket out of the closet, I paused, staring at the slender triangle of glass sticking out of my lower shin. It wasn't big—maybe an eight of an inch wide at the base, and about an inch of it was sticking out. I swallowed, then pulled it out, instantly unnerved to see that another half inch of it had been buried in my leg. But it still didn't hurt. Or bleed. At least, not blood like I was used to. A thick and dark bead slowly welled up from the cut, as if forced there by gravity more than anything else.

Taking a shaking breath, I dropped the glass into the trash can, then pressed my fingers to my neck, seeking a pulse.

I don't have one! I began to mentally wail just as I felt a low throb. Going completely still, I kept my fingers pressed to my neck as I silently counted. *One one-thousand. Two one-thousand. . . .*

The vein throbbed beneath my fingers. Two seconds later it throbbed again. I dropped my hand as unease tightened my gut. Okay, so a heartbeat every two seconds. I wasn't the greatest at math, but even I could figure out that meant my pulse rate was about thirty—and I'd been around the medical types long enough to know that thirty beats per minute wasn't considered terribly healthy. Yet I wasn't dizzy or light-headed. I was simply . . . hungry.

My mood did backflips while I pulled the mop and bucket out of the closet. I knew I should be more freaked out, but weirdly it all made sense considering everything else I'd experienced. I'd bled totally normally when the van wrecked, but I was well-fed on brains at the time.

Was I really alive at all? Or was I *more* alive when I was full on brains, and less when I wasn't?

Scowling, I swiped the mop across the floor. What difference did it make anyway? I was still moving, and that was what ultimately mattered.

Right?

Right. Being kinda dead is nothing to worry about at all, I thought.

I turned my attention to the sinkful of nasty dishes and did my best to put questions about how alive I was or wasn't out of my head. By the time the lasagna was done the floor was clean, the dishes were washed and put away, and I'd managed to replace my worry over my degree of alive-ness with a healthy distaste for how dirty the kitchen had been.

This is the cleanest this place has been in years, I thought with a grimace as I pulled the food out of the oven. Had my dad and I simply given up? *Yeah, that's exactly what we did.* It didn't happen immediately, but after Mom was gone somehow we came to a point where we accepted that there was no point in trying to keep things clean or make things right. I know I had.

But now my situation wasn't complete shit. Or rather, it was shit in different ways. I ate brains, but at least now I knew I wasn't crazy. Not after seeing the other zombie. I knew what I was—well, I was about 98% sure—even if I had no fucking idea how I'd ended up that way.

However, right now I wasn't craving brains as much as a damn clue. How the fuck did this happen to me? Shit, maybe I *did* overdose, and then . . . what? Maybe Zeke the Zombie could fill me in. I'd told him to come to the morgue, but what if he came by while I was out on this leave? Would he come back? I wasn't all that eager to share brains with him, but I was also getting desperate for some information, some sort of framework I could put this whole crazy scenario into.

Surely he'd come back. He needed brains.

And so do I. Yeah, I'm a brain eater. A zombie. That's still shit. That's not normal. I was never going to be normal again. Why the hell was I trying so hard?

Chapter 13

I practically sang for joy when I got the call at six A.M. to pick up a body.

I'd never been so eager to get back to work in my entire life. And, strangely, it wasn't only because I was completely out of brains. Yeah that was a huge part of it, especially since I was feeling more and more dead—the sky looked grey, even though it was cloudless, and I'd turned the radio off because it sounded like a bunch of tuneless jangling. Plus, I was obscenely hungry. But for the first time I actually felt as if I was "one of the gang" where I worked. Maybe it had something to do with the type of job it was. Maybe we felt closer to each other because no one else could possibly understand what it was like to be around death all the time.

I snorted. Look at me, trying to be all philosophical and shit. Maybe I simply liked my job because the money was good, the people were cool, and it wasn't in a convenience store. Either way, I was damn glad to be back at it.

As I neared the address, I let out a low whistle. This was no ordinary body pickup. The street was lined with sheriff's cars and a bunch of unmarked cars, as well as two crime scene vans. An ambulance was departing in the opposite direction as I neared the address, but it didn't seem to be in any hurry.

This is a crime scene, I realized with an absurd little thrill. A real one, not simply some guy who dropped dead in his living room. *It must be a murder!*

Okay, it wasn't as if I wanted someone to get knocked off. I wasn't that much of a sicko. But I totally loved all those forensic cop shows, and this would be my first chance to really see the whole crime scene investigation thing up close, not merely watching a bored tech snapping some pics and taking a few measurements.

The ambulance had left a convenient opening in the row of cars, and I quickly pulled the van in before anyone else could claim it. Climbing out of the van, I saw that Derrel hadn't been so fortunate and was walking up to the house from practically the other end of the block.

"Lucky bitch," he said with a good-natured grumble, nodding to my primo parking spot.

"That's me," I replied. "And I'd have double-parked the damn thing if there'd been no spot. I ain't pushing a body down to the end of the street!"

Laughing, he gave me a wink and a thumbs up before he headed into the backyard. I grinned, spirits absurdly buoyed by the silly little show of camaraderie. Yeah, I was pretty easy to please. I tugged the stretcher and body bag out of the back of the van, kicked the doors closed and headed to the backyard, whistling as I pushed the stretcher before me. Crime tape was strung across the entrance to the backyard, and I enjoyed a dorky little thrill as I signed my name on the crime scene log before ducking under the tape.

We were in the backyard of a two-story brick house in the sort of subdivision that desperately wanted to be considered upscale but couldn't manage to break out of slightly above average. Surrounded by a white picket fence, the yard was expensively landscaped—decorative trees and artistically placed clumps of flowers, a koi pond in the corner complete with a cute wooden bridge over it that led to an equally cute gazebo, and expensive-looking paving stones forming twisty paths throughout the yard. I'd long ago accepted that I would never live in a house like this. My backyard was landscaped with a couple of decrepit cars on blocks and an old washtub that held mosquito larvae instead of fish.

My whistling stopped when I saw the body. "Son of a fucking bitch," I muttered.

Detective Ben Roth glanced at me and grinned. "Bit of a shocker, isn't it? You gonna be okay?"

I nodded and plastered on a grim smile. "Of course!" I said with a nonchalant shrug. "Less for me to have to pick up."

Detective Roth let out a bark of laughter. "That's one way of looking at it!"

As soon as he turned away, I let the grim smile shift to a sour scowl. I wasn't upset at the sight of the body. Or rather, I was, but certainly not because my delicate sensibilities were shocked. No, it was obvious that, once again, the universe was back to fucking with me.

This body had no head.

The second in a month. I let out an uneven breath. Okay, this was a good thing, right? I mean, not that someone else got whacked, but at least I knew there was no way I could have killed this guy. I didn't have any gaps in my memory this time. *And if the two murders are connected, then that totally clears me of the first one.* I winced at the thought. Great. I was hoping for a serial killer.

It looked like he'd been lying down when his head had been hacked off. Deep gouges in the grass by the stump of his neck helped support that theory. I wasn't a detective but even I could figure that much out. White male, dressed in jeans and a faded *Pizza Plaza* T-shirt. It was tough to tell his approximate age with the head missing, but the skin on the hands and forearms made me think he was somewhere between teenager and old fart.

The cops and Derrel would surely find it all interesting and informative, but I really didn't give a crap about any of that. Now that I was fairly sure that I wasn't an axe-wielding murderer, what I gave a crap about was the fact that if the head was missing, so was the brain.

And I was *hunnnnnngry*, damn it!

They weren't ready for me yet, so I found a spot by the fence out of everyone's way. There were about half a dozen crime scene techs in the back yard, but none of them seemed to be doing anything more interesting than taking pictures and measurements. Three detectives were clustered by the fence on the other side of the yard, peering intently at smudges of dirt on the white paint. Beyond the fence a petite, dark-haired woman dressed in brown fatigue pants and a grey T-shirt had a German shepherd on a long lead. She didn't look like a cop, but no one was chasing them off, so I figured they were a search dog team of some sort. They must be looking for the head, I decided. That was probably a cadaver dog—trained to find dead bodies. I'd heard of them but never seen one except on TV. I watched them for a few minutes, but they weren't doing anything very interesting, and I finally gave up and returned my attention to what was going on in the yard.

I could hear a female voice rise briefly in hysterical tones from the house, cutting through the crackle of police radios. After a couple of minutes of listening to the various buzzes of conversation, I gathered that the lady who lived here had discovered the body early this morning when she let her dog out to pee. A car with a *Pizza*

Plaza sign on it had been found parked in front of an unoccupied house a few blocks away, and apparently the driver had failed to return from a late delivery last night. The victim was tentatively identified as Peter Plescia, the missing driver, though this needed to be verified with fingerprints.

I scanned the area for the missing head but didn't see it lying conveniently nearby. Or even not so nearby. There weren't any bushes that could conceal a missing head, and I even snuck a quick glance in the koi pond, hoping to see a face peering back at me, but there was nothing but a bunch of oversized goldfish darting back and forth. Then again, if it had been anywhere in the yard, the dog would surely have found it by now.

A stab of hunger tightened my gut, and I chewed a fingernail as I waited. Even with the disappointment of no-brains it was still kinda exciting to be here for this—again, exciting in a weird, morbid way. The guy's head had been *chopped off.* That sure as shit wasn't an every day thing around here.

The cops were excited too, which made me feel a little less like a sick nutjob. There weren't many murders in this area, and hardly anything as lurid and sensational as this—especially twice in barely over a month.

The entire fingernail abruptly came off in my teeth. *Crap!* I quickly spat the fingernail out and hid my nail-less finger by my side, then plastered a smile on my face as Derrel approached.

"It looks like it's going to be a few more minutes while they take some pictures of some footprints by the fence," Derrel said. "Sorry. I probably could have let you sleep another half an hour."

"It's cool," I said. "It's actually kinda neat seeing all the CSI stuff."

He tilted his head. "This is your first murder scene, isn't it?"

"Yep. Got my cherry popped with a good one," I said with a nod toward the headless corpse.

"This is definitely more exciting than some I've been to."

"So, um, do the crime scene people ever do anything more—?"

He grinned. "Interesting? Cool? Full of neon and whiz bang chrome?"

I gave him a rueful smile. "Yeah. Is it always this boring?"

"Oh, no, not at all." Derrel gestured to where a red-haired man who didn't look much older than me was crouched and peering at the grass. He had on a jacket with *SEPSO Crime Scene* emblazoned across the back, and a scowl on his face. I'd seen him on scenes before. Nice guy who didn't have a problem helping me get the occasional body into a bag. I remembered that his name was Sean though I had no clue what his last name could be. This was the first time I'd ever seen him not smiling.

"See that guy?" Derrel continued. "Someone found a cigarette butt back here, and so the major has stated that he wants any cigarette butts to be collected as possible evidence."

My gaze slid to the back porch of the house, and I winced. "Dude. That's stupid. There are ashtrays on the table. The people who live here smoke. They probably smoke out here *all the time*. What, they think the guy was enjoying a smoke while he cut the pizza guy's head off?"

Derrel gave an emphatic nod of agreement. "Could be worse. I worked a murder a couple of years ago—happened in front of a house where a big party was going on. The captain in charge told the crime scene guys to collect all the empty beer cans in case there was a chance to use DNA to put a suspect at the scene. It was a big party. There were *hundreds* of empties. It was completely moronic, because not only would it have taken forever to get all the cans tested, but it would have blown the crime scene budget for the year to pay for it all. But the techs went ahead and gritted their teeth and collected the damn beer cans, because the captain told them to do so. The damn things are probably still in the evidence locker, unprocessed."

I let out a sigh. "You're shattering all my cool illusions about forensics."

Grinning, he clapped me on the shoulder. "That took less time than I expected!"

"Fucker. So, is that dog looking for the guy's head?" I asked. I was still hoping that it had been found and someone had simply covered it up or something so that it didn't look so gross. Then again, no one had covered the headless corpse.

"That's right. No luck so far though," he said with a shrug. "Guess whoever whacked him kept it as a souvenir."

"Ew." I frowned. "Is this one like the murder that happened out on Sweet Bayou Road? And was that guy's head ever found?"

"Yes to your first question, and no to your second. The cops are already having a field day coming up with theories." He swiped a hand over his scalp. "At least we have a head start on making an ID on the guy here. Makes my job a bit easier."

"The cops don't do the ID thing?" I asked.

"Nope, it's our responsibility, as is contacting any next of kin. However, we work pretty closely with the cops since they have the fingerprint systems and stuff like that."

Someone called Derrel's name and he glanced that way. "Looks like we're up." His nose twitched and his expression turned puzzled as he looked back to me. "Have you been handling decomps?"

Crap. My smell was worse than I thought. I gave him

a grimace, thinking furiously. "Um, a cat died under my house last week. My whole bedroom reeked, and I guess it got into my clothing. Sorry," I said with a grimace. "I washed it, but the smell really clings to it. I didn't notice until I was on my way here."

To my relief he seemed to buy the story and merely shrugged and walked off. I exhaled as I grabbed the body bag and headed to the corpse. I sure as hell couldn't tell him the real reason why I stank like a decomposing corpse.

I had to wrap a sheet around the stump of the guy's neck to keep the body from oozing blood or anything else that might come out. Derrel helped me get him into the bag and onto the stretcher, then I buckled the straps to keep everything in place and trundled my gruesome cargo out to the van.

Getting the stretcher and bag into the van wasn't all that hard since the van and stretcher were the kind that could be handled solo. But when I was trying to get it out at the morgue, I managed to get my forearm pinched in the back leg of the stretcher. No big deal if I'd been a normal, living human—other than probably hurting like hell and leaving me with a nasty bruise. But I wasn't normal—and a strip of skin about an inch wide and five inches long peeled right off.

I froze, looking down at the gaping wound in my arm. I wasn't really bleeding—just a sluggish pooling of black blood—which was almost as gross as the fact that I could see bone. And it didn't hurt. I mean, I could feel it, but only in the way you could feel pressure after a part of your body was numbed up. *Dying by bits and pieces.* Cold nausea tightened my gut as I quickly yanked the trailing skin off the stretcher and hurried into the morgue with my cargo. Tossing the skin into the first bio-hazard can I saw, I shoved the stretcher ahead of me on my way to the cooler, fighting back the urge to run. The floors were always slick in here, and I didn't want to dump the body bag on the floor, or bust my ass and end up with another piece of me falling off.

"Oh, thank you hail Mary Jesus!" I breathed as I entered the cooler and saw another body bag. The hunger rose as I shoved the stretcher against the wall, then turned and yanked the zipper of the other body bag open in one move.

"SHIT!" I looked down at the body, aggravated and distressed. Sure, this body had a head, which was an improvement on the one I'd brought in. But it hadn't been autopsied yet. Its brain was still nice and safe within its skull.

I quickly zipped the bag back up, then exited the cooler and headed to the computer. After skimming the schedule I allowed myself to feel a slim measure of relief. At least the autopsy was scheduled for this morning.

My eyes dropped to the gaping hole in my forearm. "That is seriously disgusting," I muttered, then took a deep breath to try and control my flailing panic. All I had to do was hide the fact that I was falling apart until the autopsy was finished. The good news was that the smell of the morgue would hide my own lovely odor.

Yeah, that wasn't much as far as good news went, but I was willing to take anything I could get at this point.

Chapter 14

"You're certainly raring to go, Angel." Dr. Leblanc gave me a quizzical smile as he picked up his clipboard.

I was already completely decked out in the protective gear—which, thankfully, had long sleeves—and gloves to cover the fact that I'd manage to lose another fingernail. I'd nearly been forced to resort to wearing a mask as well after I'd made the mistake of scratching an itch on my cheek. I'd felt the skin begin to peel away and stopped right before giving myself a gaping crater in the side of my face. *Wouldn't that have been lovely?* Several frantic minutes in the bathroom with a combination of makeup and—god help me—hair spray had provided a temporary patch, and right now it merely looked as if I was trying to cover up some serious acne. Or leprosy.

The body was also ready: stripped of clothing, with the block beneath the shoulder blades to make it easier to open up the body and examine the innards. I didn't want a single second to be wasted.

"You know me, Doc. I love me some dead bodies!" I said it with a deliberately cheeky grin, and he gave a laugh in return.

"Fortunately, we can accommodate you." He made his notes and then commenced with the Y-incision.

I did my best to be Super Morgue Tech, ready with every piece of equipment the pathologist needed before he could ask for it. I had to bite back a whoop of joy when he finally gave me the go-ahead to cut the head open. In fact, my anticipation was so great, I had to take several deep breaths to get my hands to stop shaking so that I could make the incision across the top of the head. Luckily, Dr. Leblanc was too busy slicing organs to notice.

When I opened the skull, the smell of the brains washed over me in such a heavy wave I had to grab the edge of the table to steady myself. The hunger rose up like a rabid piranha, and I gritted my teeth against the urge that wanted me to bury my face into that convoluted surface and suck it all down. Breathing shallowly, I carefully removed the brain from the skull and set it on the scale, then passed it over to Dr. Leblanc as soon as he took note of the weight.

He murmured thanks and then bent his head to slice into it. I moved to where I was directly behind him and surreptitiously sucked the juices off my fingers. A mistake, since that merely jabbed my appetite into full wakefulness. I only *thought* I'd been hungry before.

An eternity later Dr. Leblanc dropped a sample of the brain into a tub of formalin, and then dropped the rest of it into the plastic bag. "Okay, close him up," he said as he pulled his gloves off and dropped them into the hazardous waste container. "I have a deposition to get to, so I'm going to autopsy the headless one later this afternoon."

Not trusting my voice to work, I gave him a nod, then stepped up as soon as he moved away. I didn't give a shit about the headless guy. No brain meant no interest on my part. Busying myself with the needle and string, I waited, heart pounding as I listened to Dr. Leblanc's retreating footsteps, then I quickly dipped my hand into the bag and palmed a piece of brain. It wasn't big, only about the size of a walnut, but when I knelt to pretend I was tying my shoe it went down my throat like golden honey. The hunger gave one last wail before settling, momentarily satisfied with the offering. It wouldn't be enough to put me back to normal, but at least I could think straight and finish what I was doing.

I managed to sneak one more bite before closing everything up and putting the body back in the cooler. Then I did the smart thing and made absolutely certain there was no one left in the morgue. Dr. Leblanc had gone back to the main building for his deposition, and Nick and Pete were both off. *Now* I could eat as if my life depended on it.

I quickly tugged the zipper open and untied the bag. I was getting good at finding all of the brain pieces and getting them into a jar with a minimum of mess and fuss. Standing near the open door of the cooler, I kept an ear cocked for anyone entering while I ate the brain right out of the jar. Normally I'd have waited until I was away from the morgue to eat, but not now.

A relieved sigh escaped me as I savored the rush of returning sensations—including the strange tickle as my fingernails and skin grew back. The spot on my cheek itched again, but this time it was due to the bizarre glop of makeup and hairspray stuck to it. Smiling, I peeled it off and flicked it into a trash can.

There were only a few small chunks of brain left in the jar. It didn't surprise me that I'd managed to bolt down almost the entire brain, as famished as I was. That should hold me for a few days. Surely there'd be some bodies coming through by the time I needed more. I needed to build up a stash. I couldn't afford to let myself get that desperate again.

I jerked at the sound of the door buzzer, nearly dropping the jar and the last few chunks it held. *Crap.* The buzzer was from the back door of the morgue, which meant that someone from one of the funeral homes was here to pick up a body. That was yet another part of my job. Once a body had been autopsied and released by Dr. Leblanc, then someone from the chosen funeral home would come and pick up the body from us. For bodies that were released on the scene—which was quite a few, especially with elderly victims—the funeral home picked the bodies up right there. Saved me a lot of work, since if I had to pick up every old fart who croaked I'd be running bodies nonstop.

Taking a deep breath to settle my pounding heart, I snuck a quick peek out into the hallway to make absolutely certain that I was alone, then hurriedly tipped the jar back and downed the last few bits. I wrapped the empty jar in a bunch of paper towels and dumped the whole thing into a garbage can as the buzzer sounded again.

"Coming!" I called, suppressing a burst of aggravation. Snatching another paper towel, I dragged it across my face to get rid of any blood or brain juice on my chin, then ran my tongue over my teeth to be sure I didn't have any telltale chunks in my smile. Not that I expected people to know that the food caught in my teeth was brains, but still, anything caught in teeth would be gross.

I half-jogged to the back door and shoved it open. This door opened onto a broad covered walkway about twenty feet long, and beyond that a parking lot large enough to hold about a dozen cars. I usually parked back here since I spent most of my time in the morgue anyway. About the only times I went to the main building anymore was for staff meetings or to pick up my paycheck.

A funeral home van was parked at the end of the

walkway and an Asian-looking guy leaned up against the outside wall by the door, an empty stretcher parked on the sidewalk beside him. Maybe in his mid-twenties or so, he looked more like some sort of goth-punk rocker than a funeral home worker to me. His hair was cut in a spiky mop with one long lock that draped across his face, and he was wearing black pants embellished with zippers and chains. His T-shirt was plain black, which somehow seemed conservative considering the rest of his general look, though in the next second I decided that wearing something adorned with skulls might be frowned upon by the funeral home he worked for. I probably stared rudely for a couple of seconds before he pushed off the wall and grabbed the stretcher.

"Hi. Sorry," I said, holding the door for him as he pushed the stretcher in. "I was just finishing up after an autopsy. Hope you haven't been waiting long." I pressed my lips together to keep from smiling as I noted that he had a tiny skull earring in his left ear. *Wow, darlin', you digging the death thing a bit much, huh?*

"No big deal," he said with a casual shrug. He had the barest touch of accent, telling me he probably hadn't been born here, but it was so faint I figured he must have been only a kid when he'd come to the states. "I saw the van," he continued, "so I knew someone was here. I figured you had your hands full."

"Who are you here for?" I asked, pulling the door closed behind him..

He tugged a piece of paper out of his pocket and glanced at it. "Faust, Daniel."

I controlled my smile. Faust, Daniel was the fine gentleman whose brains I'd just chowed down on. "Got it. I'll bring him right out."

I retrieved the body from the cooler and brought it and the stretcher back out to the main room, then plopped into the computer chair. I was stupidly proud of myself that I'd picked up the computer system with little trouble, though my typing still sucked ass. "Okay, Faust, Daniel. . . ." I flicked a glance up to the funeral home worker. "Which home are you with?"

"Scott Funeral Home." His tone was strangely mild, and his eyes stayed on me in a way that probably should have been unnerving, but I was high on brains and feeling too good to be down in any way.

I made the appropriate entries, then printed out the receipt. Standing, I yanked it off the printer, then handed it to him with a dorky flourish. "Sign here, and he's all yours," I said.

"You're new here, aren't you?" A slight smile played on his face as he signed the paper.

"A little over a month," I replied.

"Is there anyone else here new?"

I shook my head. "Just me."

He straightened, eyes raking me in a strangely appraising way. "So you're probably the one who can tell me where all the brains have gone."

I felt as if he'd punched me in the gut, and I know I stood there with an utterly stricken look on my face.

"I . . . uh . . . what do you mean?" I said, but I couldn't keep my voice steady. I knew I sounded guilty as hell. *Shit.* I didn't think anyone would have noticed that they were missing. Nick had told me that the funeral homes never did anything with the bag of organs.

The skin around his eyes tightened in annoyance. "What, you thought no one would notice? That's not how this works. Didn't anyone tell you?"

"Tell me what?" I managed, voice cracking.

"The brains come to me at the funeral home," he said with patronizing slowness. "Then I distribute them."

My initial shock and terror faded to be replaced by a strange relief. But I didn't dare reveal myself yet. There was always the chance that he was with some organ donation service, and if I came out and said, "Hey, you're a zombie too?" I'd look like a complete whacko.

"Who the hell are you?" I said instead. "And why do you need the brains? Who do you distribute them to?"

He leaned against a filing cabinet and tucked his thumbs into the top of his pockets. "You're new, aren't you."

"I told you," I said, scowling, "I started here a month ago."

He shook his head. "That's not what I meant. You're a new zombie, right?"

I swear my knees shook, and I had to grab at the table behind me.

"Oh, thank god!" I exclaimed before I could think. "Shit, I swear there was a part of me that thought I was fucking crazy. I mean, I'm wanting to eat . . . well, y'know." I realized I was babbling and forced myself to stop and take a deep breath. "Is that—really? Is that what I am?" Instead of horror at the confirmation all I could feel was overwhelming relief. *I'm not crazy.* There'd been that teeny tiny sliver of doubt. *Okay, so I'm a monster. And, yeah, that's more acceptable than being insane.*

He cocked his head. "You really don't know? Why did you think you were craving brains?"

My attitude slowly began to reassert itself. "Well, how the fuck was I supposed to know? I thought I was nuts!" Then I narrowed my eyes at him. "You're one too, right?"

"That's right." He stuck his hand out. "I'm John Kang. Everyone calls me Kang."

I took his hand, shook it. "Angel Crawford. Nice to meet you." He didn't feel dead or undead, or whatever. His skin was warm, and he looked totally alive to me. Did that mean he'd fed recently?

I inhaled sharply. "You left that note!"

He gave me a puzzled look. "Note?"

"Yeah, there was a note at the ER and on my van. . . ." I trailed off as his expression remained blank. Disappointment curled through me. Yeah, that would have been way too easy. I shook my head. "Never mind."

He was silent for several seconds, regarding me. "Who the hell changed you?"

"Changed me? What, you mean someone made me like this on purpose?"

"Well, yeah. It's not something that happens by accident. You have to be close to death already, then get bitten all to hell by a zombie to get the virus into you, and then you have to eat brains almost immediately to feed the virus."

"Well, I don't know these things," I nearly snarled as the frustration threatened to boil over. "I figured I'd been bit or whatever by accident. Hell, I had no idea what happened." Did that mean that whoever left the notes for me was the one who changed me? But why? And if it was a virus, was there some sort of treatment for it? "Why don't you tell me what the hell's going on!"

"Sure," Kang said. "But first, you need to ante up the brains."

I could only stare at him for several seconds. "Wait . . . you mean I have to turn all the brains over to you? Why?"

Kang's expression tightened. "Because that's how things work. I get the brains, and then I distribute them."

"To who?"

"Other zombies. Who the hell do you think?"

I narrowed my eyes. "Uh huh. And when you say distribute, do you mean you have a soup kitchen sort of thing set up for local zombies looking for a meal? Or do you sell them?" I had a feeling I already knew the answer. Zeke, the zombie who'd ambushed me with a tree, wouldn't have been so desperate if there'd been a place to get free brains.

"I sell them," he replied, practically spitting the words out. I could see that my failure to instantly buckle under was annoying him.

"Do you get them from the other funeral homes too?"

He lifted a shoulder in a shrug. He was working really hard to keep his cool, I had to give him that. "I get as much as I can. Look, this is an efficient system we have going on here. I don't need you coming in and screwing everything up."

I folded my arms across my chest. "So you're telling me that you're the only zombie who works in a funeral home?"

"I'm the only one in a position to take care of all the others," he retorted. "If you think you're going to come in here and cut into my business, you're deluded."

"Yeah, well, let's get one thing straight, asshole. I have no intention of cutting into your business, okay? But I'm also not gonna let you screw me over." I found myself smiling. I'd been in scenarios like this before, though they hadn't been about brains. Maybe my less-than-pleasant history would come in handy after all. "See, I think what you want is for me to give you all the brains from bodies that don't normally go to your funeral home. 'Cause right now you only get, what, maybe a fifth of the ones that come through the morgue?" His scowl told me I was on the right track. "But it's not like you could be short of brains. I mean, you also get all the ones from the people who y'all pick up who don't come through here. Nursing homes, hospitals, hospice deaths. . . ."

I watched a muscle in his jaw leap. "You have no idea how this works."

I shrugged. "Yeah, maybe not. But I've dealt with your type before. I know you're not the only zombie in this business." I didn't know for sure—there was always the chance that Zeke was the only other one, but the more I thought about it, the more it made sense that zombies would automatically gravitate toward jobs where they could get a hold of brains with a minimum of hassle. "And I think that right now you're just being a dick, trying to pressure me into handing everything over to you and cutting everyone else out—including myself." I threw my hands up. "Do I really look that stupid?"

Kang's lip curled into a sneer. "You didn't even know you were a zombie."

"Yeah, so? I was ignorant, but I'm not a fucking moron. Why would I give the shit to you just so I could buy it back from you later?" I leaned back against the counter. "Hon, you're fucking with the wrong chick. I've been around too many drug dealers to buy into a scheme like that."

He shocked me by bursting out laughing. "Drug dealers? Well, that's an interesting analogy." He shook his head but a sardonic smile stayed on his face. "All right, clearly I underestimated you. You're serious about not wanting a cut of the action?"

I hesitated. I was already risking enough by taking the brains for my own use. If I was somehow caught profiting from it. . . . It felt skeevy, even though I could logically see that it was no more skeevy than a restaurant charging for food. "Yeah. I don't need to do that."

"But you're still cutting into my supply," he pointed out.

"Okay, well, how 'bout I leave the brains in the bags that are going to Scott Funeral Home. So nothing changes for you. And, if I get into a bind or something, you help me out, and vice versa."

"And you're going to keep all the rest?" He raised an eyebrow.

"That's right," I replied, putting as much defiance as I could into my tone. "We don't get that many bodies through here. Y'all get a buttload more through the funeral homes."

He grimaced. "Sure, but most of them are old. Taste old too."

I resisted the urge to say something obnoxious like, "Suck it up and deal with it." It was clear he wasn't thrilled, but he also seemed to realize that this was as good a deal as he was going to get. "So, are you gonna tell me about zombies and how all this works?" I asked instead.

He started pushing the stretcher toward the door. "You're a zombie," he said, tone flat and curt. "You eat brains. What more do you need to know?"

I stared at him in shock for a split second, then scrambled to get between him and the door. "*Seriously*?" The word practically exploded from me as I planted my hands on the other end of the stretcher and stopped him. "Could you please turn off the dick mode for a few seconds? I've already said that I'm not going to cut you out. Don't make me regret that!"

He glowered at me. "Fine," he finally said. "But make it quick. I need to get back."

I bit back a smartass retort. "You said you distribute brains. Surely that means you know who the other zombies in the area are, right?"

"Only a few," he said with a shrug. "And trust me, none of the ones I know would be likely to have turned you. Too secretive, too scared of discovery. Most zombies don't want anyone to know about them." His mouth twisted. "Hell, most are pretty damn lazy. You burn fewer brains if you sit on the couch all day watching TV."

I blinked. I hadn't thought about it like that. A vision of a fat, redneck zombie sitting on his couch watching football and eating brains instead of popcorn swam up in my head, and I had to resist the urge to burst out laughing.

"And the ones I provide to, who aren't lazy fucks," he continued, "are either people who work only to make enough money to buy the brains they need, or people who don't want to get their hands dirty and can afford to pay for delivery."

"I suppose animal brains don't do the trick?" I asked.

Kang gave a dry laugh. "We'd probably have a lot more zombies if that was true. But no, human brains are the only kind that give us what we need. And, in case you were wondering, zombie brains are no good either." He shrugged. "This is why it's not good to have too many of us in one place. Brains aren't exactly easy to come by, and the last thing any of us needs is attention drawn to ourselves."

A chill walked down my back as I tried to process that last statement, but he gave the stretcher a jerk, pulling me out of my thoughts.

"Can we please do the twenty questions bullshit another time?" he said with a cocky sneer. "I need to get back to my job."

Even though I knew I had a million more questions for him, I couldn't put anything into words at that moment. I released the stretcher and stepped aside. He was out the door in the next instant, while my thoughts tumbled in an uncoordinated, frustrated loop.

Chapter 15

As annoyed as I was at Kang and his no-more-info-for-you bullshit, the entire incident *had* clued me in to several hugely important facts. I was a zombie. I wasn't crazy—or rather, not any more than I already was. There were other zombies around. And someone made me a zombie on purpose.

Which means I don't need Kang, I thought smugly as I finished cleaning up the morgue and getting everything set out for the next shift. *I can find me another zombie who'll tell me what the hell is going on. Pompous jerk.* Screw Kang. I didn't need his help.

But that brought up the big question: How the hell could I tell if someone was a zombie? I didn't know Kang was one until he told me. I'd known that Zeke was, but only because it was pretty damn obvious. In other words, probably the only way I'd be able to tell would be if someone was low on brains and starting to smell.

Great, so I simply needed to go around and sniff people to find the ones who smelled like rot and death. Yeah, that wouldn't be weird at all.

There had to be other ways I could find out more

about what I was facing, now that I knew for sure what I was. Hell, there were a zillion movies about zombies. Maybe there were some seeds of truth in all of that.

As soon as I was finished at the morgue I called Randy.

"Hey, you busy?" I asked after he picked up.

"Nah. Gotta take apart a fuel system later on, but that's about it. Why?"

"Well, I was wondering if you wanted to do a movie marathon. I'll bring the movies."

"Sure thing, babe. Sounds like fun. You'll need to get some beer too. I'm almost out."

"No problem," I said, trying to keep the grimace out of my voice. Look at me, being all cheap because I didn't want to buy beer that I wouldn't drink. It was different with my dad. That was a survival tactic. But the DVD player at home had been busted for ages, and I couldn't see spending the bucks on a new one since Randy had the latest technology. Besides, he had the big screen. "Be there in about half an hour."

"Clive's here too," he said. "So's you know."

"Oh. Yeah, sure. Okay." I found myself hesitating. Clive was who I usually got pills from. Or rather, who I used to get pills from. He and Randy went way back, and the three of us had hung out at Randy's place before, though I'd never in a million years say that I was friends with Clive. It wasn't that I disliked him or anything. It was just that . . . he was Clive. I bought drugs from him. I wasn't gonna be best buds with him or anything.

I headed for the movie rental store and grabbed about half a dozen DVDs. There was probably no way we'd be able to watch them all in one night, but I wanted to have some variety to work with. A quick trip to the SpeedE Mart near Randy's house for the beer and some too-greasy fried chicken, and I was ready to go.

*   *   *

Clive was on the couch with his feet on the coffee table and a rifle in his lap when I came in to the trailer. He wasn't much taller than me, but he probably outweighed me by about a hundred pounds—and none of that was fat. He spent several hours a day in the gym, and it was pretty obvious to anyone with eyes that Clive was as serious about his steroids as he was about his workouts.

He looked over his shoulder and gave me a slight nod. "Yo. Angel. S'up?"

"Hey, Clive. How's it goin'?" I said. I dropped the DVDs onto the table, then pushed aside some engine parts to make room for the beer. "What's with the gun?"

"Deer season starts this weekend." He accompanied this statement with a withering look as if to say I was less of a person for not knowing this. "Finishing cleaning up my baby here," he said, giving the gun a caress.

I gave him my best eye roll in response. "Whatever."

"These are all zombie movies," Randy said, looking up from the pile of DVDs with a puzzled look on his face. "What's up with that?"

I shrugged and passed him a beer. "Thought it would be fun, y'know?"

"Zombies are cool," Clive announced from the couch. I looked at him, waiting for further commentary, but apparently that was the extent of Clive's opinion on the matter.

Randy made a *hmmf* noise, then looked back at me. "Whadja do to your head?"

I reached up and felt the Band-Aid. "Oh. I was in a wreck the other night in the coroner van. I only had a cut. Didn't even need stitches. It's no big deal."

He frowned, but Clive suddenly twisted to look at me. "That was you?" Clive asked. "I heard someone to-taled the CO van."

I threw up my hands. "Jesus, is there anyone who hasn't heard about this?"

Clive shrugged. "Well, I heard about it at the gym from Emily—the receptionist, who heard about it from her sister, Edith, who's dating Keith, who drove the wrecker that picked the van up. So, no, I think everyone's heard about it by now." Then he grinned and nodded toward Randy. "Except for him. He needs to get out more."

"Wait," Randy said. "How bad was this wreck? Why didn't you call me?"

I shook my head. "It wasn't bad at all. I mean, yeah, the van went on its side, but I was wearing my seat belt. It's no big deal." I didn't answer his second question. I had no idea why I hadn't called him. It hadn't even occurred to me. *He's my boyfriend, isn't he?* "I didn't want to worry you," I finally said in an echo of my response to my dad. It was just as lame this time, too.

"Didja get fired?"

"Nope. It wasn't my fault. Some dickwad pulled a tree out into the highway, and I hit it."

"Hunh. That sucks." He popped open his beer, then glanced at the Coke in my hand. "You're not drinking?"

"Nah. I'm on call." I wasn't, but it was a damn good excuse.

He gave me a withering look. "Yeah, like one beer's gonna make a difference."

I resisted the urge to sigh. "C'mon, don't hassle me. I had the wreck only a few days ago. I can't get into any more trouble."

"You're really serious about this job, aren't you?"

"Yeah," I said, picking at the label on the Coke bottle. "It's a good job. I'm trying not to fuck it up, y'know?"

"Leave her alone, Randy," Clive said with a wink to me. "She's being good. She has a sweet gig and doesn't want to blow it."

The way he said it was odd, as if he was trying to share some inside joke with me. If so, I didn't get it, and I didn't feel like getting it, so I let it slide.

"Just as long as she doesn't turn into some sort of Goody Two-shoes," Randy muttered. He must have seen the hurt expression on my face because he leaned over to kiss me on the forehead. "I'm kidding, Angel. I know you're cool."

Now I understood. Or at least I thought I did. He was afraid that if I stopped with the drugs and the booze, I'd be on him to stop, too. "Yeah, I'm cool. C'mon, now, put one of the movies in." I handed him the one on top without even looking to see which one it was. I didn't care. I simply wanted this weird conversation to end.

I thought he was going to say something else, but to my relief he simply turned away and stuck the DVD into the player. I plopped down onto the couch, leaving room for Randy in the middle, then did my best to tune the world out and learn about zombies.

Five hours later I knew a lot more about the movie versions of zombies, and not a damn thing that would help me in my own situation. All the zombies in the movies were the enemy—mindless creatures that wanted to kill and eat flesh and brains. There were still two more DVDs in the stack, but I couldn't face the thought of watching them. Too depressing. *This isn't me*, I told myself. *That's not what I am.*

As long as I stayed well-fed, right?

Clive and Randy were still watching the end of the third movie—one of the George Romero flicks. Or at least that's what I thought it was. I'd lost track. I glanced at the clock: One A.M.

"Y'all can keep watching. I've had enough." I stood.

Randy looked at me with a frown. "You're not staying the night?"

"Nah," I said. "I need to be up early." It sounded weak, and Randy sighed and rolled his eyes.

"C'mon, Angel, stay," Clive said without taking his eyes from the screen. He was enjoying the movies way too much—cheering loudly every time a zombie got dispatched. I knew that was the point of these movies—humans overcoming the zombie menace—but, gee, for some reason it was beginning to get under my skin. "Besides," he continued, "your man here needs some hot lovin', and I ain't about to give it up for him."

Yeah, well, I wasn't about to give Randy any hot lovin' with Clive around. About a year ago Clive had made a joke about me doing both him and Randy at the same time—the kind of joke that wasn't really a joke if I'd even hinted at being willing to go for it. Which I wasn't. At all.

I tried to think of a nasty-funny comeback, but I was too worn out to come up with anything. "I need to go," I told Randy, ignoring Clive's bark of laughter. "I'll call you later, okay?"

He gave me a nod and a shrug. "Yeah, no biggie."

I kept the smile fixed on my face. No biggie. Yeah, that was us. I collected the movies we'd already watched and headed out. I didn't ask Randy to walk me out to my car, and he didn't offer. I left to the sound of Clive yelling encouragement as zombies died on the screen.

Chapter 16

The third morgue tech, Jerry, was sitting at the computer in the morgue when I came in the next morning. He lifted his hand in a wave without taking his eyes from the monitor.

"Angel," he muttered in greeting.

"Jerry," I replied, mimicking his low, gruff tone. The parody was apparently lost on him though, because he simply kept on with whatever it was that had his attention on the computer.

I put my lunchbox in the bottom drawer of the desk, rolling my eyes when I saw the solitaire game on the computer.

"Anything exciting happening?" I asked.

He gave a heavy sigh. "Busy day yesterday. Dr. Leblanc cut the headless pizza guy yesterday afternoon, as well as a heart attack and an MVA that Nick brought in after you got off." He closed the solitaire game and pulled up the page that showed which bodies were scheduled to go to which funeral homes. "Those last two will probably be picked up later today."

I peered over his shoulder at the screen. "What about the Pizza Plaza guy? Anyone picking him up?"

"There's some sort of hitch with the ID which means official notification hasn't been made, which also means there's no one who's authorized to make the funeral arrangements." He shrugged, clearly and deeply unconcerned.

"What happens if no one makes funeral arrangements?" I asked. "He stays in our morgue forever?"

He wagged his head in a no. "That would be disgusting," he stated. "Bodies still rot in there. Just takes longer. Like meat in your fridge at home."

Okay, that made sense. The morgue cooler was exactly that—a cooler, not a freezer. Early in my time at the coroner's office, I'd stupidly wondered aloud why it wasn't a freezer, until it was pointed out to me that performing an autopsy on a frozen slab of meat would be a wee bit difficult. Oh. Yeah.

"So what happens to them? State pays for them to be buried or something?"

His chin dipped in a nod. "Riverwood Funeral Home handles the pauper burials for this parish and they get reimbursed a set amount for each one. They have a plot set aside for the pauper burials—no headstones or anything, though."

I frowned. "Why not? What, poor people don't deserve a real grave?"

A whisper of amusement lit his eyes. "They get a real grave. And the exact location is recorded. But there are a lot of people who'd never pay for a funeral if they knew the state would do it for free."

"Ah. I get it," I said. "People who want to be able to visit the grave are gonna pay for it. Bet there are still people who don't care, though."

"Agreed, which seems fair enough, I suppose. Funerals can be expensive. And are for the survivors, not the decedents."

I simply nodded in response. We'd had Mom cremated after she hung herself. There'd been no funeral. No one would have come to it anyway.

"That's what happened with the other headless guy," Jerry said.

I gave him a blank look. "What happened?"

"No next of kin was found, so Riverwood took him—gave him a pauper burial."

I sat on the edge of the desk. This was the guy who'd been killed while I was stumbling down the road, high as a kite. Maybe I could milk Jerry for some info. "What was the deal with that?" I asked. "That happened right before I started here. Who was he?"

"He was identified as Adam Campbell—lived in a fishing camp down at the end of Sweet Bayou." Then he shrugged. "Wrote for magazines—tech articles, that sort of thing. Neighbors said he was a nice guy. Some teenager got lost out there a couple of months ago, and Adam let the search teams use his yard and house as a base of operations. Cooked for them too—big pots of gumbo, crawfish, jambalaya. I think everyone was disappointed when the little teen bastard was found alive and well." A smile flickered across his face.

"If he was so nice, why didn't any of those people step up and pitch in for a real funeral?" I asked, frowning.

Jerry pushed away from the desk and stood, grimacing as he audibly popped his back. "Because people suck, and everyone's always sure that someone else will take care of it." He glanced at the clock. "Time for me to drag my sorry carcass out of here. Have fun with the stiffs."

"Always," I replied as I sat in his seat and pretended to pick up where he'd left off with the game of solitaire.

I waited until I heard his car leave the parking lot,

then grabbed my lunchbox and scurried to the cooler. The MVA was scheduled to be picked up by Riverwood, which meant I suffered no guilt as I scooped the brains out of the bag and into my jars. The heart attack I left alone since it was going to Scott Funeral Home. Kang had been a dick, but I wasn't going to back out of our deal.

I poured tomato soup in on top of the brains and then quickly blended them up with my cheapo handheld blender. It didn't look terribly appetizing, but at least it wasn't instantly recognizable as brains.

My appetite gave a soft little nudge as I made my little brain concoction. I knew I needed to try to resist those first nudges of hunger, try and hold out a bit to make my supply last as long as possible.

But not right now, I told myself. *I need to be sharp for work, right?* I indulged in a few big gulps from one of the jars, then replaced the lid and stuck both jars into the lunchbox with the blue frozen thingies that would hopefully keep the brains from going bad before I got home and could put them in the fridge. I didn't have a ton of brains to spare, but I also didn't feel like dealing with the hunger right now.

The doorbell buzzed as I was putting the lunchbox back in the drawer. It was Kang, and he gave me a tight little nod as I stepped back to give him room to push the stretcher in.

"You're here for Blackwell, Travis?" I asked.

He glanced at the paper in his hand. "That's right. Is he *all* ready?" he asked.

I narrowed my eyes into a glare. "Uh huh. He's *all* ready. *All* there. *All* that good stuff."

Kang gave a slow nod. "I appreciate that."

"Yeah, sure thing," I replied as I turned and headed to the cooler to retrieve the body, not adding "asshole" even though I really wanted to. The urge to run over his toes with the stretcher when I returned was pretty strong, but I managed to resist it. I was even nice and helped him pull the bag from our stretcher onto his.

He buckled the straps holding the bag onto the stretcher, then paused and looked at me. "I didn't really think you'd keep to our deal. I apologize for misjudging you."

I shrugged in acceptance of the apology. "Yeah, well, you shouldn't be so mistrusting."

His lips twitched. "When you've been around as long as I have, you learn that trusts are easily broken."

"Oh, please. You can't be much older than me."

Kang let out a low chuckle. "Yes I can, and I am."

I frowned at him in doubt. "Oh, really? How old are you?"

He lifted an eyebrow. "Isn't that a rude question?"

"Give me a break. C'mon, fess up. How old are you?"

"I was seven years old when I lost my parents during the Korean War."

"Oh. Sorry to hear that." I struggled to remember the brief smattering of history I'd actually studied, but couldn't think of *when* the Korean War was to save my life. There was still stuff about Korea in the news, so maybe it was only twenty years ago or so? I didn't want to say anything, though, for fear of looking like a complete dumbass. "Okay, well, um, anyway, don't worry about the brains. I won't screw you. But can you please answer some questions for me?"

He crossed his arms over his chest. "I'll do my best."

"How often do I need to eat brains? I mean, I feel hungry all the time."

"If you do a lot and are active, you need brains more often," he said. "In other words, you won't ever see a zombie exercise. Under normal circumstances you'll be fine if you eat about a third to half a brain every other day. After a few days without, though, things start to go bad pretty quickly, like a downhill slide. So, if you're in a job where you have to be fairly physically active, like yours, you're going to need to eat more often. But," he said with a gesture at the morgue cooler, "at least you have access to brains."

"When there are brains to be had," I pointed out.

"People die all the time, Angel. That's one thing you can be sure of."

Sure, but would they die soon enough to satisfy my hunger?

"Okay, next question," I said. "It's a virus? Is there a treatment for it?"

He shrugged. "No idea. Virus. Parasite. I don't know. Maybe a treatment or cure is being worked on. But as far as I know, it's been around for centuries."

I pondered that for a few seconds. A parasite . . . what, like a tapeworm? That was too damn creepy. And disgusting. "Okay, well, what about, um, relations."

He gave me a blank look. "Excuse me?"

I gave a frustrated sigh. "Can we have sex?"

The skin around his eyes crinkled. "Well, we barely know each other, but I'm game."

"Shit! No. Arrgh!" I could feel my face heating. "You know what I mean." I scowled at him as he laughed, though a second later I was laughing too. "Okay, I deserved that. I mean, can we—zombies—have sex?"

He grinned. "Yes. But be sure to feed beforehand. It's much better that way. Plus, you don't want to risk having bits fall off."

I shuddered. "Okay, that's disgusting."

"It reminds me of an old joke: What did the zombie say to the whore?"

I looked at him blankly. "Um . . . what?"

He winked. "Keep the tip."

After Kang left, I pulled the internet up on the computer and did a search on the Korean War, then stared at the screen in shock when I saw the dates. *1950-1953. Holy Shit. Kang's an old man.* Had he been surviving by working in funeral homes this entire time?

But he still looks like he's in his twenties, I thought with growing amazement. Then I sighed. If I'd realized how old he was I would have asked him if he looked young because of the zombie stuff. And how long he'd actually *been* a zombie. "Don't be a fool. Stay in school," I muttered to myself.

Fortunately my job offered plenty to distract me from thinking about my general ignorance. I went out on a pickup of a bum who'd been found dead under a bridge, and then of some lady who'd managed to gas herself in her bathroom by combining bleach and ammonia. I shamelessly grabbed lunch at a drive-thru on my way back to the morgue and scarfed down a burger to satisfy my far-less annoying food hunger, while managing to completely forget the fact that I had two dead bodies in the back of the van.

By the time I made it back to the morgue and got everything put away and entered into the computer, it was close to the end of my shift. Nick would be showing up in the next twenty minutes or so, and the morgue was as spotless as I knew how to make it. I'd remembered to throw the trash from lunch out, but I knew from experience that I should probably check to make sure everything in the van was where it needed to be. Nick was an arrogant pain, and if I'd somehow dropped a single french fry, I'd never hear the end of it.

I stuffed my key card into the front pocket of my jeans and exited out the back door. The door clanged shut behind me as a sickly familiar smell washed over me. I spun around as a jab of adrenaline sent me into high alert. It only took me a second to see the figure crouched in the shadow of the wall, like a lion about to pounce.

But this time I wasn't injured and alone. And I wasn't hungry at all.

"You told me to come here," Zeke said, his voice already beginning to take on an unpleasant rasp. "You said you'd give me brains." He straightened. He'd changed clothes—now he wore a New Orleans Saints shirt and paint-spattered jeans. They looked grubby and nasty, and I didn't want to think about how long he'd been wearing them.

A flare of annoyance shot through me. "Yeah, but you didn't need to scare the crap out of me. Do you get off on that shit?"

"I'm hungry," he snarled, then he shook his head. "You don't know what it's like."

"Whatever," I said, scowling. "Y'know, you could've killed me that night."

He bared his teeth. "You're a zombie. That wouldn't have killed you."

Annoyance shifted to anger. "It fucking hurt anyway! And you didn't know I was a zombie when you caused that accident. If I'd been a normal human that wreck would have really fucked me up." A cold chill walked through me. "Or was that your plan? Did you want to kill someone?"

He took three long strides forward, but I managed to hold my ground. It helped that I was still totally sharp and focused from my recent meal.

"I saw your van go by," he said. "I knew it was the coroner's van, that you'd have to come back soon enough, and that you'd have a body in the back. Why else would you be out at that hour on that highway, except for a pickup?" He paused. His shoulders were hunched in a defensive pose. "I waited until I saw headlights. Saw that they weren't a car's."

"What if you'd been wrong?" I demanded.

He tilted his head. "Then I would have been wrong,"

he said in a tone so casual it sent goosebumps down my back.

I spun and started back toward the morgue. He seized me by the upper arm. "You promised me you'd share!" he said, desperation edging into his voice.

I slapped at his arm, almost surprised when I was able to break his grasp. "I know. I'm getting it, asshole!"

He scowled and stepped back into the shadow. I swiped my card and entered the morgue, then retrieved a jar from my lunchbox—the one I'd already taken a few gulps from. Cradling the jar with its stupid masking tape/shoe polish décor, I paused. I'd completely forgotten about this zombie and my promise to him. I probably could have set some more aside if I'd been thinking about it. But my own supply was running low. Besides, it was a promise made under duress, and those didn't count, right? And surely he was getting brains from someplace else as well. It had been five days since the wreck. He'd be a lot more rotted if he'd been without brains that entire time, especially since I hadn't given him anywhere near enough to get him fully "fresh."

And he was willing to take the chance that I'd be killed in the wreck. Suddenly I didn't want to think about where else he was getting brains.

I returned outside and handed him the jar. "It's all I have right now," I lied. "I was out of work for close to a week," I added with a scowl.

He ignored the jibe and tugged the lid off the jar, eyes closing briefly in bliss as the scent of brains washed over him. Then he looked back at me with a puzzled look. "Tomato soup?"

"Trying to keep it from being so obvious, y'know?"

"I hate tomato soup," he muttered, but he stepped back and held the jar with both hands as he drank the brain-soup down. I watched, morbidly fascinated as color returned to his skin. A few drops escaped the corner of his mouth, dribbling onto his shirt to form a Florida-shaped stain. Finally he lowered the jar and gave a sated sigh.

"Ah, god, that's good," he breathed as he wiped his mouth with the back of his hand, then wiped his hand on his shirt "Even if it was *tomato*." He held the empty jar out to me. His eyes were whole and clear again. "When can you get me some more?"

I stared at him, then snatched the jar out of his hand. "More? Are you serious? That's all I have right now."

A muscle in his jaw clenched. "That's not going to hold me for long."

"Hey, it's *your* fault I had to go through most of my supply," I continued, pissed. "That wreck fucked me up. I could have lost my job!"

A snarl twisted his mouth. "And then you'd know what I'm going through."

"Yeah, well, fuck you." I'd balled my free hand into a fist without realizing it. "You stole jewelry off dead bodies. That's fucking sick, man."

A scowl curved his mouth. "I didn't steal anything. I was set up."

"Oh, right," I scoffed. "By who, the zombie mafia?" But even as I said it, a sliver of doubt managed to work its way in. Kang had been awfully hostile until he'd been sure I wasn't going to hurt his business.

Zeke's eyes narrowed. "You could call it that. Some people couldn't handle competition. Besides, we eat brains! *That's* sick."

"That's for survival!" I retorted. "That's life or death." Or undeath.

He took a step forward and fear flashed through me. *He's going to try to take my keycard so that he can get into the morgue, steal my brains.*

"I'm not going to let myself rot away," he growled. "I'll—"

"Hey! What the hell's going on?"

I never thought I'd be so relieved to hear Nick's voice. Zeke pulled back from me, scowling. I didn't dare turn around, but I could hear the morgue door swing shut and Nick's footsteps as he walked up.

"You okay, Angel?" he asked, coming up beside me. I flicked a glance his way. His stance was totally aggressive, in a bantam rooster kinda way. His eyes were fixed on Zeke in what was probably meant to be a menacing glare.

"Yeah," I said, voice a tiny bit shaky. I thought about saying something else, like *Oh, he's just leaving*, or *He's an old friend and was stopping by*, but I didn't. I felt no desire to give Zeke any excuse or out.

Apparently, neither did Zeke. With a final glare, he turned and then headed off in a jerky run.

As soon as he was out of sight I let out an unsteady breath, then almost jumped in surprise when Nick laid a hand on my arm.

"You really okay?" he asked, and I was shocked once again to see real concern in his eyes. At my nod he dropped his hand. "That guy's a complete weirdo. Always asking how many bodies we have in the cooler. Kooky stuff like that."

That was as good an excuse as any. "Yeah, that was weird." I gave him a tentative smile. "Thanks. Dunno what would have happened if you hadn't come out right then, but . . . thanks."

The smile he gave me was the most genuine one I'd ever seen from him, and he actually puffed up a bit with pride. It probably wasn't often that he could be the knight in shining armor. "Yeah, well, no prob. I got your back."

Neither of us seemed to know what to do next and an awkward silence descended. "I, uh, should probably get back inside in case Riverwood calls," I said with a jerk of my head.

"Oh, yeah, sure," he replied, seemingly as grateful as I was that the moment was over. "Don't forget to clean the van out before you give me the keys. There were donut crumbs all over the seat last time."

I masked a grin and headed to the van, strangely relieved that this Nice Nick wasn't going to be the new norm.

Chapter 17

My decent mood lasted until I pulled up to the house and saw my dad sitting on the porch. He had a beer in his hand, and a pile of empties scattered beside his chair. I silently counted the cans, then closed my eyes and breathed a curse. Well over a dozen.

I was slow getting out of my car, as if I could infinitely delay having to deal with him.

"You stink," he muttered as I tried to walk past him.

I gritted my teeth. I knew he was only saying it to be an asshole. I'd eaten this morning.

"I know you been paid by now, Angel," he said in a growl. "You need to give me some goddamn money." He paused to spit onto the porch, then curled his lip at me. "You're only gonna blow it on pills. It's what you always do."

"I bought groceries and paid the bills, remember?" I said as I yanked open the front door and went into the house. I grimaced as I heard the scrape of his shoes as he rose.

"Don't you fuckin' walk away from me when I'm talking to you!" he hollered after me.

"I thought we were done," I shot back over my shoulder. "I spent all the money. That's why the damn cable works now and the lights are still on."

He grabbed my arm and yanked me around. "You're holding out on me, you worthless little bitch!"

"Get *off* me," I yelled. "I'm clean, goddammit! You only want me to feel like shit so you can feel better about being a stupid fucking drunk!" I slapped at his hand. "You only want my money so you can buy more booze!" I tried to twist away, more than a little surprised when I actually broke his grip. For a skinny man he was still pretty damn strong.

But all it did was piss him off more. I tried to duck away from the slap, but he got me hard across the side of the head and my ear.

"You owe me!" he yelled as he landed several more solid blows to my face and shoulders. "You owe me everything! Worthless fuckin' bitch!"

I was no kind of fighter, and all I could think to do was hunch up and try to avoid the worst of it and scream at him to stop. "Dad! Stop it! You're drunk!" I shrieked. "You're hurting me! You're being like mom!"

For an instant I thought it would work, that it would make him stop. But in the next second a black rage suffused his face. "You . . . your mother's better off dead." His fist came down but I could barely feel it anymore. "She can't see what a fuckup you are. I gave up everything for you, and for what? For you to be a goddamn loser!"

"I'm not a loser," I gasped. I could taste blood in my mouth. "I'm not on the drugs anymore. I swear!" I knew I couldn't stay hunched down like this in the hope that he'd stop. I'd never seen him like this before. For the first time, I was afraid that he wouldn't stop until I was a bloody pulp.

I managed to get my legs under me and shoved him

away hard, harder than I meant to, sending him sprawling back against the couch. There was murder in his eyes as he struggled back to his feet, but it gave me enough time to run to my room and slam the door and lock it. He pounded on it and yelled for a couple of minutes, then finally fell quiet while I hunched against the wall and shook.

I should have driven away as soon as I saw how drunk he was, I thought miserably. Dad's violence was predictable. I should have known better. Mom had been the one who'd dealt out slaps and hugs with chaotic unpredictability.

I dropped my head to my knees and wrapped my arms around my legs. I hurt all over, but at the same time I could feel everything gradually going numb. Right now that was cool with me.

I jerked at the knock on the door and froze, pulse thudding painfully even as I realized that my dad never knocked like that.

"Angel?" I heard a deep and familiar voice say. "Can you come out please? This is the Sheriff's Office."

I dropped my head back against the wall. *Fuck.* A neighbor must have heard us fighting and called the cops. My throat went tight. I was going to get arrested. I'd lose my job. *I'm totally fucked.*

"Angel. Please. I need you to open the door or I'll have to force it open to make sure you're all right."

I struggled to my feet. "I'm okay," I croaked. Yeah, I sure sounded okay. I fumbled at the lock and then pulled the door open. In front of me was a broad, uniformed chest. I didn't want to look up, but I didn't have to. Not with the nametag "M. Ivanov" at my eye level. I felt like I shrank a few inches. Yeah, let me remind him how much of a loser I am.

He turned his head and called over his shoulder to a deputy I couldn't see. "Gordon. Ten-fifteen." I didn't know what that meant, but I heard my dad make a low, whining protest. Ivanov looked back to me. "I'll need to take pictures of your injuries," he said, voice calm and even. "Do you want to go to the hospital?"

"Hunh?" Then I shook my head. "I'm not hurt. It . . . it's okay." I just wanted this whole thing to be over with. A dull throb of hunger poked at me, but I pushed it aside. I couldn't worry about that right now. I was only hungry because I was a little banged up.

He gave a low snort. "Angel, you look like hell."

I glanced at my reflection in the mirror on my dresser, chest tightening at the sight of the split lip, puffiness around my left eye, and bruises already forming on my cheek and collarbone. It would probably hurt a lot more if I wasn't a zombie. Great, my pain tolerance was high enough for me to take a beating. I swallowed. "You gonna arrest me?"

"No. We're arresting your dad though."

I jerked my head up to look into his face. "You don't need to do that. He's drunk. That's all." I didn't want him to go to jail. I didn't.

So why did I feel a weird relief at the thought? God, I was a shit daughter.

His expression tightened briefly and a wash of shame went through me. He'd probably heard this sort of thing a million times before. Wife or girlfriend gets the crap beat out of them, but they can't stand to see their loved one go to jail. Yeah, I was being that victim. "I'm sorry," I tried. "It's just—"

"Angel, I have to arrest him," he said in low, firm voice. "And since this is a domestic violence case, he'll most likely be held for at least twenty-four hours before he can post bail. I know this is hard, but I really need you to be strong for this. You don't deserve to get smacked around."

"I know that." I did, right?

"I need to get a statement from you," he continued. "Can you do that for me?"

I made myself nod. Hunger nudged at me again, almost tentatively, and I tightened my hands into fists. If I'd eaten as soon as I'd locked myself in my room I wouldn't have any bruises. There'd be no reason to arrest my dad.

Or maybe I *would have been the one arrested*, I realized with a cold chill. Right now it was pretty obvious that I'd been the loser in this fight. I swallowed hard. Maybe it was a good thing that my fridge was empty. The one jar of brains I had was still out in my lunchbox in the car. "Yeah. I can do that."

Something that might have been relief lit his eyes briefly. "That's good." He paused. "Angel, you look like you're getting your life under control. I'm really glad to see it."

I bit back a laugh. This was control? Yeah, I wasn't doing drugs anymore, but that sure as hell wasn't due to any personal strength of character or anything like that. And the only reason I still had the job was because my life depended on it.

But I managed to give him a small nod. "Thanks." Too bad I had that whole zombie thing going on as well.

His gaze raked the living room, a look of distaste naked on his face. "You should think about moving out. You can do better than this." He looked back to me. "You're better than this. Don't let your family hold you back."

I was so shocked by his statement I literally couldn't form words for several seconds. "That's bullshit," I finally managed, anger flaring at his presumption. "You . . . you have no idea what it's like. You think it's that easy? You think that all I have to do is walk out and everything will be peachy fucking keen?" I knew I was treading on thin ice going off on a cop like this, but I was too upset and off-balance to censor myself.

Chagrin swept over his face. "No, look, I know it won't be easy, but—"

"You think we're just white trash scum, right? So, yeah, I'm already a loser, so why not be more of a loser and abandon my dad."

He frowned. "No, I'm saying that you need to think about yourself at some point."

"You think I don't? Fucking shit, I'm trying, okay? Give me a fucking break! I can't do it all at once! Yeah, the house and everything is shit, but do you think I like it this way? I—"

He seized me by the shoulders and gave me a small shake, cutting me off. It hurt where his fingers were pressing onto one of the bruises, but the dismayed expression on his face kept me from trying to pull away. "I'm sorry," he said, voice oddly rough. "I was out of line. I shouldn't have said any of that about moving out, or your family. It was a shit thing to say. I'm sorry. I know you're trying. I'm on your side and rooting for you, I swear."

Well, shit. How the fuck was I supposed to stay mad and upset after that? I sniffled, suddenly pissed for a different reason as I realized I'd been crying. I hurriedly swiped my hands across my eyes. "Okay. Yeah."

He sighed and for a weird instant I thought he was going to pull me into a hug. He didn't, but I had the strangest wish that he would. "Now that we've established that I'm an insensitive dick," he said, "are you still willing to give me a statement?"

I forced out a wan smile. "Yes. But you're not insensitive."

He gave me a grin. "Still a dick, though, right?"

"You're not insensitive," I repeated.

He chuckled, looking relieved. "You know me too well already. Come on out and sit down, and we'll get all of this crap over with."

I allowed myself to be led out to the living room and obediently sat on the couch. I watched him walk out the door and to his car, I assumed to get paperwork and a camera. *Yeah, right. I'm finally getting my life together. Too bad I had to die first.*

Chapter 18

As soon as the cops left with my dad I retrieved my lunchbox from my car and scarfed down a jar of brain soup. It wasn't until I was lowering the empty jar that I realized I was going to have a hard time explaining how my bruises disappeared overnight. Then again, Ivanov was the only one who'd seen them, right? I simply had to hope I didn't run into him for a few days.

The universe, of course, had different plans for me. The next morning I got a call to go pick up a body, and as soon as I pulled up to the trailer I saw Deputy Ivanov standing outside, talking to a crime scene tech.

I scowled and dug for a pair of sunglasses in my purse. Usually people wore sunglasses to hide a black eye. I was wearing them to hide the absence of one.

It didn't help that I could tell that this scene was going to be a disgusting one. There were two crime scene techs—Sean, and a blonde woman whose name I could never remember. Both were wearing tyvek coveralls and masks, and everyone else on the scene was keeping their distance from the door of the trailer. Hopping out of the van, I yanked gloves on as I walked up to see what

I was up against. Ivanov gave me a mild nod, then headed off toward his car. I didn't know whether to be relieved or miffed.

I gave Sean a grin. "Aren't you sweating your ass off in that?"

The red-haired man gave a tortured sigh. "I keep telling myself that sweating is better than stinking."

"It's a bad one?"

He shuddered. "Let's just say, I don't envy you your job one bit. All I have to do is take pictures!"

"I'm pretty sure nobody wants my job," I said. "I guess that's job security, right?"

I headed up the trailer stairs, pushing the sunglasses on top of my head. I peered in, and got a good look at the body sprawled on the floor beside an executive chair that looked totally out of place. The guy had probably been white, though with the amount of bloating it was tough to tell. He'd probably been a bit heavy before death, but now he was so swollen with decomposition I had to wonder if we'd be able to get him into the bag. He had on faded black jeans and a light blue T-shirt, though now it was heavily stained with purge fluid that had seeped from various orifices on his body. Maggots squirmed in his mouth and nose and eyes. Seriously nasty.

And my sense of smell is at full-strength right now, I thought. *How wonderful.*

Derrel was already inside and gave me a nod as he made notes on his pad. I didn't want to interrupt his flow of concentration, so I busied myself with looking around and being nosy. Big black flies buzzed against the windows and tangled in the dingy lace curtains. A line of ants tracked up the side of the kitchen counter, most likely headed to the stack of pizza boxes that hadn't been thrown out. Other than the ants and the flies, the place really wasn't crummy or scuzzy at all. He'd kept it pretty nice and neat overall. No piles of dirty laundry in the hallway or dishes in the sink. The carpet looked fairly new, the furniture all matched, and the entertainment system was even better than Randy's.

The computer on the desk was still on, screensaver running, and I gave the mouse a nudge to see if the guy had been in the middle of typing a suicide note or something.

"Dude loved his games," Derrel said without looking up.

"Huh?"

He gestured at the screen in a vague motion. "That's *Left For Dead 2*. And if you look on the shelf he also has *Halo*, *Grand Theft Auto*, *Call of Duty,* and damn near every other popular game."

I let my gaze sweep the interior of the trailer. "Did he have any life other than this? Did he have a job? Didn't anyone miss him?"

"Oh, he had a job." A grimace passed over Derrel's face. "He has a record a mile long for dealing drugs. Pot, crack, heroin, you name it. This guy was a real prize. I guess I'm not surprised that he went so long without being found." He gave a dry chuckle. "Though I bet his regular customers were jonesing. The neighbor in the next trailer over was the one to call the cops."

"Complaining about the smell?" I said.

Derrel grinned. "Got it in one."

I crouched by the body. There was something odd, but I couldn't quite put my finger on it. I took a deep breath, aware of the stench of the decomposition, but not bothered by it.

Something's missing.

My mouth went dry as realization hit home. Okay, so it had been less than a day since I'd last had brains. I wasn't hungry and probably wouldn't start having cravings for another day and a half at least. Even so, one thing I'd discovered in the past couple of weeks was that I had a nose for brains. I could smell it in the people around me, and I could certainly smell it in dead bodies. It didn't even matter if there was so much decomposition that it'd be inedible. Brains rotted fast—after a few days outside of a cooler there usually wasn't much left but a nasty grey goo—but I should still be able to detect the scent.

Yet there was only the barest whiff of it here.

"Hey, Derrel," I said, doing my best to keep my voice nice and calm and casual, even though a strange uneasiness was working its way through my gut. "What's the guess on cause of death?"

"Hang on a sec and we're gonna see what we can find out," he replied. He jotted a few more notes on his pad, then set it down on the desk and tugged on gloves. "With the amount of decomposition and all this purge fluid surrounding him, it's going to be tough to tell how he died unless there's some obvious trauma still evident."

I didn't respond to that. I knew what we were going to find. At least, I couldn't think of any other explanation. Still when we turned the body, I felt an odd relief that I hadn't been imagining it.

"Well, how's that for 'obvious trauma'?" I asked, looking down at the caved-in back of the guy's skull. Maybe I was starting to get the hang of this whole undead thing.

Derrel let out a low whistle. "I think that qualifies."

I flicked a maggot off my glove as Derrel went outside to tell the detectives that it looked like a homicide. A large black fly buzzed in a low drone around my head, and when I waved it away it joined the others congregated against the window. I straightened as Sean entered. He gave me a pained look as he pulled the mask back onto his face.

"Angel, I have no idea how you can stand this stench,"

he said. "Derrel's been doing this for long enough that I think he doesn't have any smell receptors left, but you . . . ?" He grimaced as he snapped pictures of the skull and the injury while I held the body in position for him. "You are one tough chick." Then his eyes crinkled, and even though he had the mask on, I could tell he was grinning at me. "Or maybe you're seriously sick and twisted, in which case you are *so* in the right line of work."

I laughed. "Gotta be the second one," I said. "I'm not tough!"

He finished taking his pictures, and I walked out with him. I knew it would be a while before I could take the body since it was pretty obvious it was a homicide, which meant that the detective assigned to the case would need to go in and do whatever it was that detectives did. About all I knew was what I'd seen on TV, and considering how much of what I did differed from the TV version, I figured I was most likely misinformed on ninety percent of the details.

I pulled off my gloves, leaned up against the front of Derrel's Durango to wait. *I'm tough, huh?* That was a new one. I had to admit, I was kinda tickled at the thought.

"How are you doing, Angel?" a familiar voice asked to my right.

I turned with an automatic smile before realizing who the speaker was. *And my sunglasses are up on my damn head*, I thought with a mental cringe. "I'm all right, Deputy Ivanov," I replied, keeping the smile on my face. Fuck it. I wasn't the one who'd been arrested. I wasn't going to hang my head in shame simply because my dad could be a real piece of shit. "I'm doin' all right," I said. "Thanks."

His eyes crinkled as he gave me a smile of his own. "You know, it's all right to call me Marcus." Then his eyes swept over my face, and I had to resist the urge to stiffen. "You sure don't bruise easy, do you? I'd have thought you'd have a real shiner going there."

"Um, lucky I guess. And I, uh, put ice on it."

He grimaced at my stilted response. "Sorry, I'm doing that 'insensitive dick' thing again. I shouldn't have brought that up."

I shrugged. "Nah, it's okay. Shit happens, y'know?" An awkward silence fell and I flicked off another maggot that had managed to make it up to my forearm.

He chuckled. "I bet you never thought you'd ever be casually flinging maggots around."

I had to laugh. "Oh my god, no kidding. I used to gag if someone spit on the sidewalk in front of me."

"You know . . ." Marcus paused, and it looked as if he was getting up the nerve to say something. I waited, and a few seconds later he continued, "I was the Resource Officer at your high school for a short time. I'd only been a cop for a few years and usually those assignments are given to the guys with a lot more experience, but the department went through a phase where they were shuffling everyone around."

I had an odd feeling I knew where he was going with this, but I went ahead and said, "Oh?"

His smile looked slightly abashed. "It was about five years ago. I, uh, remember you."

It was tough but I forced myself to not look away. "You remember when I left?"

He gave a slow nod.

I made a face. "Not one of my better moments." I didn't mention the time he'd arrested me. So far that incident was unspoken between us. Taboo. I far preferred it that way.

He shrugged. "Maybe so. But, at the risk of sounding like a pompous condescending ass, you're doing a good job of getting over it."

"Took me a while." And dying.

He smiled. "I mean it. It's like you're not the same person you used to be."

God, if he only knew. "I'm not. I mean, I am . . . it's, well, um, I'm trying to figure out who I am." I winced. Holy shit, that sounded kooky. "Uh, you know what I mean."

"I do," he said with a slow nod. "I think we all have to go through that at some point."

"Yeah," I said. And some of us needed a kick in the ass first.

"Look, I know this is the last thing you want to talk about, but I wanted to ask you . . . ." He trailed off, looking strangely uneasy.

"Ask me . . . ?" Ask me to dinner? Ask me out for drinks? Ask me if I wanted to see what he looked like under that uniform? *Yow, where'd that last one come from?* But no, he'd said it was the last thing I'd want to talk about.

He took a deep breath. "I wanted to ask you to please not bail your dad out of jail."

Somehow I managed to keep my face immobile while my thoughts went crashing into a tangled heap. "Hunh?"

"Don't bail your dad out," he repeated, eyes on me. "I know this is tough on you, but you shouldn't be the one to get him out."

"'Cause I'm the victim," I managed to force out. Wow, my voice almost sounded normal.

"That's right." He scrubbed a hand over the short brush of hair on his head. "Give yourself a few days peace." He looked like he wanted to say more, but I didn't need to hear it. I knew what he wanted to say. He didn't want me to be *that victim*. He gave a shit. Maybe he was like this for everyone, but it didn't matter. I still couldn't help but relish the tiny spark of warm glow that it gave me.

"Okay," I said quietly.

The smile he gave me in return was tinged with relief and worry.

"Hey," I said before he could say anything else that would make the mood even weirder or break it entirely. "You wanna grab some coffee or something someday? I mean, some time when I'm not crawling with maggots," I added with a laugh that sounded nervous to my own ears and probably sounded desperate and pathetic to his. I totally braced myself for him to hem and haw and say that he couldn't or had a girlfriend or something. I was shocked instead when he gave me a nod.

"That sounds nice. And I'm cool with the no maggots thing too."

We were saved from any more possible awkwardness by Derrel's piercing whistle to get my attention. I looked over to see that the homicide detective was exiting the house.

"I'm up," I said, as I pushed off the front of the Durango. "It was nice talking to you."

"I'm going to hold you to that coffee," he said, surprising me by giving me a wink.

I turned away with a silly grin on my face to collect a maggot-covered body.

Chapter 19

Dad called the next morning. I was expecting it, but that didn't make it any easier.

"Angel, it's your dad," he said after I answered. Not "Dad" but "your dad." In case I wasn't sure, y'know? "Baby, I'm real sorry about what happened."

I sat on the couch and pinched the bridge of my nose with my fingers. "I know. You were drunk."

"I was wrong, honey. I . . . I dunno why I get so worked up."

Because you feel like a failure, I thought. *I'm a fuckup, which means you failed as a dad.* But I wasn't a fuckup anymore. Or at least not as much of one. He couldn't see that. Or maybe he didn't want to see it. Then he'd be the only loser in the house.

"Can you come bail me out, please? I been here a day and a half now. They keep it so goddamned cold in here, and I'm hurting bad."

Shit shit shit. I squeezed my eyes shut. "I'm sorry, Dad. Maybe if you tell them you're in pain they can take you to the clinic?"

"Why can't you come bail me out?" He sounded

tired. Old. I felt older. Yeah, he'd been a complete piece of shit, but he wasn't always like that. Not always. Sometimes he came through for me—like the day he took me to the ER with broken ribs and arm when I was twelve. I could still remember the dull pain in his voice as he told the police to go and arrest his wife, because he knew that if they didn't she'd end up killing me. She'd been mentally ill—I could see that now. But all I'd known then was that Dad was saving me and at the same time betraying my mother. I'd loved him and hated him.

Still did.

The knot in my throat made it tough to talk. "I can't," I said, my voice little more than a hoarse whisper. "Dad. I . . . don't think they'll let me bail you out," I lied. "And I don't have any money left, remember?"

He was silent for so long I thought maybe he'd hung up. It was only the noise of people talking in the background that told me he was still on the line. "Okay, baby," he finally said. "I understand."

"I'm sorry, Dad," I choked out.

Then the background noise cut off, and I knew he'd hung up.

I sat there with my head in my hands for several minutes, then called the jail up and asked to have my number blocked from the inmate phone system. He'd get out eventually, but I wasn't going to help. And I couldn't take any more calls like this.

Go me, I thought dully. *I'm not that victim.*

Chapter 20

I was starting to figure out that Derrel had a sixth sense-thing going on, where he knew exactly what to say to make people feel better. Even if sometimes that something was absolutely nothing. Not even an "I'm here if you need someone to talk to"—which is usually even more unhelpful than staying out of it completely. And that old "If you need anything, let me know," is also a total crock. You hear people say it all the time, but then you never see anyone actually call up the person who said it and say, "Hey, remember when you said to let you know if I needed anything? Well, I'm feeling really overwhelmed. Could you please come clean my kitchen, because if I could have a clean kitchen, I'd feel like I had a bit of a head start." You'll never hear someone say that, because then the person asking the other person to clean their kitchen is seen as a helpless, incompetent dick.

What would be so much better would be for the person who spouted the useless "if you need anything just ask" platitude to fucking go over to the person's house and clean their goddamn kitchen without being asked.

Go over and say, "Hey, you go take care of your kid or your work, or go take a fucking nap. And when you get done, you'll have a clean kitchen. And, no, you don't owe me a goddamn thing. Someday the shoe will be on the other foot, okay?"

And that was the sort of shit that Derrel did all the time. He never breathed a word or a hint, but he was too tapped in to the gossip to not know what was going on with my dad. He didn't ask me why I was so quiet, which was more of a relief that I could have possibly expressed. And no, he didn't come over and clean my kitchen, but when I met him at a death scene later in the morning, he stopped me before we went inside the condo and handed me an insulated cup full of hot chocolate and a paper bag with an egg and bacon biscuit in it.

"You're too skinny," he told me. "And if you don't eat it willingly, I'll hold you down and make you eat it."

I took the bag from him. I had absolutely no doubt that he would do exactly that.

"Besides," he added with a wicked smile, "you should always be well fed going into a death scene. There's nothing worse then puking on an empty stomach."

"I have never and will never puke on a death scene," I informed him around mouthfuls of bacon and egg biscuit.

He grinned. "I'm beginning to think this is true. You're getting to be pretty damn hardcore. Amazing the stuff we can survive, isn't it?"

It was the closest he ever came to saying something meant to be comforting. Yet I was more comforted and reassured and all that than I would have been if he'd given me a big ol' hug or anything weird and touchy-feely like that. Actually, if he'd given me a hug I'd have probably freaked the hell out, because, well, that would have been seriously weird. But then again, I was about as far from touchy-feely as you could get. *Unless you're fucking me, don't put your hands on me.*

I finished up the biscuit and hot chocolate, and followed Derrel into the condo with the stretcher and body bag.

There was no crime scene tape or sign-in log—only a deputy at the door who directed us toward a bedroom in the back. I left the stretcher in the foyer and followed Derrel with the bag.

We were in a condo on the south end of Tucker Point in a complex that advertised itself with terms like "luxury" and "high end." Through the bedroom window I could see the Kreeger River, and I'd seen on our way up that the bottom floor of this condo had a walkway that led to a private dock where a modest-sized boat was parked. The condo had all of the modern touches—stainless steel appliances, wood floors, marble counters. The furniture in the bedroom was solid and elegant, all in a matching dark oak—unlike the thrift-store variety selection in my own house. The bedding was a rich red and gold brocade and looked expensive as hell, though right now it was stained with vomit and saliva.

But not egg-and-bacon-biscuit vomit at least.

The source of the vomit lay sprawled on her side, eyes half-lidded and dulled by death. She looked fairly young—maybe mid to late twenties or so. Pretty and slender, she had shoulder-length brown hair subtly highlighted with red and blonde, tendrils of which snaked through the congealing mess of puke beneath her head. Bubbles of spit lingered on her mouth, and I could see the remains of a dark red lipstick. She was wearing a pink tank top and panties that looked like they came from Victoria's Secret instead of Walmart, and her nails were nicely done with a French manicure. I could see flecks of pills in the puke, and about half a dozen baggies containing more pills on the nightstand.

It wasn't too hard to figure out how she'd died.

"Theresa Anderson. Twenty-nine years old," Derrel muttered with a shake of his head.

My mouth formed a grimace as I scanned the room. "Living the dream, and it's still not enough."

"Depends on how you define 'the dream,' " he replied absently.

Snorting, I casually poked through a pile of papers and file folders on the nightstand. "What, you mean 'money isn't everything,' blah blah blah?" I shrugged. "I mean, yeah, money sure as shit helps, but—" I swept my gaze around the room again. "I mean, look at this place. It fucking rocks."

I expected Derrel to argue the point with me, make the case that even rich and successful people could get overwhelmed or whatever, but he simply gave a slight nod while he scrawled notes. "It's a waste," he said mildly.

"It's fucked up," I stated. "She has money, a great place to live." I scowled down at the papers. Legal briefs, letters. Nothing terribly ominous. Looked pretty boring to me. "Looks like she was some sort of hotshot lawyer. I bet there was never any question about her going to college."

Derrel made a noncommittal noise in his throat while he peered at the body.

I moved over to the bookcase, trailing my fingers through the thin layer of dust. A reed diffuser gave off a pleasant flowery scent that mixed oddly with the smell of puke. There were more law books here. A few books with lofty titles that sounded like they'd been featured on Oprah or some such thing. Nothing that looked fun or light-hearted. "Maybe she couldn't handle the pressure," I said with a shrug, then sighed. "I dunno. I'm talking out my ass. Was it a suicide?"

"Hard to say," he said, lifting his eyes from his clipboard. "Cops didn't find a note, but that doesn't mean a damn thing. Most suicides don't leave notes. And Dr. Leblanc is usually reluctant to rule it a suicide unless there's a fair amount of certainty. I expect this will get ruled an accidental overdose." He shook his head. "Likely started out small—the occasional anxiety med, or maybe Adderall or something to help her get through her classes. Then it grew from there until she was dependent on it."

I fell silent at that, and my emotions tumbled strangely as the two of us wrestled her into the body bag. That theory hit a little too close to home. I'd narrowly escaped being found in a similar situation—though most likely in far less lovely surroundings. But it felt strange seeing that regular, upscale people went through shit like this as well. I mean, I'd known it on a logical level, but somehow I'd still always believed that drug abuse and overdose was limited to the loser segment of the population.

I smiled without humor. No. Where I went wrong was believing that being in the loser segment had anything to do with income or social class.

Derrel bagged up the various pills, then helped me maneuver the stretcher out of the condo and into the van. *I wonder if she bought her pills from Clive.* Certainly a possibility, though I knew there was a hefty market for pain meds, and plenty of people looking to make a buck that way.

Derrel's phone rang as I was closing the back doors of the van. He made some notes on his pad and then looked up at me, expression sour. "Busy day today. Good thing there's room in there for more than one body."

The second body of the day was at the other end of the parish, in an apartment at the opposite end of the economic spectrum from Ms. Anderson's luxury condo.

An ambulance was parked outside next to a Sheriff's Office car and an unmarked one that clearly belonged to a detective. A quick glance at the unit number on the marked car told me that it wasn't Marcus's, and I couldn't decide if I was relieved or disappointed.

Inside the apartment the carpet was old and threadbare in spots, and none of the furniture matched, but it was absolutely neat as a pin and as spotless as it was possible to make such a place. A faint scent of biscuits hung in the air, mingled with a faint flowery scent. I looked around to see if there was a reed diffuser in this place as well, but then realized that the source of the flowery smell came from actual flowers in a ceramic pitcher on the dining room table.

Detective Roth stood by the doorway to the kitchen. "Your victim's in here," he said in a low voice to Derrel, stepping aside so that we could see the woman on the floor. "Sarah Jackson." Then he nodded his head toward the living room. A twenty-something black man wearing a white T-shirt, jeans, and workboots sat on the couch with his head in his hands. "That's Drew Russell, her boyfriend. They live together, but he got in from working offshore about an hour ago and found her." He grimaced.

Derrel gave him a grave nod and then moved to the living room. I stayed back while he spoke in soft tones to the boyfriend, but the grief on the man's face was so stark I had to turn away.

Stepping into the kitchen, I thought for a brief, jarring instant, that the woman was simply asleep—even though I knew that couldn't possibly be the case. Not if we were there. She was lying on her right side, left arm out in front of her, legs slightly bent as if she'd curled up to take a nap. But her eyes were open and lifeless, and when I stepped closer I could see that her right arm was twisted awkwardly beneath her.

Crouching, I tugged on gloves. The portion of the body nearest the floor was red and mottled, and I'd been on the job long enough to know that was called "lividity"—the settling of the blood in the body after the heart stopped beating. I gently poked at a spot of red on her lower arm. It didn't change color, which meant the lividity was fixed and that she'd probably been dead for several hours, at least. *At least this isn't something where the boyfriend is responsible*, I thought with a vague relief. He seemed so devastated by loss, I'd have felt cheated if it was all some sort of act.

I looked up as Derrel came into the kitchen. "Anything interesting?" he asked as he crouched beside me.

"Lividity is fixed," I replied. "That's as far as I got."

He nodded, then lifted the victim's left arm and flexed it at the elbow. "Rigor's come and gone, though that's a lousy way to determine time of death. No sign of pulmonary edema—that bubbly-spit thing that the last body had. That can be a sign of possible OD."

I didn't think this woman had overdosed, but I had nothing more than a gut feeling to back that up, so I said nothing.

"I don't think she's an OD," he said in echo of my thoughts. "But Dr. Leblanc will find out for sure."

We did a quick sweep of the apartment for meds, coming up with nothing more than some antibiotics. A neighbor came and sat with the boyfriend while Derrel gently obtained information about her legal next of kin, and then I departed with the body, leaving the emotional wreckage behind.

*   *   *

Dr. Leblanc was ready to start the autopsies almost as soon as I made it back with the bodies. With the first, Theresa Anderson, he performed a quick-test for drugs while I was still getting her propped up on the block. He peered at the results then sighed and set the test aside. He practically zoomed through the rest of the autopsy, doing cursory examinations of the organs while I struggled to keep up. I'd seen the quick test, and I figured he didn't feel like wasting time on an in-depth procedure when it was obvious to anyone with eyes that the woman had died of an overdose, whether intentionally or not. Of course there was always the consideration that it could have been staged and that it was a possible homicide, but that was for the cops to figure out. The pathologist's primary job was to determine manner and means of death.

Realistically, though, we all knew there was no foul play involved in Theresa Anderson's death. This was senseless, not sinister.

In stark contrast to the first, Dr. Leblanc took his sweet time with the second victim, Sarah Jackson. He performed a quick test on her as well, but it came back as clean as a whistle.

"Ah, well," he finally said, looking down at the heart that he'd carefully sliced open on his cutting board. "That explains it."

"What?"

He gestured me over with the blood-covered scalpel, and I obediently moved to his side. "She had an abnormally small right coronary artery. Most likely caused a fatal ventricular arrhythmia. Probably never had a single symptom." He pointed to something within the heart, but I could only take his word that whatever I was looking at was abnormal in any way.

"Wait," I said. "She never felt bad or sick from this? She just dropped dead?"

"That's probably what happened."

"That's not fair!" I blurted, then realized how dumb that sounded. But it wasn't. The rich bitch had thrown her life away, while Sarah Jackson had been working her ass off trying to make as nice a life as possible with what she had. Then she died with no warning.

Dr. Leblanc's eyes were shadowed as he met my gaze. He'd seen it too many times, I realized. He was used to it.

He gave me a sad smile. "Welcome to death."

I stood in the cooler until the cold seeped into my bones, and my fingers began to grow stiff. Death wasn't fair. Death didn't give warning. Death hit nice people and nasty people. It didn't give a shit.

My one-month anniversary of working here had come and gone, and nothing had happened. No one gave me a medal or certificate for good behavior. It didn't make a difference, I realized. Nothing had changed. I was still the same thing I was a month ago.

It wasn't until hunger began to nudge at me that I realized I was being a moron and pushing my body too far with this whole standing-in-the-cold bullshit.

After making sure I was alone in the morgue, I went through my procedure of scooping the brains into my pickle jars. I felt no qualms when I salvaged the overdose victim's brain, but when I turned to Ms. Jackson's bag, I hesitated. Her death had been unfair enough already. Now I was going to desecrate her by making her brain my dinner?

Hunger poked at me again. Tightening my jaw, I quickly put her brain into the jar. Yeah, death wasn't fair. *And I'm not gonna give it any more head starts.*

Chapter 21

"What the hell happened to this guy?"

Detective Mike Abadie turned at my question then offered a thin smile. "Lawn mower," he said, gesturing to the riding mower lying on its side a few feet away from the body. Not just any lawn mower, either, but one of the big tractor things usually used in yards that were measured in acres instead of feet.

And that certainly fit the bill here. We were in the front yard of what could almost be described as a mansion: a three-story white house with a broad curved driveway, on a piece of land that was at least five acres—the majority of which was mowed grass. The house itself was about a thousand feet from the road and, in bizarre contrast, was also less than half a mile from the trailer park where the drug dealer-gamer guy had been killed. Sometimes it cracked me up the way the super nice neighborhoods were smack up next to the total shit neighborhoods.

"Looks like he was trying to do some sort of repair on it," the detective continued. "He must have had it propped up on that piece of four by four, and when it fell it smacked onto his head and pretty much crushed it."

"Crushed the *hell* out of it," I observed. Why the hell had he been underneath the damn thing? Didn't people ever stop and think how dangerous stuff was? The guy's head was damn near flattened, with two deep impressions that would probably match up perfectly to the underside of the tractor. He'd probably been dead before the tractor had fully settled on him.

"So this was the lawn guy for the place or something?" I asked.

The detective shook his head. "Nope. That's Rob Harris himself."

I let out a whistle of surprise. Rob Harris owned a local RV dealership and was also something of a local celebrity due to a series of commercials that had run for several years and featured his numerous grandchildren. He'd passed the business on to his son recently and was supposedly enjoying his retirement.

Not so much anymore, obviously.

Stupidly annoyed at the waste, I crouched by the head and by the chunks of brain that had been squished out. Maybe, if I'd been desperate, I'd have tried to recover the bits that were on the ground, but they were so mingled with dirt and grass that I wasn't about to go there. I wanted badly to pull some of the skull pieces off and see how much was left inside, but I knew I couldn't do that with so many people around. There was "tough" and "hardcore," and then there was "sick bitch."

"Want a bite?"

I jerked my head around to see Detective Abadie standing behind me, grinning. "Hunh?" I managed, trying to not look guilty. Or hungry. Of which I was both.

He nodded his head toward the scattered chunks of brain. "That'd be a buffet for a zombie, right?"

I couldn't move, simply continued to stare at him. *He knows? How? Is he one?*

He rolled his eyes. "Oh, come on, Crawford. Don't tell me you've never seen *Dawn of the Dead*, or *Zombieland*. You know—" He rolled his eyes up into his head and assumed a slack-jawed expression. "Braaaai-innnssss."

I swallowed and struggled to control my stunned expression. "Oh. You're talking about movies." I managed to keep from saying "not real zombies."

He gave me a faintly disgusted look. "No shit, Sherlock. Wow, you have no sense of humor at all. It's not like I was asking you to really eat brains." He shook his head and turned away. As he walked off, I heard him mutter "freak" under his breath.

I stood up, fighting the desire to laugh out loud, almost surprised to realize that I wasn't bothered by the intended insult. Especially considering what the truth was.

Derrel came up beside me, casting a grimace down at Mr. Harris. "Damn. That tractor sure did a number on his skull."

"Yeah." I slid a glance to the underside of the tractor—easy to see since it was lying on its side—then cocked my head and frowned. "So, what part of the tractor do you think came down on his head to smush it like that?"

Derrel gave me a puzzled look, then followed my gaze. "That's a damn good question, Angel," he murmured.

"You got those two x-shaped impressions on his head," I said. "And there's that bit at the center of the blades that's x-shaped, so that fits. For one of them, at least."

"But how the hell would he get two right next to each other?" Derrel finished for me, eyes narrowed in thought. "Goddamn, Angel. Good eye."

I smilcd, but a sick nausca was bcginning to twist in my belly. *He was murdered. Someone dropped the tractor on his head, then dropped it down again to make sure he was dead and make sure the skull was crushed open. And it had to have been someone strong.* Zombies were strong. I'd figured that much out. Not because of any sort of superpowers, but because we didn't feel the same pain that normal people could. We could push harder, far beyond what the usual person could tolerate. Yeah, it burned us up faster. *But a brain a day keeps the rotting away,* I thought with a slight shudder.

I stood back while Derrel shared my observations with the detective. Abadie scowled and peered at the underside of the tractor, then muttered something vile. I almost felt sorry for him. Handling an accidental death was a walk in the park next to dealing with a possible homicide. The procedures didn't change much, but the attention to detail went several notches up. And if he hadn't been a dickwad I probably would've felt sorry for him. As it was, I allowed myself a perverse sense of satisfaction. Hey, I never claimed to *be* an angel.

I ended up cooling my heels for another half an hour while the area was processed in more depth by the crime scene tech, but eventually I got the signal from Derrel that I could start putting Mr. Harris into the bag.

Now was my chance to see how much brain was left in the skull, even though my zombie super senses were already telling me the answer. I carefully pulled aside a segment of skull while getting the body into the bag—completely unsurprised to see that there was no brain left inside. And there wasn't that much on the ground. Certainly not enough to fill a skull.

Suddenly the short distance between Mr. Harris's mansion and the trailer park didn't seem so funny. And the place where I had my wreck was only about five miles from here.

There was a zombie on the hunt in this area. And I had a damn good idea who it was.

As soon as I had the body loaded up and in the van, I called Scott Funeral Home and asked for Kang, breathing a sigh of relief when he came on the line.

"It's Angel, from the morgue," I said. "I really need to talk to you."

He was silent for several seconds. "Uh huh. Are you in a bind?"

"Yeah, but not the kind you're thinking." He probably thought I was low on brains and needed to bum some off him. "No, I need to talk to you about someone else in our, um, social club."

I could hear him give a soft snort—whether of laughter or annoyance, I couldn't tell. "All right. I get off at three today. Where would you like to meet?"

I thought fast. "Um, how about Double Ds?"

"I'll see you there," he said and hung up.

I scowled at my phone. "You're an asshole, Kang," I muttered. Unfortunately, he was an asshole I needed. Too bad I had way too many of those in my life already.

Chapter 22

Double Ds was actually the Double Dime Diner, but no one bothered to call it that, even though the nickname made it sound like a strip club. Or maybe because of that. I arrived at about a quarter 'til three, which not only allowed me to pick a table that was well away from the few other people there, but also gave me plenty of time to agonize and worry until Kang arrived. Not that I hadn't already been doing plenty of that.

The waitress came by, and I ordered hot chocolate. It wasn't cold outside or anything, but hot chocolate was one of my comfort foods. When it arrived I wrapped my hands around the mug and sipped slowly, forcing myself to relax as the warmth and chocolate worked their magic. At least comfort food was still comforting.

Kang walked in about five minutes after the hour. The smile on his face faded as he walked up to me. I guess my worry was showing, even though I was trying to be all casual.

"What's the dish, Angel?" he asked as he pulled a chair out and plopped down into it.

Even though there was no one else anywhere near us,

I leaned forward and kept my voice low. "I've picked up three bodies in the last week that were missing brains. Hell, one was missing his whole damn head." I quickly explained the circumstances, somewhat gratified when his expression darkened with worry. At least I wasn't being completely out-the-box paranoid. "Do you think maybe there's umm . . . a rogue zombie killing people?" I asked, feeling a bit silly with the "rogue" thing.

But Kang merely gave a slow nod and shoved his hair out of his eyes, grimacing. "It definitely sounds like a possibility." Then he let out a string of curses that made my eyebrows go up. "Sorry," he said, "but shit like that makes it tough on all of us."

I hesitated. "You know about the wreck I had, right?" He nodded, which didn't surprise me. Everyone knew about the damn wreck. "Well, it was caused by Zeke Lyons, who used to work at—"

"Billings," he said with a nod. "I know him. Stupid stubborn ass." His eyes narrowed in anger. "He was trying to get the body in your van?"

I nodded. "And possibly more, I think. I mean, he didn't know I was a zombie until after he'd caused the wreck." Then I snorted. "Hell, *I* didn't even know I was a zombie until then. That was the first time I'd ever seen another one." I fought back a shiver at the memory—the sick horror that I might become like that some day. Rotted. Desperate.

"I ended up giving him some of the stash I had with me," I went on, swallowing back the lingering unease. "He came by the morgue, and I gave him more, but," I grimaced, "he was a bit of a dick, and he hasn't been back since."

"You don't need to fucking give your stash away, Angel," he told me. "Zeke knows he can buy from me."

"With what? He doesn't have a job anymore, remember?"

Kang's lip curled. "He should have thought of that before he screwed up the job he had." He shrugged. "But even so, I'd be willing to work something out with him."

I spread my hands on the table, gave a slight nod. "That's cool. Zeke said he was set up, that he didn't steal anything." *Were you the one who cost him his job?* I thought. I didn't want to come out and say it, though. I wasn't quite ready to piss Kang off.

He snorted. "Of course. The guilty man is never really guilty. He was lucky they only fired him."

"Well, maybe whoever's doing this is someone new," I suggested. "I mean, if I hadn't been given this morgue job, I don't know what I would have done."

The scowl stayed on Kang's face as he leaned back. "And that's exactly why there aren't many zombies. You don't make one just for shits and giggles, because the next thing you know you have dozens of them, desperate for brains. And brains are pretty hard to come by without causing a fuss, as you know."

My mouth felt dry. "So, how bad does it get? The hunger, I mean. Would *any* of us be driven to kill to get brains?"

I could see that Kang wanted to deny it, but I'd already seen the wince of discomfort. "It can get bad," he admitted. "And the hungrier you get, the less control you have. You're not . . . you're not you."

"Have you—" I clamped my lips shut on the question. "Never mind. I'm sorry."

He exhaled a long slow breath and didn't answer. That told me more than I wanted to know. *It could happen to me. If I got hungry enough, I wouldn't simply die. I'd become a monster first.*

"Is there anything that can be done?" I asked, fumbling for anything to say to get past this horrific topic. "I mean, about this, um, rogue. Whoever it is."

Kang looked up, and it seemed to take him a couple of seconds to focus on me, as if I was drawing him out of a terrible place. "I don't know," he said. "I don't exactly have a directory of the local zombies." His shoulders lifted in a shrug. "Let's hope that whoever it is sticks to killing losers and old farts."

A flare of anger coiled in my belly. "Wait. That's it? Sit back and hope he doesn't kill anyone important? Kang, that's bullshit."

"What the hell do you want me to do about it?"

"I don't know! You're the expert here. You said yourself that this sort of thing could draw unwanted attention to us."

"So would making a big stink about deaths that are completely unrelated in every other way. There's no link except for the missing brains, and that's easy enough to explain away." His face twisted into a sneer. "Go on, I dare you to go to the police. Tell them that these people were all killed by the same person."

"Go fuck yourself," I said dully. I hated him right now, but I also hated the fact that he was right.

He stood, then leaned forward and put his hands on the table. "There's nothing we can do, Angel. Sometimes shit happens that way. One way or another, this will get worked out. It always does. This zombie will either move on, or someone will take him out."

With that he straightened and spun. A second later he was out the door while I stared after him in confusion and anger.

Would this zombie move on? How long would it take before people started to wonder about all of the "accidental" deaths? And would anyone ever notice that the victims were all low on brains? I clutched the mug like a damn lifeline, thoughts tumbling in jangled disarray.

All he needs to do is start hiding the bodies so they aren't found for a while—enough time for them to de-

compose. Then no one would ever realize that the victims had been killed for their brains. Half of this parish is fucking swamp, too. It's not like it's tough to hide a body around here.

Of course, that thought also gave me a chill. How did I know there weren't bodies slowly rotting in the swamp already? Prey on people who wouldn't be missed. It would be so easy to get away with it.

The very fact that I was working out how to do it left me nauseated.

The waitress came by, and I went ahead and ordered another hot chocolate, along with a piece of apple pie. The comfort food was going to be working overtime.

On the other hand, Zeke had been so out in the open with these three murders that I kinda had a hard time believing he had a secret pile of bodies hidden in the swamp. That made me feel ever so slightly better. I could maybe believe that the murder of the drug dealer had been planned—I mean, even I could get behind the idea that if you have to kill someone, make it someone who was a piece of shit. I, the former druggie, endorsed this. Now that was damn funny.

And the murder of Mr. Harris with the lawn mower had to have been spur-of-the-moment. Zeke was hungry, saw the guy outside working on his mower, and seized an opportunity.

"Angel?"

I jerked and nearly spilled my hot chocolate. Standing by my table were Ed and Marcus, both looking at me with questioning smiles. The two men were dressed casually in jeans and T-shirts, which probably explained why I hadn't noticed them coming into the diner since I'd only ever seen them in uniform before. That and the fact that I was so deeply absorbed in my thoughts they could have paraded around nude and it might not have registered.

My mind wanted to continue exploring that line of thought, but I ruthlessly yanked it back to the here and now. "Hi. Sorry. I was a million miles away," I said, smiling weakly.

"You looked like you were doing some serious thinking there," Ed said. "Everything all right?"

"Yeah, just letting my mind wander." I waved toward the empty chairs around the table. "Y'all wanna sit? I'm killing some time."

In answer, both men seized chairs and sat. The waitress materialized and slid my pie in front of me, then turned to Ed and Marcus. "Y'all eatin'?"

Ed smiled. "Yes, ma'am. I'll have the double bacon cheeseburger with fries, loaded baked potato, cinnamon apples, mac and cheese, and a side salad with ranch dressing. Oh, and a Barq's."

"And I'll have a Diet Coke," Marcus said as soon as the waitress had finished scrawling down Ed's incredible order. "Also a turkey club with extra bacon, a cup of gumbo, garlic bread, and an Italian salad—with extra olive oil."

I stared at the two of them as the poor woman finished writing and hurried off. "Holy shit. And I was feeling guilty for indulging in *pie*."

Marcus grinned. "I can't hold a candle to Ed. This is a light snack for him. He has the metabolism of a hummingbird."

Ed spread his hands and gave a rueful shrug. "He speaks the truth. I have an overachieving appetite. But surely you could eat more than that," he said with a nod to my pie. "You don't have a spare ounce of fat on you."

"The word is 'scrawny,'" I retorted. "And I think I'd barf if I tried to eat as much as either of you."

Ed raised an eyebrow. "You of the legendary Iron Stomach? I think not."

I cast a doubtful glance at him. "Legendary?"

Marcus grinned. "It's true. Everyone knows that nothing bothers you on a scene."

"But that's not true!" I blurted in surprise. I could feel my face heating, and I quickly jabbed a fork at my pie in an effort to cover my sudden embarrassment. I kinda liked being thought of as hardcore, but I wasn't keen on being known as some sort of heartless robot. "Stuff bothers me," I muttered.

"Easy, Angel," Marcus said, touching the back of my hand briefly. "No one's implying you're cold or made of stone. You're as human as any of us." He offered me a slight smile. "Please trust me when I say it's a good thing when cops and paramedics say that you're tough."

"I don't feel tough," I said, unable to completely keep the sour note from my voice.

"Yeah, well, you fake it well," Ed told me, then smiled at the waitress as she poured his coffee. "Thanks, ma'am."

"So what are you two up to today?" Yes, I wanted to change the subject.

"Deer season opens this weekend," Marcus replied. "We're going to go check out the property where we usually hunt and make sure everything's in order."

The pie was good, but I had the faintest hint that I was missing something in the flavor. Then I realized. *A day without brains is like a day without sunshine.* My last brains had been early yesterday.

"You two don't strike me as the good ol' boy deer-hunter type," I said.

Ed chuckled. "And you would be right. But every now and then we feel the urge to give it a try. I think we're suckers for punishment."

"My uncle owns a fairly large parcel of land at the north end of the parish," Marcus explained.

"His uncle owns half the parish," Ed interjected.

Marcus grinned. "Not quite. But he is pretty well-off."

At a sidelong glance from Ed he chuckled. "Okay, he's filthy stinking rich. Anyway. He used to take the two of us hunting when we were kids, and now it's a stupid tradition that we continue." His mouth twitched into a smile. "Some of that male bonding crap."

"Uh huh." I gave them both a dubious look. "Do y'all ever actually kill any deer?"

Ed cast his eyes upward and tapped his chin with his fingers. "Hmm . . . that's a tough question."

Marcus gave a laugh. "The answer is 'almost never.' Mostly it gives us an excuse to go ride around on four-wheelers, play with big guns, and then spend the next few days picking ticks off our bodies."

"Wow," I said. "I am *so* glad I'm not a guy."

"It's much better that you're not," Ed said, expression suddenly serious.

I blinked. "Er, okay. Why do you say that?"

"Well, you'd be a very funny looking boy," he said. "I mean, with the boobies and all."

I let out a bark of laughter and threw my napkin at him. "You idiot."

Marcus laughed. "For what it's worth, I have to agree with Ed, though I won't use the word 'boobies.'"

"You just did," I pointed out with a mock glare.

He raised his hands in surrender. "Guilty as charged."

"So, do either of you have girlfriends who have to put up with you?" I asked, hoping it sounded nice and casual. Because that's all it was, right? A casual getting-to-know-you question. I hid a grimace. Nope, it was totally desperate and awkward. Ugh.

"Marcus has yet to find anyone to tolerate his presence on a somewhat permanent basis," Ed said, casting a teasing look at the other man. "But I'm willingly under the thumb of a fine woman who I probably don't deserve."

"You might have seen her the other day at the crime

scene for the pizza guy," Marcus said. "She had the ca
daver dog. They were looking for the head."

"Oh, right!" I remembered her. Cute and petite.

"What about you?" Ed asked with a tilt of his head.
"Is there a lucky guy in your life?"

I don't know why I was unprepared for the question,
especially since I was the one who'd brought the whole
subject up in the first place. "Um, kinda," I said, fumbling for an answer. "I mean, there's this guy I've been
going out with for about four years . . . ."

"Four years?" Marcus said. "Sounds serious. Any
wedding plans in the near future?"

"No!" I said, then felt a surge of embarrassment at
how quick I was to deny that possibility. "I mean, we're
not that kind of serious. We're kinda on and off." Shame
flowed through me at my lack of loyalty, but marry
Randy? I couldn't see that happening in a million years.
So why the hell am I still with him?

"Speaking of the cadaver dog," I said in what was
probably an incredibly obvious attempt to change the
subject, "did they ever find the guy's head?"

"Not sure," Marcus answered. "Some hunters found a
fire pit out in the swamp that had what looked like skull
fragments and teeth, but it was all pretty well burned up.
The lab's going to see if they can do a DNA match to the
pizza guy or the victim from Sweet Bayou." He frowned.
"There's a lot of weird buzz going on about that case.
It's a strange one."

"You mean *other* than the fact that the guy had his
head chopped off?" Ed said, raising an eyebrow.

Their food arrived then, and the conversation was
briefly suspended while room was found on the table for
the ridiculous number of plates.

As soon as the waitress stepped away Marcus continued. "It's looking like a setup of some kind. The guy was
delivering pizzas, but the address was a house that had

been foreclosed on last year, and empty even longer. His car was found in front of the house, and the bag with the pizza was on the ground in the front yard."

Tension knotted in my stomach, and I had to force myself to maintain an even expression. "You're saying he was lured there and then attacked." Goddammit. Zeke ordered out for a meal all right.

"And he wasn't robbed either," Marcus added. "The detectives are trying to figure out if there was anything special about this guy that would have someone wanting to lop his head off."

There was a brain in it, I thought grimly. Zeke probably chased him down, chopped the guy's head off, then took his meal and ran.

"That's pretty weird," I said, trying hard to keep my tone even.

"Yeah, Marianne's pretty freaked by it too," Ed said around his cheeseburger. I was shocked to see that he'd already plowed through all of his fries and was nearly finished with his burger. To my relief he took a few seconds to chew and swallow before continuing. "She lives a few streets away. That's how she was able to be on the scene so quickly with her dog."

"I don't blame her," I said. "I think I'd be freaked if someone was chopping off heads in my neighborhood too." I continued to slowly pick at the pie while the two men ate, my thoughts still tumbling, though not quite as jagged as before. Kang was right. There was no way I could tell anyone that all of the recent deaths were connected. Going to the cops was out. And I wasn't qualified in any way to take it upon myself to solve the case and stop the killer, as dramatic and cool as that might sound. It was beside the point that I was pretty damn sure who the killer was. I could probably even find him if I really bent my mind to it. The pizza guy had been killed south of Tucker Point, and Sweet Bayou wasn't far from my house, but the drug dealer, the lawn mower guy, and my accident had all been out past Longville on Highway 1790—which was right in between Nice and Tucker Point. Hell, maybe I could drive down the highway and wave a piece of brain out the window to see if he'd come running.

The image that summoned almost sent me into a fit of giggles, and I had to fake a cough to cover it.

Great, so I knew who the rogue zombie was, and I could probably find him if I tried hard enough. But what good would that do? I didn't have the faintest idea how to stop him. Or rather, I did have an idea. And it wasn't anything I could ever see myself doing.

I'm not a killer. I can't go there. I won't do that.

I fought back a sense of anxiety as I scraped up the last pieces of my pie with my fork. Not a killer. Sure. I believed that now. But would I continue to believe it if I ever got hungry enough?

Chapter 23

After parting ways with Marcus and Ed, I drove home. Or at least I thought I was driving home but somehow I ended up out on Highway 1790.

I slowed as I approached the spot where I'd hit the tree. I could see it on the side of the road where it had been pulled aside by road crews. I could also see the long scrape and scar in the asphalt where the van had overturned and slid.

I parked on the side of the road, shut the engine off, got out of my car.

Broken glass sparkled along the edge of the highway, catching the sun in what could have been a lovely display. I shivered, reminded of the way the glass and broken mirrors had reflected the moonlight.

Blood and teeth. Sightless eyes. A head twisted too far. Bones and flesh.

I blinked and shook my head, momentarily robbed of breath by the sudden images. I'd been in another accident. Before the one in the van. I squeezed my eyes shut, struggling to recall, but the scattered memories slipped away as soon as I tried to focus on them.

Opening my eyes, I walked to the tree, shoes crunching gravel and glass. *When I woke up in the ER I was convinced that I was seriously hurt. Yet there wasn't a mark on me, and I was a zombie.* If I'd been hurt that badly, surely it would have taken a huge amount of brains to fix me up.

A quick burst of anger surged through me. *Who the fuck made me like this?*

A breeze swirled along the highway, rustling the grass and briefly quieting the insects. I scowled and rubbed my temples. I hated that I might never find out who made me a zombie. The one-month mark had passed right on by without an explanation or note or anything that might have cleared things up. But now that I'd come this far I understood why the one month thing had been so important. I needed to stick with the job for that long to be sure that I'd be around brains when the drinks ran out, and to be sure I could maintain a supply. Whoever'd decided to get me started in this direction was apparently satisfied with his or her work and had probably moved on to the next victim. Or charity case. Whatever the hell I was.

"Or monster," I muttered. No, not a monster yet. I hadn't killed anyone. Not like Zeke. He'd killed those four people. I was certain of it. And if I'd given him the damn body, maybe he wouldn't have had to kill anyone.

Guilt tugged at my gut even as I tried to fight it off. I couldn't be responsible for Zeke's actions. But was he even responsible for his own? Surely he had to be deep into the hunger to be driven to murder. Yet, even as I thought it, I couldn't help but wonder. Sure, one murder I could see—sort of. But after that. . . . Maybe he'd realized how easy it was.

I frowned. The victim from Sweet Bayou Road had been murdered *before* Zeke lost his job at the funeral home, which meant that he might have already discovered that it was easier to get his food fresh. And as de-composed as the drug dealer was, he had to have been killed before Zeke caused my wreck. *Let's not forget that he was trying to kill me, too.* The guilt vanished, swept away by anger. He didn't know I was a zombie when he pulled the tree onto the road. He probably figured he was getting a two-for-one deal. The brain in the body bag, with me as a chaser.

"Fucker," I growled. There was no way I was giving him any more brains out of my stash.

But if I didn't help him get brains, was I helping to drive him to more murder? Maybe I needed to do the exact opposite. Maybe I should try and hunt him down and give him brains out of my stash—never mind what Kang said.

Besides, what if this ever happened to me? Sure, I was fed and sated right now. But how could I know that I wouldn't end up like Zeke if I lost my job and my access to brains.

I *didn't* know.

And it scared the shit out of me.

My dad was sitting on the couch when I walked into the house. I stopped dead in the doorway, my hand still on the knob as I took in the sight of him. He looked a bit thinner, or maybe that was my imagination.

He looked up as I entered, a flicker of apprehension—or was it worry?—in his eyes. "Hey, Angelkins," he said in a low rough voice.

My shoulders unconsciously hunched at the childhood nickname. He always used it when he was feeling beaten down. Maybe it was his way of trying to recapture those glimpses of the past that weren't made of shit. "Who bailed you out?" I asked, closing the door behind me. It probably wasn't the nicest welcome home I could have given him, but to his credit he didn't seem to be surprised by the hostility in my voice.

He looked down at his hands. They were empty no beer, no cigarettes. "Got a PR."

Personal recognizance. All he'd had to do was promise to come to court for his arraignment. I'd kinda figured he'd end up getting one. At least that took the pressure off me. I didn't ask how he'd made it home. I knew he still had a few buddies who'd be willing to give him a ride. He'd done for it others often enough.

"Okay." I stood there for a few seconds more, then finally decided I didn't really have anything to say to him. Or nothing that wouldn't start a whole new round of shit.

I started toward the hallway to my bedroom.

He stood up. "Baby, I'm sorry. I said . . . and did . . . some terrible things."

His words stopped me, and I pivoted back to him. "I'm not gonna drink anymore, Angel," he said, meeting my gaze. He looked earnest, but I knew he was saying it right now because he'd been scared. He'd spent two days in jail, and right now he was willing to do or say anything to not go back there. I understood that completely. It was why I'd taken a job in the morgue.

I also knew that after a while that fear would fade. Another week or month or so, and he'd start to forget how bad it had been, and he'd want a drink. I'd heard this announcement before. And I'd seen how well his willpower held out.

But there was no point in throwing that in his face right now. It wouldn't accomplish anything except to hurt and demoralize him. "That's great, Dad," I said instead. "I hope that works."

I turned away and continued to my bedroom. He didn't stop me again.

I heard him moving around the house. After a little while the front door opened and closed, followed by the sound of his beater pickup starting up.

As soon as the sound of crunching beer cans faded away I came out of my room and went outside to the big trash can by the side of the house. As I'd suspected, there were several bottles of liquor plus a couple of six-packs of beer. It would be admirable if I hadn't been through this bullshit before. He'd promise to change, then try and go cold turkey, zero to sixty as soon as possible. No rehab, no counseling or support groups, 'cause he was tougher than that, right?

Except that in a few days he'd start to feel it, and he'd hate it, and he'd get mean and resentful, and somehow it would be my fault that he felt so shitty because he was only trying to get sober for me. And my life would become a complete living hell, or I'd simply avoid coming home. He'd never hit me like that before—once or twice, yeah, but never a full-out beating. It was possible that him snapping like that was a one time thing. It was also possible that it would only get worse from here.

Maybe this time will be different. Too bad I couldn't make myself believe it. I pulled the bottles and beer out of the trash can, then walked to the shed behind the house and dumped them onto the workbench.

I wasn't going to sabotage him. I wasn't going to put it all back in the house or anything like that. But I was sure as hell gonna have it close at hand for the next time the shit hit the fan.

Chapter 24

My cell phone chimed with an incoming text message as I was carefully writing the date on the side of a jar. I stuck the jar in the fridge next to the five others already in there, stood and snagged my phone off the top of my dresser.

Good morning my Angel of Death. Time to go play!
—Derrel

As if in response to his text, I felt a little bump of hunger. Great, I thought with a mental sigh. Now my body knows when I'm going to be more active. It had been a busy week in the morgue, which meant that my stash was comfortably large right now. In fact I was damn close to running out of room in my little fridge. I'd realized this morning that I probably needed to become organized and write dates on the jars to keep track of which ones had been in there the longest. I'd recently managed to pry a small amount of info from Kang, such as the fact that three weeks seemed to be the longest a brain stayed "viable" in the fridge. Allowing any of them to spoil was a waste I couldn't afford. I had a nice buffer right now, but there was no guarantee that anyone worth autopsying would die in the next couple of weeks.

Look at me, being all responsible and shit, I thought with a low laugh. Hell, if I exerted a little self-control and waited a bit longer between meals, I'd probably never have to worry about my stash again. Kang had also told me that brains could be frozen and still be worth eating after, but my little fridge didn't have a freezer compartment. And there was no way I was risking putting brains in the kitchen freezer.

I thumbed in a reply to Derrel's text. My kinda fun. Gimme addy, meet u there.

The hunger nudged at me again, and I hesitated, my hand on the door of the fridge. Yeah, I'd eaten just yesterday and I could surely hold out at least another day before things started to feel dull and lifeless. But I didn't want any of it to go bad, I rationalized as I pulled a jar out, ignoring the little voice that told me that even the oldest brains in my stash had been in there less than a week. I was going out to pick up a body, which meant I'd be doing a bunch of lifting and carrying. I could start going longer between meals when I wasn't working. Not today. I took one big swallow before I could change my mind, but even as I replaced the jar in the fridge an old but familiar burn of shame formed in my gut. So much for self-control.

Sighing, I replaced the jar and closed the fridge. I needed to stop being so hard on myself. It was one damn swallow—barely enough for me to feel any difference. And everything else was going all right. In fact I had enough stash that I could afford to try and track down Zeke and give him some. I'd been resisting the idea and finding ways to talk myself out of it, but no new brainless bodies had shown up this whole week. Which meant that either he found a legitimate source, or he was hungry and on the hunt right now.

And if I could somehow prevent another murder, I really didn't have a choice. It wasn't a long term solution to the problem of Zeke, but at least it might buy him some time until he could find a source of brains that didn't involve getting them from living people.

And maybe if I was ever in the same boat, he'd do the same for me.

The address Derrel texted wasn't so much an address as a general location. Despite the vagueness of his directions—*Beaker St, 1 mile south of the hwy*—the number of vehicles clustered in one spot let me know without a doubt where I needed to go.

The area was an odd mix of rural and subdivision, with clumps of cookie-cutter houses interspersed with large plots of land complete with cows and goats. Several of the larger plots looked as if they were being developed into more clusters of houses, and a retention pond had been dug on the west side of the road. A dirt berm about five feet high separated the road from the pond and I could see a knot of people in uniform gathered at the top of it. The street was already blocked by a zillion cars, police units, and crime scene vans—far more than had been on the scene for the murder of the pizza guy. This time there were no obvious places to park anywhere near the crime scene tape, and I ended up parking the van damn near a quarter mile down the road.

The road was uneven and full of potholes, and there was no way for me to know how far beyond the berm the body was. The stretcher would probably be more of a pain in the ass than it was worth. After a brief internal debate, I decided to leave the stretcher in the van for the time being and grabbed the body bag, gloves, and an extra sheet in case I was dealing with something messy. One way or another, Derrel and I were going to be carrying a body bag.

Let's hope this victim is someone nice and small and light. A midget. Yeah, that would work. I hid a smile as I continued on foot toward the knot of people. Then again, I was probably strong enough to carry a two hundred pound body by myself if I had to. I bit back a laugh. Yeah, that would draw some attention—little, scrawny me, all of five foot three and a hundred five pounds soaking wet. SuperZombiePowers activate!

Too bad the superpowers came with insane hunger. Emphasis on the insane part.

My amusement faded, and I began to get a bad feeling as I clambered over the berm and took note of the number of people clustered right beyond the crime scene tape. I'd never met most of them, but I'd seen their faces in the news enough to know that one of the knots of people was the Sheriff and his immediate cronies— which meant that this was some sort of special crime scene: a multiple homicide, or a local celebrity . . . or a kid. My stomach clenched at the last option. There'd only been a few of them so far, but every time we had to do an autopsy on a kid, it damn near killed me. There'd been two infants who'd died right after being born, and a little girl with some sort of birth defect. But the worst had been a twelve-year-old who'd committed suicide. I'd gone into the cooler and cried like a baby after we were done with that one, and when I'd come back out— braced to be teased by Nick—I was weirdly humbled to see that his eyes were red as well. I guess some things fucked you up no matter what.

I made my way carefully over the uneven ground, breathing a silent sigh of relief when I saw, through the group of people, the lower half of a body lying face-down. Definitely an adult. Damn good. I didn't even mind that I'd have to carry him over all that ground.

Then the people moved, and I saw why the upper ranks were at the scene.

Oh, shiiiiiiit.

I moved forward toward the headless body, anger and bile filling my gut—at Zeke for not finding another way to control his hunger, and at Kang for his callous acceptance that a zombie could go rogue like this. I knew I was being pretty smug and sanctimonious, especially considering I had a fairly reliable source of brains, but even though the job had been handed to me I still worked my ass off and did what I had to do to keep it. Not like Zeke, who'd stolen from goddamn bodies. What the hell had he been thinking? Why would anyone whose existence depended on a job choose to fuck it up like that?

I shook my head. Yeah, I was fully aware of the irony of my train of thoughts. Maybe I was beginning to learn a thing or two.

"Less for you to carry again, Angel."

I glanced up to see Detective Roth giving me a sour smile. "Yeah, but this whole losing your head thing is getting old," I replied.

"Tell me about it." He ran a hand through his bristly hair and grimaced.

I let my gaze sweep the surroundings. "Who found the body?"

His grimace deepened. "A couple of kids taking a shortcut to their bus stop. High school age, but still. . . ."

"That'll give 'em nightmares," I said with a shudder.

"No shit." Ben rubbed his eyes. "Fuck. And three headless bodies means we mostly likely have a serial killer, which means the rank is going *nuts* right now."

I suddenly felt for him. All I had to do was pick up the body and go. He'd probably be out here all day and all night, and then likely spend a few more hours talking to everyone who lived around here in an effort to scare up any possible clue.

Maybe I could help point him in the direction of

Zeke as a suspect. I had no idea how I could do that, but I needed to figure out a way, and fast. Five people were dead—that I knew of—and I had every reason to believe that there'd be more. It wasn't as if Zeke was going to suddenly wake up one day and decide he didn't want to eat brains any more. He could have come by the morgue at any time instead of stooping to murder.

And there was no way I could stop him on my own. *But can the cops?* I wondered. A shiver traced its way down my spine. Even if they found him and arrested him . . . what then? They wouldn't be feeding him what he needed in jail. He'd rot, and get hungry, and. . . .

"You ready to turn him over?"

I pulled myself out of the spiral of my thoughts to see Derrel and the crime scene tech looking at me expectantly.

"Oh, yeah," I said. "Sorry." Tugging on the gloves, I crouched by the body, trying to position myself away from the messy stump of the neck. I didn't want blood or anything else gross that might come out of there splorting on me. I took hold of the victim's hip and shoulder and carefully rolled, then allowed the body to settle onto its back.

Oh Shit. Fuck. Damn.

I straightened, blood pounding in my ears as all of my carefully constructed theories came crashing down around me. White male, dressed in worn and dirty jeans and a faded New Orleans Saints T-shirt that celebrated the fact that they'd been divisions champs around a decade or so ago. Barefoot with mud on his feet and staining the bottom couple of inches of his jeans.

But I was only barely aware of those details. My attention was completely fixed on the Florida-shaped stain on the front of the shirt. *Tomato and brain soup.*

The crime scene tech leaned in close to photograph the front of the body. Each snap of the flash seemed to slice through me, jarring my thoughts into more disorder. The buzz of conversation between Derrel and the detectives wrapped around me. They would need to get fingerprints. The dog was searching the area for the head. They were considering calling out the dive team to search through the retention pond.

"I know who he is," I blurted. The detectives and Derrel pivoted to me in unison as if it had been choreographed. If I hadn't been so off-kilter I'd have probably laughed.

"Seriously?" Detective Abadie said, expression betraying nothing but doubt and impatience that I was wasting their time. "Recognize his face?" The skin around his eyes tightened as he gestured toward the body.

The feeling of being off-kilter suddenly vanished, and I straightened. Maybe a few weeks ago I'd have slunk back and mumbled an apology for wasting their time. But not this time. Now I was annoyed.

"Yeah, seriously," I shot back. "And I don't have to recognize his face. I ran into this guy a couple of days ago, and he was wearing the same damn clothes. But, y'know, if you want to be a cocky asstard know-it-all, that's fine. Don't let me waste your time." I crossed my arms defiantly across my chest in emphasis.

I heard a low chuckle that I was pretty sure came from Derrel, but I was too busy giving Mike a death glare to confirm it.

Roth let out a bark of laughter. "Hey, Mike, she knows you pretty well!" He gave me an encouraging smile. "Miz Angel, would you please be so kind as to share any info you have with us?"

I dropped my arms and gave the burly detective a sweet smile. "Why, sugar, I'd be delighted," I drawled. "This guy is Zeke Lyons. He used to work at Billings Funeral Home until he was fired a few weeks back for stealing jewelry off bodies. And I recognize his clothing because he came by the morgue the other day and was hassling me."

"Are you sure it's him?" Roth asked.

"One hundred percent? No," I said. "But I'll go with at least ninety-nine percent sure. I recognize the stain on his shirt." No sense explaining why I'd remember a thing like that.

"Ah, my Angel of Death comes through for me yet again," Derrel said with a grin as he scribbled on his pad. "You are a goddess."

Roth gave an emphatic nod. "We'll verify with prints, but that gives us a big head start." His lips twitched. "So to speak," he added. Then he gave me a wink right before elbowing his partner. "C'mon, Mike, what do you say?"

Abadie gave a sour sigh. "I'm sorry I doubted you," he said in the kind of monotone used by six-year-olds when forced to give an apology. "Thank you for saving us from tedious legwork."

The two turned away to report this information to their superiors, and Derrel sidled up to me, amusement dancing in his eyes.

"My god, Angel," he said in a low voice. "It was worth getting up early for that alone." At my perplexed look he grinned. "I've been waiting for an excuse to call Mike a cocky asstard for ages. I loved it."

I laughed weakly. "I didn't exactly plan it. But sometimes it burns me the way they. . . ." I couldn't figure out how to say what I wanted to say.

"The way they dismiss you because you're not one of them? And in your case it doesn't help that you're a convicted felon, which in the eyes of idiots like Mike, puts you several levels below him."

I flushed at the reminder of my history, and Derrel lightly thwapped me on the head with his pen. "Stop it.

You're a smart chick. The people who matter have noticed that fact. Mike's a dick. Besides," he jerked his head toward the body on the ground, "you saved me a bunch of work. I'm pretty cool with that."

I didn't know how to respond to that, but I was saved by a small commotion from the south end of the pond. I looked over to see a couple of uniformed deputies along with a woman with a dog on a leash—all looking fairly pleased about something. I recognized the woman as the same dog handler who'd been at the other headless body crime scene: Marianne, Ed's girlfriend.

"I'll be right back, Angel," Derrel said. "Unless you need help getting him into the bag?"

I shook my head. "I can handle this one." I'd learned the trick of rolling bodies into bags my first week. I wouldn't even need to use my zombie super strength.

He gave me a parting wink, then headed in the direction of the detectives. I crouched and began to wrap the stump of Zeke's neck in the sheet. *So if Zeke isn't the rogue, who is?* I wondered in uneasy frustration. Or maybe I was wrong about the whole thing. Kang said there weren't very many zombies, so what were the chances of two zombies being hard up for brains in the same area? Then again, I had no idea what Kang meant by "not many." Could be five, could be a hundred.

I opened the body bag, smoothly rolled the body into it, snapped the toe tag onto the right foot. *Probably not a hundred*, I decided. *There's no way enough people could die to support that many.* I tried to do some mental math in an attempt to figure out how many zombies could live on the number of people who died in St. Edwards Parish, but gave up as soon as I realized I would need to do division in my head.

Pulling the zipper closed, I glanced up in time to see Marianne headed my way, pulled along by a very eager dog.

"You must be Angel," the petite woman said breathlessly as the dog stopped in front of me. "Ed and Marcus have told me about you. So nice to finally meet you!"

I straightened and gave her a smile. "Hi, yeah, I'm Angel. You're Marianne, right?"

She bobbed her head in a yes, then dipped her chin toward the dog who was sitting and staring at me intently. "And this here is Kudzu." She frowned at the dog, then rolled her eyes. "Oh, you silly mutt. She's not a corpse."

I could feel the blood drain from my face, but thankfully Marianne kept right on talking and didn't seem to notice. "She's a cadaver dog, see? And she's smelling the body you have in the bag, and probably your clothes as well since you wear them in the morgue, right?" I nodded but she kept on going. Damn good thing since I wasn't quite sure if I'd recovered the ability to speak yet. "We came out to see if we could find this poor guy's head, but instead we stumbled across a little campsite where he's probably been living." She shook her head. "What an awful, awful thing." She tugged at the leash and the dog obediently returned to her side.

Well, now I knew where Zeke had been staying. Not that it mattered anymore. "Yeah, I think the cops are freaking out a bit," I said, relieved that my voice didn't show any of my earlier shock. "I guess they're thinking it's a serial killer."

Marianne rubbed her arms. "I've been making Ed stay at my place every night ever since the last body was found so close to where I live." Then she grinned. "Though that's not much of a change from the usual. He has a nice enough apartment over in Longville, but it's furnished like a dorm room. Whereas I actually have silly things like beds and chairs and couches."

"And hopefully a large refrigerator, too," I said, thinking of his incredible appetite, then felt silly for saying it since she'd probably have no idea what I meant by that.

To my relief, she let out a peal of laughter, though she quickly covered her mouth and looked around guiltily. "Oh, gawd, look at me giggling over a dead body. People will start thinking I'm horrible and cold. But, yes, I have a large fridge. That man goes through groceries like nobody's business! If I ate the way he did, I'd weigh about a thousand pounds!"

Someone called her name, and she whipped her head around. I followed her gaze to see Ed at the top of the berm. He gave me a wave, and I lifted my hand in reply.

"Speak of the devil!" she said. "He's going to help me take Kudzu on a long run around this area. It always helps to have someone else with me." She looked back to me. "It was so great meeting you. You'll have to come over the next time we have a get-together! We have a fish fry or a barbecue at least every other weekend. I'll make sure Ed or Marcus gives you a call! " Then she was trotting off with Kudzu before I could do more than give a weak smile in return.

I let out a long breath. One thing was for sure—I needed to stay the hell away from that dog.

To my shock and surprise, Ben and Mike both helped Derrel and me carry the body bag back to the road. Most of the ranking officers had left which meant I could get the van up close so that we didn't have to haul the damn thing down the road as well. I gave both detectives super nice smiles in thanks, even though Ben was the one who'd stepped up to help and had then guilted Mike into taking another strap. I wasn't going to bitch. Sure, I could carry it myself, but why burn up the brains if I didn't have to?

As I closed the back of the van I saw Marcus out on the street talking on his phone, but I didn't have a chance to do more than give him a little nod and smile. His expression remained fairly grim, though he returned the nod, and I felt instantly silly for being all smiley and cheerful on such a gruesome murder scene. At least Marianne had caught herself and realized how awful it was to laugh at a death scene. Me, I didn't even think about it. I'd become totally jaded already. I barely thought of dead bodies as former people anymore.

The thought left me cold. Was that part of the zombie insanity? Maybe it had nothing to do with hunger. Maybe it was part of this virus or whatever, and the longer it was in me the less I'd think of people as people, and it would eventually seem natural to want to bash their heads in.

No, I was being completely stupid. I mean, Kang was still pretty normal, and he was old.

Still, it continued to bother me throughout the day—enough for Dr. Leblanc to notice how quiet I was.

"Something bugging you, Angel?"

I looked up from the computer and began to give a general No, I'm fine denial, then paused. "Well, sort of, but I'm afraid you'll, um, think I'm weird."

His eyes flashed with kind humor. "Weirder, you mean?"

I gave a weak laugh. "Yeah, more than usual."

"What's up?"

I took a deep breath as I tried to figure out how to say it without sounding like a freak. I really liked Dr. Leblanc—not in a sexy way or anything. Ew! But simply as a nice person who seemed to be willing to try and understand me. I trusted him, and even I could admit that I wasn't the type to trust many people. I could do that bit of analysis on myself just fine.

"Well, I think I'm becoming kinda cold," I said. "I mean, I pick up these bodies, and I don't even think about the fact they were once living people. It doesn't bug me, and I think it should." I met his eyes. "Shouldn't it?"

He patted my shoulder. "Angel, you have a tough and crusty exterior, but you have the kindest, mushiest heart I've ever seen. You're not cold. Thinking of the bodies as non-people is simply a defense mechanism your brain engages to protect you from the horribleness of what we have to do. We all do it." The smile he gave me was warm and gentle. "We crack jokes and we're terribly inappropriate because, if we focus on the loss, we'll lose our minds and won't be able to do what needs to be done." He gave my shoulder a squeeze. "Besides, I know you're not cold."

"How do you know?" I challenged.

"Because you cry when we get kids through here," he stated. "No one jokes about the kids. Those are the ones that get to us the most."

I felt a knot form in my throat. "Yeah," I said, voice suddenly hoarse.

"You're human, Angel. Don't worry. I wouldn't have you here if you weren't." He turned and walked away as I stared after him in surprise.

So maybe there were different degrees of monster. I was a monster with a mushy heart.

Chapter 25

I finished up my paperwork, then checked the computer to see if there were any bodies scheduled to be picked up by a funeral home today. None were, but I frowned when I saw that the body of the pizza guy was still in our cooler. It had been almost two weeks. Surely some next of kin had been found by now?

I went looking for Derrel and found him hunched behind the desk in the investigator's office, his eyes flicking between the screen and the keyboard as he painstakingly pecked out letters.

"Hey, Derrel, ya got a sec?"

He looked up with an almost grateful expression. "If it keeps me from having to fight my way through writing this report, sure."

I laughed and plopped into the chair in front of the desk. "I'll try. What's the deal with the pizza guy? Still no next of kin?"

A grimace flickered across his face. "Well, we're not sure. There's some sort of screw-up."

"Like how?"

He sighed and sat back. "We ran his prints and it came back to a Peter Plescia."

I nodded. "Right. The pizza guy. So what's the deal?"

Derrel lifted his broad shoulders in a shrug. "The problem is that Peter Plescia is eighty-seven. That is, he would be if he wasn't supposedly already dead."

I felt as if a cold wind dove down my spine. *And Kang looks like he's my age. . . .* "What do you mean?" I asked as calmly as I could.

"I mean," he said, leaning forward again, "that the records must be screwed up somewhere along the line. It happens with identity theft, sometimes. The pizza guy is probably someone who stole the real Mr. Plescia's identity. Pizza guy's real name is probably buried somewhere. Since his fingerprints match the fingerprint records that come up for the original Mr. Plescia, that means he was never fingerprinted while the fake one was—while using Plescia's stolen identity. We may never know who pizza guy really is."

"Wow." I paused as I tried to get my jumbled thoughts in order "But how do you know that this isn't the real Peter Plescia? Maybe he faked his own death or something."

"The age," Derrel replied. "The people at Pizza Plaza said he was only in his thirties or so, plus Dr. Leblanc says there's no way that the guy was in his late eighties. He can tell by looking at the bones and that sort of thing." Then he chuckled. "Besides, I can't see an eighty-seven year old delivering pizzas."

He could if he was a zombie. So he wasn't killed by a rogue—at least not for his brains. *An eighty-seven-year-old zombie. Holy shit.* The brains healed me of any injury and made me feel like a million bucks. It made sense that brains would somehow heal the stuff that made us get old. Kang was probably close to seventy and sure as hell didn't look it. An odd chill skimmed over me. I'd realized he was old, but the full impact of it hadn't hit me until now. Had Kang been forced to fake his death at some point? Did he have to move before people got suspicious? And how long would it be before people noticed I wasn't aging? And how long did it last? Would the virus or parasite eventually die off on its own? Great . . . I wasn't really alive, but the good news was that I could be that way for a really long time.

"So, what will you do now?" I asked, masking my inner turmoil as much as I could. "Check into this old guy's death? Maybe the imposter was a friend or the real Peter Plescia's kid or something."

He gave me a nod and a smile. "You'd be good at this. That's exactly what I'm doing now. The original Peter Plescia lived in Littleton, Colorado. I called the Coroner's Office over there yesterday and asked if they could pull any records and get copies to me. They should be faxing it all this afternoon. But unfortunately that doesn't necessarily give us any info on the guy in our cooler."

"What about getting information on the pizza guy . . . like where he's been living," I suggested. "Even though the name might not be his"—which I figured it probably *was*, but I wasn't going to argue that point—"there should be info in Lexis Nexis under that name, right? So maybe you could at least track down possible acquaintances or stuff like that, find someone who knew him and might know more about the real him."

His smile widened. "Damn, Angel, you should be a cop!"

I gave a casual shrug that didn't feel terribly casual. "Can't. Convicted felon, remember?"

Derrel looked briefly abashed. "Sorry." Then he gave me a wink. "Well, that means we get to keep you."

A warm flush spread through me as I tried not to

show how much the comment meant to me. "You mean, you're stuck with me!" I teased.

"Either works." He tugged the keyboard toward him. "But I still like your idea about Lexis Nexis." He fell silent while he did the hunt and peck thing again. A part of me wanted to yank the keyboard away from him and do it myself, but the more rational part pointed out that I sucked at typing even worse, and it wouldn't speed things up at all.

"You have good ideas," he said after a moment. "The original Peter Plescia died in 1988 and this one showed up here in 1990." He clicked a few more keys. "Lived at various apartment complexes."

"Is there a way to find out where he worked?" I leaned forward eagerly. "I mean, other than Pizza Plaza." If he'd ever worked in a morgue or funeral home, that would clinch my theory that he was a zombie. Plus that would surely make it easier to fake his death.

Derrel gave me a funny look but didn't question my interest. "Not on here. The system we use tells us stuff like residence history, possible relatives, phone numbers, that sort of thing. Basically, anything available in a public record search. That's pretty much all we need, since the main reason we use it is for locating next of kin."

I sat back and nodded. "Okay, that's cool." It didn't matter anyway. I was pretty damn positive that the dude was a zombie. "What about the guy we picked up this morning? Has the ID on him been confirmed yet? Was it Zeke Lyons?"

"Yep. That came through about an hour ago. Zeke Lyons, forty-three years old, white male. No hiccups with that one at least."

Okay, so he wasn't an old zombie. I had no idea if he'd really looked forty-three, since I'd never seen him at his "best."

"How 'bout the guy from Sweet Bayou Road?" I pressed. "And the two guys this week who died of head injuries?" I asked. "Was there anything strange about them?"

This time he gave me a funny look. "You're stretching now, girl," he said, though with enough of a smile to take any sting out of it. "The victim from Sweet Bayou was Adam Campbell, fifty-three years old, and no apparent anomalies there either. But as far as the other two—totally different means of death with those."

"But—" I stopped myself before saying anything about the missing brains, took a deep breath instead, and made myself nod. "Yeah, I guess."

"However, to answer your question, no. Nothing weird about those two. No connection or similarities. Families were notified. All the usual stuff."

They were within a few miles of each other. But for the first time I had to wonder if I was seeing something that wasn't there. Squished-head guy's brains might have been picked up by a damn dog for all I knew. And decomp drug dealer dude . . . well, his brains could have liquefied and leaked out by the time we arrived.

Damn it. I'd been so certain that Zeke had killed those two. Was I missing something obvious? But even if those deaths really had been accidental, there sure as shit wasn't anything accidental about Zeke and Peter and Adam getting their heads whacked off.

"All right," I said. "Well I figured it was worth thinking about."

"Keep it up and you'll get promoted to Investigator," Derrel said. Then his eyes flashed with amusement. "And we all know how much that would piss Nick off."

"Ooh, something to shoot for!" I said, laughing.

* * *

I'd lost track of time and had to run back to the morgue to get everything set up for the autopsy before Dr. Leblanc got there.

I hadn't assisted at the autopsy of the other headless body, and I felt kind of useless without a head to deal with. Usually as soon as Dr. Leblanc finished his removal of the organs, I'd start on the head while he did the more meticulous examinations and dissections. But since there was no head, I pretty much stood there and watched, all the time feeling as if I was forgetting to do something.

"So it's pretty obvious it's a serial killer, right?" I asked Dr. Leblanc.

He glanced up, scalpel poised above a kidney. "Why do you say that? Do you think it is?"

I was starting to get used to Dr. Leblanc and his way of answering questions with questions of his own. Derrel had told me a while back that Dr. Leblanc was a fan of the Socratic Method, which made absolutely zero sense to me at the time. In fact, I didn't even realize he'd said "Socratic" and thought he'd said "secreting," which had me just as confused. It wasn't until I said something about "the secreting method" that Derrel explained—after laughing his ass off at me first—that the Socratic Method was a way of teaching by using questions. I didn't understand the whole thing, but there were times when I really wished Dr. Leblanc would give me a straight answer.

However, I was willing to go along with it for the moment. "Well, sure. I mean, in the last couple of months we've had three people with heads cut off and two others who died of pretty major head injuries."

He lowered the scalpel and regarded me. "Three," he said after a few seconds.

"Three what?"

"Three who died of major head injuries," he said. "Right before you were hired we had an MVA fatality where cause of death was multiple traumatic injuries, most notably decapitation."

A bizarre chill walked down my spine at this for no reason I could understand. "Okay," I said, shaking it off. "So. Six total."

He didn't lift his scalpel again and continued to look at me. "But what makes you think any of the accidental deaths could be related to the decapitations?"

I sighed and shrugged. "Never mind. I'm being silly."

A smile flickered across his mouth. "I'm not going to let you off that easily. You think there might be a connection. What led you to that theory?"

I fidgeted. I could hardly say that my zombie supersense told me that there were brains missing from squished-head guy and decomposed-guy. "Okay, um, the three men who got decapitated. Not the one from the car wreck—" Memory flickered but was gone before I could focus on it. "—but the pizza guy, Sweet Bayou guy, and this one are connected because the heads were chopped off."

Dr. Leblanc gave me an approving nod. "That is definitely a telling detail. And I believe the fine folks at the Sheriff's Office are quite inclined to agree with you." But he still made no move to begin the dissection of the kidney. "Now what leads you to believe that the other three deaths are connected?"

All I could do was shrug helplessly. "I got nuthin'," I said. "Just seemed weird, so many guys with their brains falling out."

He smiled and began his cut. "It's funny how sometimes things seem to have an odd synchronicity." At my blank look he explained, "Those times when the same word or phrase or incident seem to repeat. Most of the time a closer examination reveals little more than coincidence. And, of course, decapitation is such an unusual and shocking way to die, that when such occurs, it tends to stick in our memory." A thoughtful expression came over his face. "In fact, about ten years ago or so, a couple of skeletons were found out in the swamp. The skulls were missing, and there was trauma to the spinal column that indicated they'd been decapitated with several blows to the back of the neck." He shook his head. "It caused a huge stir, obviously, but the case went nowhere. Theories ranged from a psychopath haunting the swamp and collecting heads, to an especially gruesome mob hit."

I could only stare at him. More people had been decapitated?

Dr. Leblanc smiled, almost as if he could see the thoughts ticking through my head. "But that same year three other bodies were found in the swamp as well—one was a hunter who died of a heart attack, one was a drug dealer from New Orleans who'd been shot and dumped, and the last was the husband of a woman who figured poison would be less of a hassle than divorce. Yet no one remembers those."

"You did," I pointed out.

He chuckled. "I did the autopsies. I highly doubt anyone else remembers, though I would imagine there are quite a few who remember the two headless bodies. It made quite a splash in the news for a while."

"Okay," I said with a nod. "I see your point." I did, too. But, still, could those two have been somehow connected to these? Maybe it was a serial killer who decided to take a long break?

I fell silent while I pondered this. Zombies could live a long time, so it wasn't outrageous at all to think that whoever was doing the beheading stuff now might have also been doing it ten years ago.

"Did you ever figure out who those two were?" I asked.

He gave a slight shrug. "ID was made from items found in what clothing remained. It was a fairly young couple who'd recently moved to the area. The police had a great deal of trouble finding out much about them, and there was a healthy suspicion that they were part of some sort of witness relocation program." He gave a slight grimace. "Which, of course, added weight to the theory that it was a mob hit or something of that ilk."

I frowned as a nasty certainty began to form in my gut. *I've had tunnel vision. I'm looking at this all wrong.* "Well that sucks the shit from a dead rat's ass," I muttered.

Dr. Leblanc gave a dry chuckle as he sliced into the kidney. "Angel, you truly have a way with words."

I grinned sheepishly. I hadn't meant for him to hear that. "Hey, go with your strengths, right?"

"You have more strengths than that."

"Aww, Doc, you're gonna make me blush."

After the autopsy I put the body back in the cooler, turned my attention to cleaning up, and allowed my mind to wander and sort through all this new information.

First off was the biggie: I'd definitely been looking at this all wrong. I needed to stop trying to force a connection where there probably wasn't one. What if Zeke did kill those two people? He had to have been getting brains from somewhere, and he'd been living in that area. Then what if someone *else* chopped off his head and the heads of the other two men? That made a lot more sense.

Therefore, *why* were Zeke and Peter Plescia and Adam Campbell murdered? I knew Zeke was a zombie, I was pretty sure Peter was one, and I didn't really know anything about Adam, but I sure did have a big ol' hunch. But let's assume for the moment that he was. Zombies couldn't eat other zombie brains, which meant it was doubtful that this was a zombie doing the head-chopping. Or rather, it wasn't a zombie driven by hunger.

There was only one answer I could come up with.

Someone was hunting zombies.

Chapter 26

I drove home in a cold sweat, arguing with myself the whole way. I was jumping to conclusions. I didn't know for sure that Peter Plescia and Adam Campbell were zombies. Maybe it's a serial killer who happens to be going after bums. And pizza delivery guys. And technical writers.

Yeah, right. My hideous gut feeling was that my first theory was the right one.

The churning of my thoughts came to a screeching halt the second I walked into the house.

Horror sliced through me, but I was frozen in place, framed in the doorway as the distinct scent twined around me. I could see the broken glass in the hallway, the liquid and tapioca-like chunks in congealing puddles.

No. Oh, god no. I should have given him money. I should have put a lock on the fridge.

My pulse pounded loud behind my eyes and I could barely hear the rantings of my father. I heard my name. Heard some insults and cursing. They didn't register. All I could focus on was the carefully hoarded stash now soaking into the already nasty carpet of the hallway.

I felt myself moving forward, every footstep feeling surreal and deliberate. My dad appeared in the hallway, face twisted into anger, one of my jars in his hand.

"You fuckin' worthless bitch," he yelled. "Where are you hiding it? I know you got booze! What the fuck is this shit? You tryin' to poison me?" He flung the jar down to shatter and mingle with the rest.

"Those weren't yours," I said, and I shocked myself at how calm and mild I sounded. Inside I was shrieking.

For an instant he seemed shocked as well, but then he rallied. "Everythin' in this house is mine!" he frothed, desperation and rage battling it out on his face. "If I wanna look for a drink in your room, I will! You took my beer out of the trash. You goddamn druggie." Misery darkened his eyes for an instant. "Damn you. Gave her up for you. Then you go and turn out like this." A shudder racked him, then his gaze snapped to me again and his mouth curved into a crooked sneer. "You *always* have booze, always have drugs. Well, I want a goddamn drink. So where the fuck are you hiding it now?"

I continued walking forward, eyes on him. My chest was clenched so tightly I wasn't sure how I could possibly breathe, but somehow I kept moving. He'd given up his wife to protect me and then I'd turned out like shit. *And whose fucking fault is that*? I wanted to scream.

The fury in his face flickered for an instant, and he took a half step back. He flushed as soon as he did and sneered. "You're on some new drugs, right? I was right to break it all."

"Those were mine," I said, still not raising my voice, but I could feel the air vibrate. "Mine. Not drugs."

"You're a goddamned liar! I know you're always popping pills. I heard Clive talking!" he said, taking another step back. "I have every right to go through your shit. I'm your father and this is my house!"

I was in front of him with my hand entwined in his

shirt. I didn't even remember closing the distance between us. "I'm clean. I have a job. And Mom was *mentally ill*," I said through clenched teeth. Yeah, he was so worried about me now. Why hadn't he stopped me from dropping out of school, or hanging out with the shitbags I'd gotten drugs from? No, he simply wanted a damn drink, and he'd used a sudden burst of fatherly concern as an excuse to go through my shit. "I'm not a loser. But you sure as fuck are!"

He let out a gasping shriek, and I suddenly realized that I'd lifted him off the floor several inches and had him pinned against the wall. One-handed.

I let him drop and stepped back, heartbeat slamming. His eyes were wide, the red-streaked whites enormous in his sallow face. The smell of the brains swirled around me like a taunting cloud as we faced each other.

I spun and stormed into my bedroom. The fridge was on its side, door hanging open. There weren't any jars left in the fridge. He'd done a thorough job of trashing everything in it. *I should have found a way to lock it*, I thought, then instantly dismissed it. He'd have found a way to get it open—taken a sledgehammer to it if necessary.

I barely noticed that he'd trashed the rest of my room as well. The mattress was half-off the bed, and the drawers of my dresser had been pulled out and dumped onto the floor. I grabbed a plastic shopping bag from the floor and started throwing clothes into it. Jeans, underwear, bras. I made sure that all of my coroner's office shirts and cargo pants were in there. It took about two minutes to stuff everything I thought I might need into three sacks. That was almost as depressing as the loss of my brains.

I turned to leave and stopped dead at the sight of my dad in the doorway of my bedroom. We stood there looking at each other for what felt like forever, though it was probably only a few seconds.

"Where you goin'?" he finally asked, voice low and cracked.

"Anywhere but here," I threw back at him. "You're a worthless, drunk, mean piece of shit. I don't need to be where you're gonna slap on me, or tell me what a fuckup I am. You've always hated me because Mom went to jail, but that wasn't my fucking fault! And y'know what? I don't think I'm as much of a loser as you think. I got me a job, and I'm getting my shit together. I don't need you."

He visibly flinched at the harsh words, then silently drew back. He looked suddenly old, wrinkles caving into canyons on his face. I stormed past him and headed out, slamming the door behind me like an eight-year-old. The house shook and a shingle slid off the roof and landed with a plop in the overgrown grass.

I climbed into my car and gunned it out of there. I looked back in the rearview mirror, expecting to see my dad in the doorway, watching me go, like you'd see in one of those tearjerker Lifetime movies, but the door stayed closed.

I was crying by the time I reached the end of the driveway. By the time I hit the highway I totally hated myself.

Who was the loser here?

Chapter 27

Hunger prodded me, as if to taunt me about the loss of my brains. I let out a harsh laugh—*yeah, I was brainless*—then scrubbed at my face with the back of my hand and made myself take several deep breaths. Great, so I finally stood up to my dad. Told him all the things that I'd been wanting to tell him. Told him stuff I knew would hurt him. Now I felt like total shit, and I had no place to go.

I slowed down to the speed limit. The last thing I needed was to get pulled over. Plus, it wasn't like I was in a hurry to get anywhere. Where the hell was I going, anyway? I could probably afford a hotel for one night, but more than that would eat my savings up pretty quickly. I needed to be thinking like a damn grownup. Budgets and shit like that.

I pulled into the parking lot of a SpeedE Mart and tugged my phone out of my purse. I started to punch in Randy's number, but then I hesitated. I barely even thought about him anymore. I said he was my boyfriend, but when was the last time he called me? My finger hovered over the keypad as I chewed my lip. Okay, so we'd never had that sort of super-deep, madly in love kind of relationship where we called each other up and talked on the phone just to talk. Mostly we hung out together. *It's comfortable*, I admitted to myself. But who else was I going to call? *Marcus?* I let out a bark of laughter. Yeah, right. Even if I had his number, there was no way I was going to ask him to get involved with my fucked up personal life. He'd already seen enough of that. Besides, he'd probably get on me again about getting away from my dad.

Well I was finally away from him. Go me. Now what the fuck was I supposed to do?

I sighed and finished punching in the number.

"Hey, Randy," I said when he answered. "I'm fighting with my dad. Can I come by?"

He greeted me with his usual hug and kiss then went back to working on a Toyota Camry. I went on into the trailer, dropped my purse on the end of the couch, and stood there for a moment, looking around as if I was seeing it for the first time.

Randy's trailer was far from nice, but it was a shitload better than my house. Still, he had dishes piled up by the sink and laundry in a pile in the hallway. It had always been like that, I realized, but this was the first time I'd really *seen* it. Maybe it was because I'd spent the last couple of months where half my job was cleaning—and I didn't mind it. Or maybe it was that I'd finally had the chance to see that most normal people didn't live like complete pigs. In the past several weeks I'd been inside dozens of houses. I'd been in million dollar homes and barely standing shacks, and I'd seen the difference between the places where the people took pride in themselves and their homes, and the shit dumps—like where I lived with my dad. And the price of the house didn't mean a damn thing.

I was drying the last dish when Randy walked in. He gave me a funny look.

"What are you doing?"

I stacked the plate in the cabinet. "Doing your dishes. Duh."

He gave a dry laugh. "Okay. Just never seen you do that before."

"I figured I'd help out, y'know?"

"Um, okay. If you say so. Doesn't fucking matter to me."

I found myself scowling. Did anything matter to him? I used to love how laid-back he was. About the only times he ever seemed to get worked up was when another guy showed interest in me, and even that never lasted for long—only until he was sure I wasn't going anywhere. Then he'd be back to being all calm and laid-back, comfortable, with everything the way he liked it.

I was beginning to see that "laid-back" was simply a nice way of saying "doesn't give a shit."

"I'm trying to get my fucking life back on track," I said. Then I shook my head. "No, it's never been *on* track. I'm sick of being a loser."

He plopped down onto the couch and shrugged. "I don't think you're a loser. You don't rape old ladies or steal from welfare moms, right?"

I wiped the water off the counter. "No, but that's not being a loser. That's being evil."

"I s'pose. Hey, grab me a beer since you're up?"

I pulled the fridge open, snagged a beer, and handed it to him. "See, I think losers are people who don't want anything for themselves. Or who don't do the shit that needs to be done to get anywhere in life." I handed him the beer.

He cracked it open, then glanced at me. "You're not drinking?"

"Nah. I'm wiped," I lied. "If I drink I'll fall asleep." I paused. "So what do you think?"

He took a swig and then gave me a sideways glance. "About what?"

"About being a loser."

"Oh." He took another swig. "Yeah, I guess that makes sense." He shrugged again. "I dunno. I think if you're not hurting anybody, it's all good."

"But maybe being a loser is about hurting yourself," I pressed, but I could see that I'd already lost him.

"Jesus, Angel, you're being awfully deep." He laughed. "C'mon, look at us. We have fun. We fight, make up, fuck. We grab a beer, smoke a joint, knock back some pills. No one gets hurt. We're not robbing convenience stores for money."

"But some of those pills are stolen from people who need them."

His mouth twisted. "Maybe some, but most are prescribed to people who go from doctor to doctor. The docs don't care, 'cause they get their money."

I blew out my breath. "I dunno. Maybe so. You should see the drugs and pills I come across in my job now. Seems like everybody and their mom is on painkillers or anxiety drugs."

"Whaddya mean? How do you see them?"

"Oh, when someone dies we collect any leftover prescription drugs, and then they get destroyed."

He hadn't moved. "So they throw out all those pills?"

"They get incinerated," I told him. "But they get counted first," I added, suddenly feeling strange telling Randy about the drugs. "Anyway, thanks for letting me come by," I said, trying to change the subject. "My dad's out of jail and being his usual dickish self."

"You know you can always come stay here." He pushed off the couch and went into the kitchen, returning a half minute later with the bag of pot.

He lit a joint and passed it to me. I sighed to myself and took the hit even though I knew it wouldn't do anything. It tasted like shit, and I instantly regretted doing it as the taste faded and the color in the room dimmed. *I'm fucking poisoning myself, using up my brains*, I thought sourly. *These are my brains on drugs.*

I passed the joint back to him. "I don't want anymore," I said. "Toldya, I'm tired. It's been a shitty day."

He eyed me for a second, then leaned his head back and took a long hit. "You're not turning into one of those squeaky-clean, moralistic fuckers, are you?"

I scowled. "Gimme a fucking break, all right? Would I be here if I was?" *And would it matter if I did?*

"Dunno. Would you? You're only here right now 'cause you need crash space."

I stood and grabbed my bag. "I don't need this tonight. I'll find a goddamned hotel."

He made a noise of frustration and snagged my arm. "Lighten up, willya? I don't give a fuck why you stay."

I stared at him for several seconds. Why didn't he give a fuck? Shouldn't he? Wasn't that how normal people acted around each other? They should want the other person to be there for them. Did he really want me, or did he simply not want me to be with anyone else?

"Do you love me?" I blurted.

An expression of pure bafflement crossed his face. "You know I do, baby."

The crazy thing was that I was fairly sure he did, in his own strange way. And I loved him, in a strange, dependent, who-the-fuck-else-would-want-me kinda way.

He stood and ran his hands up my arms, then pulled my purse out of my hand and set it back on the couch. "Is that what's been screwing your head up? You think I don't love you enough?"

I shook my head. "That's not it." He loved me enough. As much as he could ever love me, I realized. There'd never be anything more or deeper between us. It was better than nothing, though, right? *But who's to say that "nothing" is my only other option?*

He slipped his arms around me. "Look, I've told you before that you can stay here anytime you want. All the time if you need to. It's cool."

I looked up at him. "So you're asking me to move in with you?"

He looked briefly puzzled. "Huh? Well, yeah. I guess. I mean, I'm here by myself, and we're already fucking, so it'd make sense if you wanted to stay here too."

Wow. That was romantic. I didn't have to look around. I knew what the trailer held. Was this really the best I could do?

"Um, I need to think about it," I mumbled.

He gave me a squeeze. "Okay. Offer stands." He slipped his hands lower and pulled me close to him. "I'll even let you work off the rent," he said with a laugh.

I knew he wasn't trying to sound like a sleaze, so I didn't call him on it. "I can pay," I said.

He lifted his head. "What's that supposed to mean? You don't like fucking me anymore?"

Shit, that really hadn't come out like I'd meant. "Sorry. I mean, I have a job now and can split costs with you. I'm not a leech." I fought back the grimace as the words came out of my mouth. Shit, was I agreeing to live here with him? *It's temporary*, I told myself. *It's better than living with my dad.*

"Um, okay," he said, then dipped his head to nuzzle my neck. "If that makes you feel better."

"Yeah, look, babe, I'm super tired," I said, putting my hands on his chest. Fucking him would use up my brains like crazy. And I didn't have any to spare. But if I moved in with him I'd need to stay tanked up on brains. Where the hell would I store brains here, anyway? Maybe get a storage unit and a freezer. Shit, there was no way this would work.

"I'll make it up to you," I said, realizing it was a lie as the words left my mouth. I had no desire to screw him anymore. I didn't want to move in with him. I was using him for the night. Yeah, classy.

Luckily he didn't seem to be offended, simply dropped his hands with a soft sigh. "Okay, I won't be a dick. You do look pretty worn out."

"Gee, thanks," I said, managing a smile. He gave me a lopsided one in return, but his expression was guarded, as if he was debating whether or not to say more. I didn't feel like prying it out of him, whatever it was. "Okay, um, I'm gonna go grab a shower, okay?"

He gave me a slow nod, then plopped back down on the couch and picked up the remote. I turned away and headed down to the bathroom, feeling like there was something hanging in the air between us, with neither of us giving enough of a fuck to care.

The morning light seemed dull and filtered as it speared through the streaked window. Dust moved sluggishly along the track of light as if reluctantly being sucked up to some higher dust heaven. I could feel Randy pressed up against me, his face tucked into the nape of my neck. His breath was warm against me, but even that felt muted. I closed my eyes and sighed. My last full meal of brains had been two days ago. By later today I'd start to smell. In another day or so I'd begin to fall apart.

I eased away from him and checked the time on my phone. Maybe I could go on in to the morgue with the excuse that I left something there. Check and see if any bodies came in.

I'm still a junkie looking for a fix, I thought with a scowl. *Only now my life depends on that fix.*

Randy was pretty well dead to the world, and I was able to pull clothes on and slip out before he woke up. A weird sense of relief washed over me as I drove away. Once again, I checked my rear view mirror to see if anyone was watching me go. Once again, real life failed to pay attention to how things were depicted in the movies.

It was barely eight A.M. when I pulled up to the back door of the morgue. I did my best to not act like I was slinking, but I sure felt as if I was pulling some sort of heist. My mouth was dry, and my hands shook as I swiped my card in the reader. I had no reason to be so nervous, though, right? I mean, all I had to say was that I was looking for something I'd lost. *My watch.* That would work. I hurriedly yanked mine off and stuffed it deep into a pocket.

I closed the door behind me and listened hard. There was only the low hum of the cooler and the scent of Pine-Sol and formalin. I headed down the hallway, cringing at the absurdly loud echo of my footsteps on the linoleum.

Pulling open the door of the cooler, I quickly slipped inside, relief swimming through me at the sight of a bag on a stretcher. I paused. Took a deep breath.

Shit.

Even before opening the bag, I knew what I would find. Still, I pulled the zipper open, confirming with my eyes what my nose had already told me. The woman had probably been pretty in life, and even through the bloat I could see that she'd maintained herself well. Toned and slender body with some fake boobs that had probably set her back quite a few grand. Carefully waxed eyebrows. I could even see the remnants of makeup. I had no idea how she'd died, but whatever the circumstance no one had found her for several days. She wasn't crawling with maggots or anything like that, but the first few layers of her skin were already beginning to slip off and I knew that there wouldn't be any brains worth salvaging.

"Angel? What the hell are you doing?"

I jerked in shock and whirled to see Nick standing in the doorway of the cooler. *Shit!* I'd been so absorbed in my pity party I hadn't heard the cooler door.

"Jesus, dude, you scared the crap out of me!" I yanked the zipper closed, then moved to exit the cooler. I thought for a second that Nick was going to block my way, but at the last instant he stepped aside, giving me a baffled look.

"What were you doing, Angel?" Suspicion and worry darkened his voice.

I paused, took a deep breath and turned back to him. "I was looking for my watch." I twisted my face into a grimace. "I remember having it on the last time I was here, and I've looked everywhere. Stupid me was thinking that maybe I dropped it in a bag. . . ." I trailed off. God, this was the dumbest thing I'd ever come up with. There was no way he was going to buy this.

But, shockingly, the suspicion in his face cleared. "Oh," he said, brows drawing together in a slight frown. "That must be one special watch if you were willing to wear it again after it was in the bag with a decomp."

I mustered a weak smile. "I didn't know that was a decomp. I guess the last one I worked on has already been picked up. I mean, it's not a really nice watch or anything, but I hate the thought of springing for a new one, y'know?" The lie came to me with the ease of too much practice.

He shrugged. "I guess," he said in a tone that told me he'd never really had to worry about money. "You seriously came in on your day off to look for a watch?"

I gave him what I hoped looked like a sheepish smile. "Yeah. Hey, I have no life, y'know?" And if I didn't find brains soon, I wouldn't have any life.

He rolled his eyes. "Obviously."

I mumbled something and then made my escape.

Chapter 28

I sat in my car and bit my lower lip as I considered my situation. I was scheduled to work the following morning, so there was no reason for me to start panicking yet about my next brain-meal. It had only been two days since my last—longer than I usually liked to go, but I was only barely beginning to smell, and I was getting weirdly used to the gradual dulling of my senses. As long as I didn't go crazy with activity it should be at least another full day before I started actively rotting.

Somebody would surely die in time for me to get a meal. I was going to be fine. Really.

I groaned and rested my forehead on the steering wheel. *I suck as a motivational speaker.*

Screw it. I had nothing to do and nowhere to go, so maybe this was a sign that it was time for me to take the first step and see how much it would really cost to find a new place to live. Time to be a grown-up, right?

I drove to an apartment complex about five minutes from work—a nice place that looked clean and safe. It didn't have super-fancy landscaping or a guarded gate or anything like that, so hopefully it wouldn't be too expensive. I parked in front of the leasing office and tried to control the nervous flutters in my stomach, shamed by how clueless I was about the process. Normal people would learn this stuff from their parents. Or maybe even in school. There'd been a class called Life Skills when I was in high school—the sort of class that had once been called Home Ec, but wasn't called that anymore because that would be politically incorrect or some crap like that. I'd even taken that class and made it through the part about how to boil eggs. But the section on how to do stuff like balance a checkbook and make a budget had been at the end of the semester. After I dropped out.

Sick anger swam dully through me. Where were the people who were supposed to make sure I grew up right and not a complete fuckup? My parents? Yeah, that was a joke. Mom couldn't stand to be around me. Dad had actually been all right at basic dad stuff until he had to do it all himself. Then it was like he gave up doing anything at all. By that time I'd been self-sufficient enough to make sure I got fed and had clothes to wear. But there was more to growing up than that.

This is stupid, I chided myself. Taking a deep breath, I held it until spots swam before my eyes then let it out. "Yeah, well I'm a goddamned grown-up now," I muttered. I picked up dead bodies for a living. I could handle this. Okay, so I got screwed in the parenting department. But there was no getting that time back. I could whine and bitch about it all I wanted, and it wouldn't change a damn thing. Everything that happened from here on out was my own doing.

With that attitude firmly in hand, I got out of my car and headed up to the leasing office.

By mid-afternoon my positive attitude had taken a hard beating. The rent on the first place was half a month's salary. Plus the security deposit. And fees for getting the power turned on. And if I wanted cable there was a deposit for that. I knew I could live without the TV but not without power. On top of that there was a form to fill out for the background check. . . .

I slunk out of there without filling out any applications or paperwork. I looked at three other apartment complexes, and the only one that I thought I might be able to afford had cars on blocks in the parking lot and groups of shifty-eyed young men who watched me in ominous silence as I walked up to the office. Simply visiting the place left me freaked out and scared. I couldn't imagine living there.

Anything that isn't total scuz is going to be too expensive, I realized with tired resignation. But I sure as hell wasn't giving up yet. I still had options before settling for being homeless, right? I could go back and live with my dad, or I could take Randy up on his offer

Not Randy. The speed of the thought surprised me. My dad had a million issues, but if I stayed with Randy, I'd go nowhere. I'd be in that trailer, stagnating. And that was without factoring in the whole I'm-a-zombie thing.

And then there was my dad. If I rented a storage unit and bought a fridge, maybe I could store brains there. I wouldn't have to worry about him messing with my stash again.

But I'd have to worry about him messing with *me*. I still wasn't ready to face him. Not yet.

I could do what Zeke did and live out in the woods or sleep in my car. Get a gym membership so that I had a place to clean up. *And be scared all the time that someone would screw with me while I was asleep.* No, I needed some place with a door that locked.

Hunger coiled in my stomach, a constant background growl, reminding me of my more pressing need. Compared to needing brains, worrying about where to stay seemed almost pointless. *One more day,* I told myself. *I can tough this out.* A humorless laugh bubbled up. It wasn't as if I really had a choice.

Or rather, I didn't have a choice that I was willing to take.

Yet.

I ended up blowing about eighty bucks at a hotel in Tucker Point which got me a room with clean sheets and a toilet with no stains. I didn't need anything fancy or exotic. I only needed a safe, quiet place where I could spend the next twelve hours or so doing as little as possible. No need to burn up any more brains than absolutely necessary. With that in mind I indulged in a long, hot bath, watched TV for a few hours, and then fell asleep.

When I woke up it took me nearly a minute to figure out where I was. It didn't help that I could feel my movements becoming more sluggish and uncoordinated. The smell was starting to kick in too. Great, so I couldn't smell anything else, but I sure as hell could smell myself.

I clenched my teeth against the coiling of hunger and headed down to the free continental breakfast that the hotel offered. Maybe if I could really fill up on regular food it would slow the rotting a bit.

There were a few other people in the lobby, but I did my best to keep my distance from them—not only to keep anyone from noticing my smell, but also because I was becoming more and more aware of the scent of brains in living people.

And it was beginning to seriously freak me the hell out.

Scarfing down a bagel managed to still one hunger, but did nothing for the one that snarled for something I didn't have. How bad would it be if I had to go several more days like this? My gut tightened into a knot at the thought. I didn't even want to consider that possibility.

Already I craved sensation. I wanted to feel and taste properly again. I wanted music to have a tune. I wanted—desperately—to feel *alive* again.

I can see how someone could go rogue, the thought whispered to me, and the sudden understanding left me cold.

Chapter 29

I headed in to the morgue early, hoping to god that another body had been brought in while I was off. I checked the log as soon as I got in and nearly wilted in relief at the sight of an autopsy scheduled for the day. Sixty-three-year-old white female. This would get me through the weekend. All I needed was one brain. Next week I could start building my stash up again, once I figured out where the hell I was going to live.

Turning away from the log, I paused at the sight of a small paper bag with a sticky note with my name on it. What the hell? Picking up the note, I quickly read the overly neat script.

Hey, Angel— found this watch when I was cleaning up. Figured it was yours. If it's not, you might as well keep it since it probably belonged to a corpse, and they won't need it anymore. Ha Ha. Nick.

I tipped the watch out into my hand and turned it over. *Oh, Nick . . . you are so busted.* This was a brand new watch. It wasn't anything super fancy or expensive, but I figured he'd probably spent about thirty dollars on it. He'd taken it out of the package and removed the price tag, but forgotten to pull the little tab to start the battery.

Guilt flashed through me at the fact that I hadn't really lost my watch at all ... but. Wow. This completely floored me. Of course I couldn't possibly tell him now that I'd "found" my watch or anything like that. He'd done this cool thing and gone out of his way to keep me from thinking he'd bought a watch for me. But why? Was the whole "prick" thing simply a front? Well, no matter the reason, I wasn't going to ruin the moment for him.

I must have stood there looking down at the watch in my hand for a solid minute, with a goofy smile on my face and a warm fuzzy purring in my middle. How the hell was I supposed to think of him as Nick the Prick any more?

I quickly pulled the little tab and set it, then slipped my old watch off and the new one on.

Despite my ravenous hunger I hummed to myself as I readied the cutting room. Had all the instruments out and placed all nice and pretty, the floor and table cleaned as much as they could be cleaned. By the time Dr. Leblanc came into the morgue, I even had the body of a Miss Twyla Faciane laid out on the table, ready to go. Moreover, the scent of the morgue covered up my own less-than-fresh scent. Or so I hoped.

The doc gave me a bemused smile as he pulled on his smock and saw me at the ready. "I think I may start to worry about you, Angel," he said with a dry chuckle. At my baffled expression he gave me a kind smile. "Not many are as eager to dig into a dead body."

I flushed. Shit, what if he thought I was some kinda weirdo? I mean, I *was*, but not in the way he was probably thinking.

"Sorry," I said. "I mean, I'm just trying to do a good

job. . . ." I trailed off into a mumble and winced. Now I sounded like a suckup.

"Relax, Angel," he said with a wink. "I can see that you want to do well. It's nice to see a strong work ethic."

I could feel my face heating again and made myself busy with straightening the instruments while he made notes on his clipboard. Now I felt like a heel since my eagerness had more to do with the hunger clawing at me than any desire to be a super-employee. Not that I didn't want to do a good job, 'cause actually I really did kinda like it when the doc gave me one of those approving smiles. Yeah, I was like an eager puppy. Give me a smile and a pat on the head, and I was good to go.

I went through the motions of the autopsy, moving as quickly as I could while concentrating hard on not dropping anything. The sooner this autopsy was over, the sooner the bag would be in the cooler, and the sooner I could stop feeling like my stomach was about to leap out of my body and go on a rampage through the town.

As soon as Dr. Leblanc gave me the nod, I propped Miz Faciane's head up on the block and separated her hair. I made the cut quickly, doing my best to not cut too much of the lady's hair. It was impossible to not cut through some of it, but I didn't want her to be half bald in the casket. I managed to nick my own finger in my haste, though. The blood that slowly welled up was thick and dark, and I quickly grabbed another glove and jammed it on over the first before Dr. Leblanc could notice.

On the upside, I was getting better at peeling the scalp back and was able to do it without taking half the damn day. And the bone saw didn't feel like it was going to shake my arm off. Look at me, actually getting the hang of this silly job.

I pulled the top of the skull off and couldn't resist

taking a deep breath as the aroma of the brain filled the air. Not too much longer. . . .

A chill washed over me as I looked at the brain. *No. No. This can't be happening.*

I took a steadying breath. "Hey, Dr. Leblanc," I said, using every ounce of control I had to keep my voice sounding normal and casual, and not at all terrified and sick. Because this brain didn't look right, and I had a bad feeling that it wasn't good news for me. "I think there's something wrong with this brain."

He stepped over, peered at the brain, let out a soft sigh. "Well, that explains it. What you're looking at is a tumor."

Shit. Could I eat that? Probably not. But surely I could eat around it. I was famished enough to give it a try. All I needed was a couple of bites.

Dr. Leblanc was speaking and his words didn't fully register at first. "Wait, what?" I asked, hoping I'd misheard.

"Save the brain," he said, gesturing with his scalpel to the skull. "There are some large plastic tubs in the specimen room. Grab one of those and fill it halfway with formalin, then put the brain in there. I haven't seen a tumor like that in a long time, and I'll want to examine it more thoroughly later on."

He turned back to his work on the body, a good thing since I knew I was staring at him in horror. I couldn't eat a brain after it had been stored in formalin. The poison of the preservative would more than counter any benefit I'd get from the brain itself. And he'd notice for sure if I cut any of it off. I could feel tears of frustration starting behind my eyes, and I quickly spun and headed to the specimen room before he could see and wonder what the hell was wrong with me. *Shit. Shit!* Today was Friday. There were no other bodies in the cooler which meant that even if another one came in this afternoon or over the weekend, it would almost certainly be Monday before there was another autopsy. There was no way I could last that long.

I didn't have a choice. I was going to have to ask Kang for brains. *I've kept up my side of the bargain*, I told myself. *He'll come through for me. I only need enough to tide me over.*

And if Kang wouldn't come through for me I was dead meat.

Literally.

Chapter 30

As soon as Dr. Leblanc finished up and returned to the main building I called Scott Funeral Home and asked for Kang, only to be told he wasn't coming in until noon and no, they could not give me his personal information or cell phone number. I left a message asking him to call me. I didn't know what else I could do.

I cleaned everything I could possibly think to clean in the morgue, obsessively checking the clock every five minutes. I could feel my coordination going to shit the more I did, but I was too wired and nervous to sit still. At 12:05 I called again. It took forever for him to come to the phone, and I was beginning to think I should have given a name other than my own.

"Angel, what's the matter now?" Kang said curtly after he finally picked up the line. I fought back the wave of annoyance and took a deep breath.

"Two things," I said, speaking quickly. "First, I dunno if you've seen the news, but another headless body was found the other day."

"I saw. So?"

Another deep breath. "They haven't released the

names of these last two," I said. "But, they were both, um, like us." God, I hoped no one was listening on the line.

He was silent for a few seconds, and I felt a little bit of satisfaction that I'd made a dent in his attitude.

"Probably coincidence," he said, deflating my satisfaction completely.

"Are you *kidding me*?" I said, struggling to keep from shouting. "This last one was Zeke! They all had their goddamned heads chopped off. And you think it's coincidence?"

"Fine," he replied, voice taut. "It's a problem. What do you want me to do about it?"

You're an asshole! I wanted to scream, but I hadn't asked him for the brains yet. I took a deep breath to get my temper in check. "Nothing. I simply figured you might want to be aware. Okay? So you could, um, watch out and shit."

I heard him exhale. "I see. All right. I appreciate your concern, though it's misplaced. No one knows about me."

And the three victims probably thought the same thing, I thought, but I wasn't going to waste energy arguing with Kang about this. I'd warned him. Hopefully he'd at least watch his back now.

"What's your second thing?" Kang asked.

"I, uh, I'm in a bind with my supply. Lost my whole stash. I need some to tide me over."

He made a noise that sounded scornful. "Figured. Fine, come by the funeral home after we close at seven P.M. I need to work late anyway."

Shit. I was starving, and I didn't want to have to wait until this evening. It had been three days since I'd last eaten. But I also didn't really have any choice. Kang was so damn twitchy I didn't dare push the issue. "Cool," I said. "I appreciate it."

"Uh huh. Come after seven." And with that he hung up.

The next seven hours were the longest hours of my entire fucking life. I drove to the park, found a shady place and sat curled up in the front seat of my car—trying unsuccessfully to nap and not move or do anything that might burn me out faster than absolutely necessary. I had the windows rolled down to keep the car from getting too stifling, but as the day progressed the scent of joggers and people walking their dogs grew more and more noticeable. Hunger roiled within me every time someone went by and the scent of their brains wafted through the car. I finally rolled the windows up and forced myself to endure the stuffiness and my own stench.

The hunger wound through every cell of my body—so much a part of me, I felt as if everyone could see it. Colors and sounds felt muted, but one thing cut through my sense of smell: brains. Brains in everyone around me. Pulsing with life and flavor. God almighty, all I needed was to club one of them down, feed while it was still warm . . .

I shuddered, clenching my jaw against the urges. I wasn't that far gone yet. I was still aware. Surely I had a couple more days until the hunger ruled me? Zeke had been out of work for a couple of weeks, right? Except I already knew he hadn't been without brains that entire time. I was pretty damn positive he'd killed that drug dealer and Mr. Harris. And if he'd had a stash he might have only been without brains for a few days.

But according to Kang that's all it would take—he'd said that things started to go south pretty quickly after only a few days.

That's me—going south.

I closed my eyes and tried to breathe through my

mouth, but that only caused my lower lip to crack in a disgusting fissure that made me look like I had some sort of hideous deformity. I would have cried but my eyes could barely maintain enough moisture to allow me to see.

At a quarter 'til seven I uncurled and started the car, nursing a dull fury as I drove over to the funeral home. Kang was being a complete dick making me wait like this. And I didn't have a fucking choice but to take it, which pissed me off even more. He had access to more brains than I did by a long shot. Most deaths didn't require autopsy. In the less than six weeks I'd been working for the Coroner's Office, I'd seen at least half the bodies released on scene, plus the funeral homes got everyone who died at the nursing homes and hospitals. Sure, most of those were natural deaths, which usually meant they were older. And okay, so older brains didn't taste as great, but, seriously, once you added some flavor or spice—like my soup—it didn't make that much difference.

The thought made me giggle in a silly, almost hysterical way. Maybe I needed to start making recipes for brains. Something more than throwing some tomato soup or coffee in. And maybe there was something that could be done for brains that were decomposing and liquefying. Brain soup? Vichyssoise? I didn't know if decomposing brains still had the enzyme, or whatever the hell it was, that zombies needed, but at some point I'd probably have to try it. What was the worst that could happen? I'd die?

I snickered again as I pulled around to the back of the funeral home. There was only one car parked there. I hoped and assumed it was Kang's. I hadn't even considered that other people could be working at this time—simply assumed that had to be why he wanted me to come by this late, after everyone else was gone. Hell, I hadn't been thinking about much at all, trying to rely on stupid instinct. And right now my instinct wanted me to club passing joggers down and scoop their brains out.

I should have come to Kang sooner, I realized. I was desperate now, and he'd see it. He'd ask for anything, and I'd give it to him. Already my skin felt as if it was about to slip off my bones.

Fuck it. Lesson learned. I was getting a lot of those lately.

I rapped on the back door, waited, mentally rehearsing what I was going to say. Or rather, trying to mentally rehearse. It was kinda tough to do since I had no idea what I wanted to say.

I rapped again, tried the handle. To my relief it was unlocked. I sure as hell didn't want to turn around and leave. I didn't have anywhere else to go at this point.

"Hey, Kang?" I called tentatively as I stepped in. He'd better have the brains here for me. I'd fight him for them if I had to.

I suddenly realized that my hands were tightened into fists. I forced myself to unclench them. Kang would come through for me. I knew that much. He'd charge me through the nose, but he'd come through for me.

I got a faint whiff of brains as I came down the hall, but it was mixed with an undercurrent of something I couldn't immediately pin down. I entered the embalming room and wrinkled my nose. I knew what that other scent was now. There was a body on the table that had apparently recently been embalmed. When a body came straight to the funeral home the brains stayed nice and safe in the skull. They weren't conveniently sliced up and put in a bag, ready for the taking. But I could barely smell brains in this body, which made me think that most of them had already been removed.

How does Kang get the brains out? I suddenly wondered, frowning down at the body. I didn't see any sign that he'd drilled a hole in the skull. It would be easy enough to fill something like that in with wax or putty or something, but then there'd be the risk that someone else might notice. Maybe through the nose? Wasn't that how the Egyptians did it? Now I was curious.

"Kang?" I called again. I moved through the embalming room, surrounded by the low hum of the cooler. I frowned as another odor cut through the faint scent of brains. Coppery and. . . .

Blood. A sliver of fear wormed through me. That had to be a lot of blood for it to get through my dulled senses.

I came around the corner and let out an involuntary scream that would have done any horror movie teenage camper proud. Gasping raggedly for breath, I shuffled backwards, away from the headless corpse and the broad dark pool surrounding it. *He hasn't been dead long*, an oddly rational part of my mind informed me. The blood didn't look like it had coagulated much, and still dripped from the stump of neck in large, slow plops. Not even an hour, probably.

That's Kang, a more freaked-out part of my mind shrieked. *That's Kang*.

Someone was definitely hunting zombies. There was no way I could deny it now.

I backed away as panic and horror closed my throat. *Where am I going to get brains?* I thought, instantly shamed and miserable that I was so concerned with myself at this moment.

What if the cops thought I did this? That was probably a bigger concern right now. I needed to get the hell out of here. Wipe down the doorknobs for fingerprints.

Oh, Angel, you are so fucked.

I couldn't stay and call the cops. I knew that. Not with me falling apart and smelling like this. I knew that running away from the scene would only make me look guilty as fucking hell if anyone ever knew I was here, but I didn't see that I had a choice. Besides, no one would really think that I managed to do this, right? I mean, for fuck's sake, he outweighed me by at least fifty pounds. At the worst I'd get in trouble for not reporting it, and I could claim that I was afraid the killer was still nearby.

Oh, god . . . . That thought nearly sent me into a blind panic. I reached for the wall, took several heaving breaths to keep from freaking out. *No, stop*. I needed to try and think like someone with a fucking ounce of intelligence.

But, god, I was so hungry.

Taking a shaking breath, I straightened. He'd told me to meet him here. Surely that meant he had brains to give me.

I spun and returned to the embalming room. I'd seen gloves in a box on the wall. I quickly snagged a pair and pulled them on, tugged another pair on over those. I'd seen something on one of my nifty crime shows where the cops had recovered prints even though the perp had worn latex gloves. I had no idea if that was true but I didn't see any reason to risk it.

Moving as quickly as I could, I searched for anything that looked like it might contain brains—cooler, refrigerator, anything. I could feel a clock ticking in the back of my head, telling me I'd already been there too long, and I needed to get the hell out.Kang had been convinced no one knew he was a zombie, but he'd been wrong. Hell, everyone who bought brains from him had to know, right? And the only one who knew *I* was one was Kang . . . *and whoever made me*, I reluctantly reminded myself. But whoever was doing this must have had some way of discovering that Zeke and Pizza Guy and Sweet Bayou Road dude were zombies. And maybe the reason my zombie-daddy never contacted me was because he'd been whacked by this killer.

Panic rose as I searched everywhere I could think of and still couldn't find any brains. *I've been here too long,* I told myself, nearly sobbing at the realization that I was going to have to leave empty-handed.

Maybe he hadn't planned on giving me any. I forced myself to consider the thought. But the whole brain thing was his business, which meant he had to have some saved up *somewhere*, right? Maybe they were at his house—wherever the fuck that was.

I made myself go back into the hallway, somehow avoiding stepping in the pool of blood while I tugged Kang's wallet out of his back pocket. I memorized the address on his license and replaced his wallet. I just had to hope the address was current.

Grabbing a towel, I hurriedly wiped down every surface I could have possibly touched before I'd pulled on the gloves. I cautiously peeked out the back door to make sure no one was nearby, walked oh-so casually to my car, pulse slamming in near panic the entire distance. There wasn't another soul around—I was so hungry that if any living human had been within fifty yards I'd have been able to smell them. Great, one more zombie super power—I was a goddamn life detector when I was hungry enough.

I dropped the towel into the back seat, peeled off the gloves, got the hell out of there. I drove in random directions for about fifteen minutes, gritting my teeth against the awareness of brains all around me. I finally ducked behind a grocery store and tossed the gloves and the towel into a dumpster.

I drove away, hands gripping the steering wheel tightly as the hunger thrashed and growled. A glance at myself in the rear view mirror sent a chill through me. Skin was peeling off my forehead, and my complexion had a greenish-grey cast. My left eye was starting to cloud over, which explained why I was having some trouble seeing out of it. Thank god it was dusk. Somehow I'd completely lost the flesh off the pinky and ring fingers on my right hand. Probably when I'd pulled the gloves off.

Brains. The thought consumed me. I drove hunched down in the seat to keep anyone from seeing me, operating the car on instinct more than anything. Luckily I was familiar with Kang's neighborhood. I wasn't sure I had the mental focus right now to be able to read a map.

Slowing at a corner, I watched as an elderly woman pulled a wheeled cart of groceries down the sidewalk. *She'd be easy to take down.* Probably couldn't run or anything. I could break her neck before she could make much noise, drag her into that backyard. There was no one else nearby right now. I could bust her skull open with a brick or one of those stones bordering the flowerbed. God, it would taste like heaven.

The honk from behind me jerked me back to myself. My gaze shot to the rear view mirror to see a Lexus and a glowering man behind the steering wheel. To my shock I realized that I'd opened my door. *Oh god . . . I was about to do it. I was going to attack that woman.*

The man behind me honked again. I hurriedly slammed my door shut and stomped on the gas, terror and panic briefly overwhelming the hunger. *Get to Kang's house,* I repeated to myself, clinging to that thought like a lifeline. *Don't look at anyone. Don't give the hunger a reason to take over.* This was how a zombie went rogue. Now I understood. With terrifying clarity, I understood.

I managed to maintain enough self-preservation to park on the next street over instead of pulling into Kang's driveway. Tugging my jacket down over my rotting hands, I stepped out of the car. There were a few people in the area, but no one outside. Hopefully no one was looking out a window. Walking as casually as I could, I ducked between the houses. A ditch separated Kang's backyard from that of the house behind his, but daylight was almost gone and there were trees which would give me some cover.

I paused before covering the distance to his back door, took a deep breath, scenting. No one in the house as far as I could tell. No one in the adjacent houses either. A couple of houses down there was a man in his backyard having a smoke behind a privacy fence.

"Get to Kang's," I muttered, forcing myself forward instead of toward the man in his backyard. I'd never had anything resembling willpower before now. Never been able to convince myself to stop taking the pills, or keep a job, or clean up my house. But I was going to fucking break my willpower in right now. *I won't become a monster. I can't.*

The back door was solid, but also had window panes in it. Silently praying that Kang didn't have an alarm system, I pulled my jacket sleeve all the way over my hand and punched through the glass in one of the panes. Reaching through to unlock the door, I could feel dimly that the glass had sliced into my hand and arm. But it didn't hurt. Dark, thick blood welled up sluggishly from the slices then stopped. I tucked my arm further up into my sleeve. I wasn't about to put myself in any danger of dripping blood anywhere.

I wasn't greeted with a shrieking siren when I pushed the door open, and I didn't see a control pad anywhere, so at least that much was going all right. I made my way to the kitchen and went straight to the fridge. He had it well-stocked and it was obvious that he enjoyed cooking, but my zombie super-sense of smell didn't twig to any stash of brains in there. Still, I opened every container and took a deep whiff to be sure. I checked the freezer next, heart sinking at the sight of about a dozen boxes of frozen pizza but no bags or containers or anything that could hold brains.

This didn't make sense. Where the hell did he keep his stash? Fighting panic, I prowled through the house, searching for anything that could function as a cooler or a fridge. I thought I struck gold when I found the deep freeze out in the garage, but disappointment threatened to crush me again when I saw that it was full of more frozen dinners.

I stumbled back into the house. If I'd been able to cry I'd have been sobbing in frustration. This couldn't be happening to me. He had to have brains somewhere. What if he kept them somewhere else? A storage unit or something like that? If that was the case, I was totally fucked. I couldn't go outside again. I barely made it in here without giving in to the hunger and killing someone. I slowly sat down on the kitchen floor, staring dully at the high quality pots and pans hanging from the rack above the range. *Maybe it would be for the best if the zombie killer got me*, I thought dully. I didn't want to be a murderer. Best to take me out before I killed anyone. It wouldn't be hard to find me. Follow the brains. Hell, if I was hunting zombies, that's what I'd do—find their food source.

Food.

I clambered back to my feet. Why the hell would someone who loved to cook have so many frozen dinners? I pulled the freezer open and yanked the top box off the stack, noting absently that it was for some sort of diet entrée. *Moron. That should have been your first clue*. I ripped the top of the box off, pulled the plastic open, inhaled. I hadn't smelled it earlier because they were frozen and sealed in plastic, but now I knew I'd struck gold.

I didn't bother heating it. I didn't care if they were

frozen, though I giggled stupidly as I shoved the frozen brains into my mouth. *Brain freeze!* Sensation returned in my mouth first, protesting the cold that I was forcing into my body. I was dimly aware that there was real food mixed in—rice and meat and flavoring. Properly heated it would probably be fantastic. I didn't care about fantastic at the moment. The real food in it was almost annoying since it got in the way of the brains, but I continued to cram it into my mouth as fast as I could. Slowly the bliss began to spread through my body, and I found myself crying from the agonizing relief. I felt like one of those shirts that only show color in sunlight—and I was getting a tan now, baby.

I ate until I couldn't possibly stuff in another bite and the hunger had curled into sated, sleepy comfort. The rest of me followed suit shortly after.

I experienced an instant of sheer panic when I woke and found myself on an unfamiliar kitchen floor. Memory clicked into place a few seconds later at the sight of several empty Lean Menu boxes scattered around me, and I allowed myself to relax a bit. It was still dark outside and the clock on the stove read 3:17. *And I haven't been beheaded by a zombie killer yet,* I thought with a shaky smile. *Things are looking better.*

I crumpled the empty boxes into the trash, then found a large clean garbage bag. *That's probably why I couldn't find the brains at the funeral home*, I realized with chagrin as I dumped the "frozen dinners" from both freezers into the bag. I could barely smell them packaged and frozen like this. Oh, well. I sure as hell wasn't going to go back to the funeral home and look for them. I had no idea if Kang's body had been found yet, but considering that no cops had shown up here, I was going to keep operating on the theory that it hadn't been. Guilt tightened my stomach at the thought of his body still lying in that hallway. *But there was no way for me to report the murder without getting myself into trouble*, I told myself. Certainly not last night when I was rotting and falling apart. And I couldn't do it now. What excuse would I have for finding him at three in the morning?

I sent up a silent apology to Kang. He'd have understood. *He'd have done the same thing*, I thought with a sad smile. He was too much of a mercenary to put himself at risk.

Pausing at the back door, I grimaced at the broken glass. That looked suspicious as all hell. I sighed and swept my gaze around. I'd been a moron and gone all over the place with no gloves. Screw it. If by some chance the cops came here and found my prints, I'd just lie and say that Kang and I were friends and I'd been here before.

Working quickly, I swept up the glass and dumped it under the empty frozen dinner boxes in the trash. Next, I fashioned a repair for the back window out of duct tape and cardboard that would hopefully have any cops believing it was old damage. After all, what intruder would bother to patch the hole they'd made in glass? Plus, if they searched the house, they wouldn't find any valuables missing.

I hefted the bag of brains, locked the back door at the knob and closed it behind me, took a deep breath to see if anyone was nearby. I blew it out a second later with a roll of my eyes. Zombie super-smell didn't work anywhere near as well when I wasn't starving. *Yeah, well, I'll gladly trade not-rotten for super-smell*, I decided as I took off in a sprint for my car. I was fully tanked up now, and even with what was probably thirty pounds of frozen brain-dinners weighing me down, I ran like the wind. I figured it was better to look suspicious because I was running with a garbage bag than to look suspicious because I was walking with a garbage bag, because at least there'd be less time for anyone to notice me while I was running.

My car was still where I'd left it. A moment later I was driving away, grinning in relief and triumph.

Chapter 31

Making my getaway was the first step. But now I had a bag full of frozen brains, and this was south Louisiana. Even in late October it could get pretty warm during the day, and I sure as hell didn't want to lose a stash of this magnitude.

I found an open gas station that sold cheap styrofoam coolers and bought way more ice than I probably needed. I pulled the plastic bags of brains out of the cardboard boxes so that I could fit them all into the cooler, and in short order I had the whole lot iced down. I figured I had maybe a day or so before they thawed.

Okay, Angel, you have a cooler full of stuff that is vital to your fucking survival. Which meant that I needed to make some hard decisions. Hard decisions weren't my strength. Avoiding them was my usual method, but that would prove pretty disastrous here.

As far as I could tell, my current options were to a) magically find an affordable and non-skeevy apartment within the next day, b) take Randy up on his offer, c) go back and deal with my dad, or d) rent a storage unit and sleep in my car until I could figure out a better solution.

I returned to the same spot in the park where I'd waited before going to see Kang, leaned the seat back and closed my eyes. It wasn't really that hard to make a decision, I realized. Sure, I wasn't exactly thrilled to be planning out how to handle being homeless, but the more I thought about it, the more I realized that it was really the only option that left me with any self-respect. I wasn't prepared to deal with my dad, I couldn't afford an apartment, and living with Randy was . . . well, there was so much baggage attached to that it wasn't even funny.

Did I even love him anymore? I frowned. I'd asked him if he loved me but hadn't really thought about the other half of the equation.

I don't think I do. A strange pang went through me. I'd called him my boyfriend for so many years that I suddenly found it hard to believe that he might not be anymore. So what was I supposed to do now? Break up with him? Or just let it drift away?

I must have fallen asleep because the next thing I knew I was jerking awake at the sound of my cell phone, and sun was shining right onto me. I squinted against the glare and fumbled for my phone. This spot that was so lovely and shady later in the afternoon was in blinding sun at—I glanced at my watch—nine A.M. Wow, I must have been wiped out. Maybe my body needed the rest to recover from being so rotted?

I finally dug my phone out of my purse, more than a little surprised to see Randy's ID. *Some of that synchronicity Dr. Leblanc was talking about.*

"Hey, babe," he said after I answered. "Where y'at? I got an idea that might help you out with your whole living situation."

I scrubbed a hand over my face. No doubt he was going to ask me again to live with him. I knew I didn't want to, but I'd been hoping to avoid actually *telling* him that.

Confrontations weren't really my thing. But why would he be calling me up to press the issue? Pursuing me wasn't *his thing* either. "Um. I'm in Tucker Point. What's up?"

"Thought of a way you could get your own place." He sounded pleased with himself and a little amused, which put my defenses on alert. A tiny knot of tension unwound as I realized he wasn't going to pressure me about moving in with him, though a silly little twinge of disappointment replaced it. Even though I'd admitted to myself that it was over between us, it would have been nice to be wanted like that.

I took a deep breath, pushed the stupid disappointment aside. "Randy, I swear to god, if this is some big joke about me giving blow jobs in the Pillar's parking lot—"

"No! It's not that. Meet me at Double Ds. I'll tell ya what I got."

I hesitated, then sighed. "Sure." What else did I have to do? Maybe he had a line on a place I could rent that wasn't complete shit.

I made a quick detour to a McDonalds and did a quick washing up in their bathroom. I changed clothes as well—into cargo pants and long-sleeved shirt, simply because those were the first things I grabbed out of the bags containing my worldly possessions. There was no way to wash my hair, so I simply brushed it back as neat as I could manage. If this thing with Randy didn't pan out into a place to live, my next move was going to be to join a gym. Not because I had any desire to get fit—which didn't really matter anymore now that I was a zombie—but for less than a hundred bucks a month I'd have a place to shower and change clothes every day. I'd still have to sleep in my car, though. And I'd have to buy a freezer and keep my brains in a storage unit.

Okay, so what if I'm too broke to live on my own, I thought fiercely as I pulled into the parking lot of the

diner. *It'll suck, but I'll get through it.* Still, it would definitely make my day if Randy could find me a place to
sleep other than my car.

After making sure the cooler was tightly closed in the
trunk, I headed inside, inhaling deeply of the scent of
waffles and eggs and coffee. As tanked up on brains as I
was, breakfast was going to taste fantastic.

Randy was in the booth farthest from the door, seated
so that he could see anyone coming in. I slid onto the
cracked vinyl seat across from him and gave the waitress
a smile as she stepped up.

"Coffee, orange juice, three pancakes, two eggs over
easy, bacon, and grits," I rattled off, hiding a grin at the
memory of Ed ordering a similarly massive amount of
food.

"Damn, Angel, when did you last eat?" Randy asked
with a laugh as the waitress scribbled down the order
and hurried away. "There's no way you'll eat all that."

I shrugged. "I'm hungry." The hunger for real and
normal food felt insanely tame compared to the clawing
of the Hunger. And when I was Hungry, it was tough to
eat real food since I could barely taste anything. Food
only tasted decent for about one day out of three unless
I had an unlimited supply of brains. I wasn't about to
waste this opportunity to actually enjoy it. And this
place had good, southern, comfort food, dripping with
butter and calories—worth gorging on. Why the hell
couldn't I crave something less weird than brains?
Chocolate zombie, that would be cool. Must have
chocolate . . . .

I turned the giggle into a cough, then looked over at
Randy. "Okay, what gives?" I asked.

He started to speak and then paused as the waitress
returned and poured my coffee. I added milk and sugar,
cupped the mug in both hands and sipped. *Coffee zombie would make more sense.* I looked at him expectantly.

"Damn, you look like you've never had coffee before."

I smiled slightly. "I've decided to appreciate the good things in life." Especially since I wasn't always able to experience them. Besides, I needed to make sure I continued to eat real food to keep me from needing the brains quite so often, right? Kang's warning about burning up the brains came back to me, and my throat tightened briefly at the reminder of him. Kang and I hadn't been the best of friends or anything like that, but I felt as if I'd lost a companion in arms or something equally dorky.

I was on my own now with this whole zombie thing. Flying solo. Fuck it. I could do this.

Randy gave a shrug. "So I was talking with Clive and telling him about your job. And some of the stuff you told me."

I looked at him blankly. "What stuff? About the bodies?"

He leaned forward and a chill of foreboding came over me. "No, I mean what you were telling me about," he lowered his voice and flicked a glance around, "the pills."

I kept my hands wrapped around the mug as an uncomfortable knot began to form in my stomach. "Yeah?" I couldn't make myself say anything else. I knew where he was going with this.

"Yeah. He said that—" He abruptly paused and straightened as the waitress returned and slid a plate of pancakes and a bowl of grits onto the table in front of me.

"Eggs and bacon'll be right out, hon," she said with a smile before scurrying off again.

I carefully set my mug down and picked up my fork, controlling the tremor in my hand as best I could.

Randy kept his voice low. "He already knew about

the stuff with the CO people seizing the pills. He said that all you had to do was slide some of that stuff his way and he'd take care of you. You wouldn't have to do any selling or anything like that. There's no way you could get into trouble. I mean, they destroy the stuff anyway, right? So what difference does it make?"

I stayed silent, carefully cutting off pieces of pancake with my fork and bringing them to my mouth. The very act of chewing and swallowing seemed strangely exaggerated. "I'd get in trouble if I was caught taking the drugs," I finally said.

"So don't get caught!" he replied with a laugh, as if that solved everything. Then he cocked his head. "Angel, what's the deal? You said yourself that they destroy the stuff. It's not stealing from anyone who needs it. And you *do* need the money. What, you're gonna live with your white trash loser dad for the rest of your life?"

"He's not a white trash loser," I snapped.

Stark disbelief filled his eyes. "Right. Y'all live in a fucking shack, he smacks you around, and he drinks all the time." He took a deep breath. "Look, I'm sorry I insulted your dad." Then he spoiled the apology by rolling his eyes. "But you need to think about *you*. Clive'll take care of all the hard work and give you half what he makes."

I put my fork down. Suddenly the pancake didn't taste so great. "And what do you get?"

Wary surprise flashed across his face, then he gave me a wry shrug and smile. "I get a small cut, too. I'm like the middleman, see? Since I'm hooking you two up and all."

I gave a short nod. Maybe . . . maybe I wouldn't have to be homeless. A weird relief filled me at the thought, and I suddenly realized how nervous I'd been at the thought of having to sleep in my car. Maybe I was being stupid and reckless to think that I could make it on my own. "How . . . ." I cleared my throat and tried again. "How much does he think he can get?"

Randy spread his hands. "That depends on what you can get him. But you know how much the stuff goes for on the street." He tapped the table, leaning forward a bit more. "Babe, I'm thinking about you. You should too. Hell, this doesn't have to be a long-term thing. Maybe for only a few weeks? In that time you could get more than you'd earn at the Coroner's Office in a fucking year. Then you wouldn't have to keep working there." He chuckled. "And you wouldn't smell like dead bodies anymore."

His words were like a bucket of ice water. I took a shuddering breath. How could I even be considering this? I had everything to lose. Yeah, Randy was right. I needed to think about myself.

"I remember one time when another buddy of yours hooked me up with a really great deal." I said. "I couldn't lose. Remember? Five hundred bucks, and I got a car that was practically new." I met his eyes with a hard gaze of my own. "Remember that? Remember me going to jail?"

He winced. "Yeah, well, that was fucked up. Everything that coulda gone wrong did."

I shook my head. "No, the first thing that went wrong is that I believed something that was too good to be true."

He let out an exaggerated breath. "Shit happens, but this—"

"No, Randy!" I interrupted. "Shit doesn't just *happen*. Someone has to make a boneheaded decision first. And y'know what? I happen to *like* my job."

Anger darkened his eyes. "Look, Angel, I've put up with a lot of your fucked up, neurotic shit over the years. I've given you crash space whenever you've wanted it, and listened to you whine about how your folks were *so* awful. You're being pretty selfish here."

"Selfish?" The word exploded from me. I was aware that people near us had turned to look, but I didn't care. "Jesus, Randy, if I was caught, I'd go to jail! Did you even think about that?"

"Don't give me that holier-than-thou crap," he said, sneering. "Clive says you haven't bought anything from him in almost two months. And there's no way you went cold turkey and quit using. So I *know* you've been skimming those pills from work. What's the deal? You're already selling 'em on your own? You don't want to give me a cut after everything I've fucking done for you?"

Fury seared through me, white and hot. "Don't you *ever* fucking accuse me of that," I said, voice low, intense. "I've never stolen anything from work, especially not drugs. I'm *not* using any more. I'm trying to turn my life around. Maybe you don't understand that, but that's not my problem, and I'm not going to let you drag me down anymore."

Randy let out a harsh bark of laughter. "Me, drag *you* down? That's rich. Man, you've become one hell of an arrogant little bitch. Oh yeah, you're such a model of goddamn virtue. Is that why you went off and fucked that guy you met at Pillars the last time we were there? How much didja make off him?"

I stared at him. "What the *hell* are you talking about?"

His eyes narrowed. "When you left with that dickwad who'd been buying you drinks all night. I went out to see what the fuck was going on, and your drunk ass was all over him. You told me you wanted a good hard ride. And then the two of you peeled out in his Porsche."

Bitter flashes of memory clicked into place. "I don't remember much from that night . . . but I didn't fuck him."

He snorted. "Yeah, sure."

I shook my head, feeling almost dizzy for an instant. "No," I said, more memories suddenly crowding in. I hadn't tried to walk home from the bar. "No, I was talk-

ing about his car. I'd never ridden in a Porsche before."
I dragged my eyes up to him. "You're the one who'd
been ignoring me all night for that other twit. He bought
me a couple of drinks." I stared at him as shock and be-
trayal surged through me. "I was falling down drunk,
and you let me go off with him? Did you know him? Did
I? It didn't occur to you to watch out for me?"

Randy's scowl deepened, but there was a flicker of
shame in his eyes. "I thought you knew him," he muttered. He was lying. He'd known perfectly well that I'd
had no idea who the guy was.

I wrapped my hands around my mug. "I think you
need to go, Randy," I said, rather amazed at how calmly
I was able to get the words out.

His brow creased in puzzlement. "Angel . . . ?"

I spoke quietly, but with the entire force of my will
behind it. "Let me rephrase it: Go fuck yourself." This
was the closure that I'd been wanting and then some.
"I'm not going to steal drugs for you or anyone else,
and if you try to start a rumor that says I am, I will *Fuck.
You. Up*."

He drew back. Maybe he could see in my eyes that I
had no fear of him in any way and that I meant every
word. Hell, I was dead already. I ate *brains*, for god's
sake.

"You're fucking crazy," he mumbled, but there was
no heat in his words.

I allowed myself a small smile. "No. It's much worse
than that. Now please, go fuck yourself. I don't ever
want to see you again."

It was obvious he wanted to say something else—
some sort of stinging retort that would make me recon-
sider, cause me to doubt myself. But he didn't. Maybe he
knew he'd be wasting his breath.

Slamming up from the table, he settled for storming
out of the diner. I didn't turn to watch him leave. I could

hear his muttered cursing as he walked away. A couple of seconds later I heard the ringing of the bell over the front door.

I picked up my fork and continued to eat my pancakes as more and more pieces of memory fell into place. By the time I finished breakfast I knew where to start looking for the rest.

Chapter 32

After checking the styrofoam cooler to be sure everything was still pretty frozen, I headed to the hospital.
The volunteer at the front desk was a hundred years old
and gave the worst directions ever, but after a number
of wrong turns and the interrogation of a cute orderly I
finally found the medical records department. I had to
pay a copying fee, but ten minutes later I had a stack of
papers that comprised all of the records and charts and
reports from my visit to the ER two months ago.

Returning to my car, I cranked it to get the AC going,
pushed my seat back and started flipping through the
papers. There weren't too many surprises, which was a
bit of a disappointment. I wanted to find some sort of
confirmation that my memories weren't completely off
the deep end, or that the theory nagging at me was
wrong, but the gist of the report was that I'd been
brought in suffering from an apparent overdose. No injuries had been noted.

I leaned back in the seat, catching sight of myself in
the rear view mirror. I barely recognized myself—but in
a kinda good way. My usually frizzy hair was combed

and fairly neat. I had no makeup on but instead of looking like death warmed over, I looked . . . fresh. I experimented with a smile and felt an odd pleasure at the resulting look. Sure, I was topped off with brains right now, but even beyond that I looked all right. Pretty good in fact. Cripes, when was the last time I looked in the mirror and was proud of what I saw?

Still smiling, I continued flipping through the papers, stopping when I came to the lab reports. Most of it was in terms I couldn't understand, but the tox screen had drug names that I recognized. I sighed as I read through the list. It was a wonder I'd never overdosed before. Of course I hadn't really given a shit about surviving back then. I wasn't the sort to ever take the step of committing suicide, but I'd sure been trying to do it in a passive way. Story of my life. Or rather, it *was* the story of my life.

Flunitrazepam. That was a drug I didn't recognize, but I vaguely remembered Dr. Leblanc muttering something about it when looking through tox reports on autopsies. I frowned. I'd smoked some pot—that was the cannabinoids—and I'd taken a Lortab. And then, of course, I'd been drinking. I'd scored a Percocet from the bartender, but I hadn't taken anything else except for a Xanax the night before. I was sure of it.

Puzzled, I drove back to the morgue, parked my car in the shade, headed inside and went straight to the investigator's office. Derrel wasn't in, but Monica was, her fingers flying across the keyboard in absurd contrast to the painstaking hunt-and-peck technique that I utilized.

I tapped lightly on the doorframe. "Hey, Monica, ya gotta sec?"

She glanced up and gave me a brisk nod. "Sure. What brings you in on your day off?

I settled into the chair in front of her desk, suddenly unsure how to ask what I wanted to know. "Well, I've been doing some reading and stuff. Y'know, trying to learn more about this business and all."

A smile lit her face. "That's cool. You're a smart chick. You don't want to be a van driver forever, I'm sure. Heck, you'd do great as a paramedic or nurse."

That shocked me out of my train of thought and it took me a second to respond. "Me?" I laughed and shook my head. "Monica, I don't even have my GED."

"*Pffthh*. So what? You could get that in nothing flat. Hell, you could probably pass it right now without even studying. And then you could go train to be an EMT Basic. You could get through that in just a few months."

"Really? But you're a paramedic, right?"

"Yep. That's a two year program, though sometimes there are accelerated programs where you can get it in under a year."

"Do death investigators have to have medical backgrounds?" I asked, suddenly intrigued at the thought of having an actual *career*.

She shook her head. "This particular office likes for us to have medical background since it makes it easier to understand stuff and work with the pathologist, but it's not a requirement."

I sat back, thoughts whirling. I didn't want to be a van driver forever. I was tied to the morgue because of the access to brains, but what if I went to school for other stuff so that I could be an investigator? That would be more money, I'd still be where I could get to the brains, and—

"So, did you have a question for me?" Monica asked, yanking me back to reality.

"Oh, yeah, sorry." With difficulty I wrenched my train of thought back onto its tracks, filing away the thought of becoming an investigator for another time. "How hard is it to overdose on alcohol and painkillers like, say, Percocet or Lortab?"

She spread her hands and grimaced. "Wow, that depends on a lot of factors. Weight, health, medical history, you name it."

"But say someone healthy and normal had a couple of beers, and just had one Perc and one Lortab, that wouldn't be dangerous, right?"

She pursed her lips. "Without repeating my earlier bit about all the other factors, I think it's unlikely that someone in good health could OD on that alone."

I pulled the slip of paper out of my pocket. "Okay, next question. What's flunitrazepam?"

An expression of distaste twisted her mouth. "That's Rohypnol. The date rape drug," she explained.

I stared at her, shock and horror undoubtedly stamped across my face. A sudden understanding flared in her eyes, and I realized she knew exactly why I was asking.

"That one is easy to overdose on," she said in a tone so gentle that I *knew* she knew. "Especially if someone had been taking other drugs prior."

I could feel a flush of humiliation climbing up my neck. I'd suspected that there were more than a few people at the coroner's office who were aware of my background and what had happened to me. There were privacy regs all over the place, but people still gossiped.

"Yeah, I know all about your history," Monica said with a dismissive wave. "Big fucking deal. That's exactly what it is—history. In the past." She looked angry, and it was with a shock that I realized she wasn't angry at me, but *for* me.

I fumbled for something to say but apparently she wasn't finished. "It's none of my business, and you can tell me to fuck off if you want," she said, tone suddenly clipped and harder than usual, "and I don't know if it'll make you feel any better," her mouth tightened into a thin line, "but the asshole who did that to you won't be doing it to anyone else."

"What?" I couldn't manage anything beyond that.

Her eyes grew hard. "I worked a scene that night. An MVA. Only the one occupant. It was a messy accident. Ejection and decapitation. But he had a bottle of pills in his pocket. No markings on the bottle." She abruptly stood, started shuffling papers. I got the impression she wasn't looking for anything, simply wanted to do something with her hands. "Anyway, the victim's tox screen came back clean, other than some alcohol—and not much of that. But I sent the pills off for testing and they came back as flunitrazepam." She gave her head a sharp shake. "Only one reason why he'd have them. But I didn't think about it much until . . . now."

I could only stare, stunned into silence. Monica took a deep breath, released it, then gave me a more normal smile. "Y'know, if you're really interested in becoming an investigator you should go into some of the old case files and see how they were written up. You can pull reports up by date, if you want." The look she gave me was strangely penetrating. "I need to go run an errand. Feel free to use my computer. Log out when you're done, okay?"

She was almost out the door before I could manage a response. "Monica, wait," I croaked.

She stopped in the doorway, slowly turned back.

"I . . . why do you . . . ?" Shit. I couldn't say what I knew I wanted to say. *Why are you angry for my sake when this was something I did to myself? Why are you pissed on my behalf when I was the moron who got drunk and got into the car with him? Why don't you hate me as much as I hate myself?*

Monica's expression softened though her mouth stayed hard. "Nobody deserves rape. *Nobody*."

"But . . . but I wasn't raped," I blurted.

Her eyes darkened. "Not every rape is physical," she said in a quiet voice. Then she was out the door.

I sat where I was for at least a full minute before I stood and slowly made my way to her chair. The report program was already on screen. All I had to do was input the date. There were three death reports from that day, but only one that was listed as an MVA—motor vehicle accident.

I printed it all out without reading it—reports, pictures, everything—then logged out of the computer, retrieved my printouts, and headed out.

Chapter 33

I ended up going back to the diner, simply because I couldn't think of anywhere else to go where I would have the room to spread out and look everything over. I felt a little silly as the waitress came up to me, but apparently it wasn't the first time she'd seen a booth used as a temporary work desk. She merely poured me coffee and gave me a warm smile.

I sipped my coffee and started flipping quickly through the thick sheaf of papers. Right now there was only one thing I was really interested in.

Decedent—Herbert Singleton. White male, thirty-seven years old, lived in Longville. Only next of kin was an ex-wife who lived in Lafayette. There was a driver's license picture, and I peered at it for close to a minute while more memories flashed into place. Yeah, this was the guy. I'd probably seen him at Pillar's once or twice before. Not a local. Just someone who wanted a drink and a good time. Maybe too good a time.

So, Herbert, were you the one who made me like this? Were you a zombie? That he'd roofied me, I had no doubt. But he hadn't counted on the fact that I already had a nice high rocking when he started buying me drinks and adding his special little touch of Rohypnol to them. The full effect must not have hit me until I was in his car. Maybe he realized I was overdosing and he panicked? Then why drive out to the middle of nowhere instead of a hospital?

Because, if he'd gone to the hospital, they'd have figured out that he was probably the one who'd roofied me. But if he made me a zombie, he could walk away from the whole thing. I was dying, so he did whatever zombies do and then dumped me on the side of the road.

I frowned. No, that didn't hold water. I would have had to eat brains immediately, right? Okay, so he might have had his own stash. And then after dumping me he got into a wreck, or was hunted down by the zombie killer. . . .

My frown deepened. Nope. It still didn't work. Someone had sent me the clothing and brain-drinks in the ER, and had arranged for the job at the morgue. *Well, maybe there's a big Protect New Zombies conspiracy going on?*

I scrubbed a hand over my face. This was stupid. If this guy had been a zombie, why would he have gone to the trouble of making me one too simply because I was overdosing? It was far more likely that he'd taken me out to that remote highway to bash my head in and scoop out some nice fresh brains. Drug the white trash skank, take her out to the swamp, chow down.

And then what? The zombie killer had saved me?

I made a noise of frustration. None of this made sense. But I'd had it with being in the dark. I had the reports, and I was going to find the damn answer if it took me the rest of my undead life.

Well armed with coffee and workspace, I spread the pages of the death report out and began my search for any possible clues that could help me figure out what the hell had happened. On a separate piece of paper, I made notes of anything that might help things make sense. According to the state police accident report it appeared that dear old Herbert lost control of the vehicle on a curve and went off the road, at which time the car flipped once and hit a tree. The driver had been ejected and decapitated, and fragments of the skull had been found on the highway. Toxicology reports showed that Herbert's blood alcohol was .06—technically not over the legal limit, but probably enough to impair his reactions on that curve.

But no mention of a passenger.

"Working hard?"

I looked up to see Ed with a coffee cup in his hand and a smile on his face.

"Because if you are," he continued, "I feel somehow obligated to interrupt you."

I grinned. "Aw, you're so thoughtful." I pulled the papers closer to me in order to make some room on the table. "C'mon, interrupt away. I'm just trying to figure out some stuff that's been bugging me. What are you up to?"

He sat and set his coffee cup down. "I'm waiting for Marianne so I can give her the keys to my apartment, then I'm going to pick up Marcus, and we'll be on our way for our annual fruitless attempt to murder Bambi's parents."

I laughed. "Male bonding at its best."

"Testosterone heaven," he added, grinning. "As well as a nifty excuse to play with ATVs." He nodded toward the window. I followed his gaze to see a pickup with two four-wheelers strapped onto a platform across the back.

"So, what am I interrupting here?" Ed asked, peering down at the papers spread across the table. "Ew. Looks like work stuff." He made a face.

"Well, it's actually a sorta weird personal thing, to be honest."

He lifted an eyebrow. "Oh, I'm totally into weird personal things. Is it dirty as well?"

I laughed. "You wish!" I shook my head. "Actually, this accident happened the same night that you . . ." I sighed and screwed my face into a grimace, "saved me from killing myself from an overdose."

"Ouch. Yeah. Strange night, that one. You're talking about the fatality out by the parish line?" At my nod he leaned back. "I'd come on shift only about half an hour earlier. My unit was dispatched to that scene but it was pretty clear they weren't going to need our services. The cops were pretty well tied up between that accident and then the murder scene out on Sweet Bayou Road." He winced. "Which is where Marcus found you. We'd just left the accident scene when we got the call to his location. You lucked into it there."

"How so?"

"Well, Marcus was actually assigned to be patrolling the district by the state line—where the accident occurred. He told me the only reason he was near Sweet Bayou was because he'd dribbled something on his uniform and had to run home to change."

I had to smile at that. "A spot on his shirt? The horror!"

Ed laughed. "Yeah, for a tough guy he can be a bit of a priss. So, why are you so interested in this MVA?"

"Okay, this is going to sound crazy, but I'm pretty sure I was in that car. I left the bar with this guy that night." I tapped the page with Herbert's driver's license information.

Ed shook his head firmly. "There's no way you could have been in that car when it wrecked. You didn't have a scratch on you. Or clothing," he added with an apologetic grimace. "Besides, the accident was almost twenty miles away from where you were."

"Yeah, there's no way. I know that, but. . . . I don't re-member a lot from that night though, so maybe he pulled over and let me out. . . ." I trailed off as images of glass and metal and blood flickered haphazardly in my memory.

He frowned. "In the middle of the swamp? Naked?" His expression abruptly turned stricken and all traces of humor vanished. "Oh, fuck, Angel, I'm sorry. I didn't mean to joke. Oh, man."

I flushed and shook my head. "No, it's okay. I . . . I wasn't, um, attacked. At least that's what the nurse in the ER said." Monica's words flashed through my head. I wasn't raped. *But I was drugged.* I wouldn't have got-ten into his car, and I probably wouldn't have overdosed. And I *was* attacked—turned into a zombie against my will. I sure as shit hadn't been given a choice about that.

Ed was silent for several seconds, then nodded to-ward the printouts with the pictures. "May I look?"

I pushed them his way. "I haven't done more than glance at them yet. But I haven't found 'Angel was here' scrawled on the dashboard or anything."

He chuckled, then started flipping through the pages. After about half a minute he paused, attention fixed on one picture. "It's funny," he said. "Marcus was on his way back out to help with the accident—after changing his shirt—when he saw you."

"Like you said, I'm lucky," I replied. Then I laughed. "If he hadn't found me it probably would have been De-tective Abadie. And he probably would have pushed me into the ditch!"

Ed's expression stayed strangely sober. "How did you get the job at the Coroner's Office, Angel?" he asked, not looking up. His voice sounded odd, as if he was working hard to keep control of himself.

I hesitated, briefly tempted to tell him the fiction about my probation officer arranging it. But I suddenly didn't want to deal with evasions and lies. "I'm not really sure," I admitted. "I, uh, got a letter telling me there was a job waiting for me. I asked around a bit, but the most I could find out was a rumor that someone with political connections arranged it for me." I spread my hands and shrugged. "I don't know why I would rate that, though. I wish I had a better answer for you."

As I spoke, his face seemed to cave in, grief flooding in so intensely that it nearly took my breath away. I watched him, baffled. What memories could this picture be dredging up to make him look so stricken? And why would my explanation about my job seem to make it worse?

A few seconds later Ed took a shaking breath and set the picture down. The horrible grief in his eyes was gone, replaced by what looked like a weary acceptance.

"You okay?" I asked tentatively.

"I'm fine," he said quietly.

"You don't look fine," I said, frowning. "Is something wrong?"

Lifting his gaze, he gave me a smile that completely lacked its usual spark. "I, uh, lost my parents in an accident like this. It just hit me all of a sudden."

"I'm so sorry," I said, reaching to touch the back of his hand. "Is that why you became a paramedic?"

His eyes dropped to my fingers on his hand. He made no move to pull away but I had the weirdest impression that he wanted to. "I suppose you could say that," he said. "When they died . . . it changed my outlook on a lot of things." His gaze never shifted from where I was touching him. Suddenly self-conscious, I broke contact and pretended to scratch an itch on my arm.

"It'll all be fine." He took a deep breath, looked back up at me. "You're right," he continued, tapping the picture. "If you were in the car, you didn't leave yourself a convenient note." He glanced at his watch and grimaced.

"Hey, uh, I really need to get on my way. Are you going to be here for a while?"

"Sure," I replied. "You want me to give Marianne the keys?"

"If you could, that would be great," he said, already getting up from the booth. He fished in his pocket then dropped the keys on the table. "I'll see you soon," he said without looking at me, then turned and walked away without another word. I watched him as he climbed into his truck and drove away, then pulled the picture to me—a shot of the blood-spattered interior of the car. Gruesome, to be sure. I shivered and rubbed my arms. It had to be torture for him to work accident scenes. I couldn't imagine having a job that constantly reminded me of a tragedy in my life.

Marianne walked in a couple of minutes later, gaze scanning the diner. I gave her a wave as I held up the keys, and her expression cleared. She headed my way and slid into the booth, giving me a perky smile.

"So, Ed has you doing his grunt work now?" she asked with a chuckle.

"Yeah, I don't mind," I said. "You missed him by only a couple of minutes. He seemed to be in a real hurry to get out of here." I paused. "He was looking at some of the pics from this accident and got real upset," I grimaced. "I feel bad. If I'd known his folks died in a car wreck I wouldn't have kept all these pics out on the table like this."

A baffled look came over her face. "They didn't die in a car wreck. Ed doesn't like to talk about it, but the story I've always heard is that his dad was killed in a boating accident, and his mom committed suicide a few years later."

"Oh," I said, suddenly baffled as well. "Well, that's pretty awful too." So why did he lie to me? And if they didn't die in a car crash, why did the picture of the blood in the car trigger such a reaction?

Marianne gave a sigh. "Look, sometimes he can be kind of moody. Whatever upset him probably had nothing to do with his parents at all. I think that sometimes he lets things from work get to him. He's a fun and funny guy, but he also has a really big heart." Then she grinned. "Almost as big as his stomach. That boy sure can put away some food."

I smiled. "I've seen him eat. It's a sight for the record books." My gaze fell to the picture again. It was taken from the driver's side and showed the front seats. I could see the passenger seatbelt dangling, obviously unused. Blood lay pooled in both seats, smeared across the doors and soaked into the carpet. It looked as if a pig had been slaughtered.

I jerked my head up to look at Marianne. "I'm sorry, what did you say?"

"I was saying how Ed can put away an entire pizza on his own," she said with a laugh. "I always have to order a large one for him and a small one for me!"

Cold shock rippled over me. "Your dog, Kudzu, does it, um, stay in a pen or a kennel?"

Marianne gave me a perplexed look. "Huh? No, she has free run of the house. She's very well-trained. She's practically my baby. Why?"

"Pizza Plaza, right?"

The confusion on her face increased.

"When you order pizza, do you ever order from Pizza Plaza?" I asked as I threw the papers into a rough pile. I knew I sounded impatient and a little demanding but I suddenly didn't have time for niceties.

"Yes." Marianne narrowed her eyes. "Angel, what the heck is going on?"

I shoved the keys toward her. "I'm sorry. I really am.

But I have to go." I dropped a five dollar bill on the table to cover my coffee, grabbed the pile of papers, and dashed for the door.

I knew exactly what had happened that night. I knew who'd made me a zombie. And I knew who the zombie killer was.

Chapter 34

Herbert Singleton wasn't a zombie—just an asshole who could only get laid if the girl was too wasted to say no. That piece of shit had slipped me some date rape drugs and taken me for a drive so he could score some one-sided action. I could be charitable and say that he hadn't planned on dumping me out in the middle of no-where after raping me—probably in some hotel room, or maybe some local parking lot. But when he saw I was starting to seize or have trouble breathing, he panicked and headed to someplace remote where he could dump my body.

The picture showed a fuckload of blood in the car. Yet the report said the driver had been ejected.

In other words, the report was wrong.

When Herbert lost it on that curve, neither of us were thrown from the car. Maybe Herbert was killed in the accident, but I was still alive—though pretty badly fucked up.

But there'd been someone else out there who'd either seen the accident or come upon it before I managed to finish dying. Someone who knew me. Someone who thought that maybe I could use a second chance. Someone who made up a story about having to change his shirt so that he could get me away from the accident scene.

I drove like a bat out of hell with one hand on the steering wheel and the other working my cell phone. The dispatcher at the Sheriff's Office refused to give me any of Marcus's contact info at first. I finally told her I worked for the Coroner's Office and lied and said I needed to get his cell phone number for a report. She reluctantly gave it to me but only after putting me on hold for an interminable length of time, during which I was pretty sure she called the Coroner's Office to be sure I actually worked there and wasn't some sort of psycho stalker chick who had a major crush on Marcus and was doing a really sloppy job of stalking him.

Okay, I probably did have a crush on him, but if I was going to stalk him I'd be a lot better at it than this.

I called Marcus, cursing when it went straight to voice mail. I left a message asking him to call me as soon as possible, stressing that it was *really* important. But I had a feeling I was wasting my breath. Somehow I suspected that Ed wasn't going to give anyone the chance to warn Marcus that he was in danger. Ed—who somehow knew about zombies and who realized the pizza delivery guy was one when Marianne's dog indicated that he was a corpse.

He'd seen the blood in the picture from the accident scene and realized that I *had* been in the car. He knew there was an explanation for how I'd survived, realized that Marianne's dog had indicated on me because I *was* a corpse—not because I handled corpses. And that wasn't the first time he'd found a zombie that way. He'd probably been part of that search team on Sweet Bayou Road when that teenager went missing, and Adam Campbell had been so hospitable to the search teams. At some point Ed saw Kudzu indicate on Adam.

Ed had also realized that there was only one person with the motive and opportunity to turn me into a zombie—one person who obviously also had the means to do so. And who had a relative with the connections and influence to get me the job I needed.

That explains the grief, I thought, sick with worry. *He realized that Marcus—his best friend— is a zombie. And for some reason he feels compelled to kill zombies.* I didn't know why, but I knew I was right. But would Ed really be able to bring himself to kill his best friend?

That wasn't something I was willing to gamble on.

Unfortunately, right now I was dead in the water. I didn't know where the hell I was going. I had no idea where Marcus lived, and I was damn positive there was no way I'd be able to squeeze that info out of the dispatcher. I even called information, but I wasn't very surprised to find he was unlisted and unpublished. There weren't many cops who made it easy for people to find them. I could understand that, but right now it was pissing me the fuck off. Shit, at this point I wished I *was* a psycho stalker who followed him home from work and that sort of thing. At least then I'd know where he lived.

Wait. I was being stupid. I needed to slow down and think this through logically.

Marcus was off-duty. He was going to be off for the next couple of days. He and Ed were supposed to go hunting. Ed wasn't going to chop his head off at his house. No, Ed would want to do it someplace remote, where he could find a way to make it look like an accident, or dispose of the body.

I drove to the library as fast as I could get away with. I'd learned a trick or two from working with Derrel, and the one that was most useful to me now was the trick about how to find information. I still wasn't the sharpest knife in the drawer when it came to computers, but I was hoping I didn't need to be.

There were several empty terminals in the library computer room which saved me the trouble of physically tossing someone off of one. The computer was slow as molasses, and I jiggled my foot impatiently as the website loaded, but thankfully the parish website had been designed with idiots like me in mind, and the link for the property tax search was clearly marked on a nice big button.

Pecking out the letters as quickly as I could, I typed I-V-A-N-O-V, praying that the uncle who owned the land they always went hunting on was on Marcus's father's side. If he had a name other than Ivanov, I was out of luck. And so was Marcus.

My luck held. There was a listing for an "Ivanov, Marcus." But more importantly, there was also an "Ivanov, Pietro," for a large chunk of property at the north end of the parish.

Fingers shaking, I pulled up Google Maps, stuck in the address of Uncle Pietro's property, printed out the resulting map, and got the hell out of there.

I knew there was still a very real chance I was completely wrong, and Ed wouldn't bother going all the way to the north end of the parish. It was quite possible that he was currently in the process of taking Marcus out to some nearby back road for some head-lopping. But if that was the case, I had no chance of finding them in time anyway. So I might as well commit to stopping him where I think he might be.

Yeah, I know, my logic left a lot to be desired. But my intuition screamed that I was on the right track. I knew the murder of a cop would be taken a hell of a lot more seriously than that of a pizza delivery guy, or a mortuary worker. It wasn't fair, but it was the truth and Ed knew it, which meant that he needed to find some way to make it look like an accident. Like, say, on a hunting trip. In the middle of bum-fuck nowhere.

Before hitting the road I'd quickly made up two bottles of brain "slush." Those were now filling the cup holders in the console, plus I had the cooler full of "brain food" in the back seat. Even though I was already pretty full up on brains, I went ahead and sucked down one of the slushies while I drove like a madwoman and prayed that there weren't any state troopers on the back highways. I'd never gone this far overboard on brains before. It would have been an insane waste under normal circumstances, but right now I didn't give a fuck about conserving my stash. I only wanted to be sure I was fully tanked up, but as soon as I tossed the empty bottle aside I discovered something amazingly cool. Suddenly my senses were sharper than they'd ever been in my life, and my reflexes could have given Dale Earnhardt a run for his money.

I grinned and increased my speed. Zombie super powers could come in handy at times.

It was a good thing I had those heightened reflexes and senses. If not for them, I'd have totally missed the twisted sign by the little dirt road. Slamming on the brakes, I somehow managed to wrench the car around in time to make the turn without going into the ditch.

I could see fresh tracks in the mud which relieved my worry that I might be headed in the wrong direction, but my poor little Honda shimmied and gave out some ominous noises as I forced it over the ruts and through puddles. This road was meant to be navigated by a truck with much higher clearance, and certainly not at the speeds I was attempting. I was barely a mile down the road when the car gave a sudden lurch into a rut, and I came up hard against the seat belt.

"No! Shit!" I jammed it into reverse, but I could hear the tires spinning. I was stuck, and good.

Shutting the engine off, I quickly thought through my options and plans. Hell, I didn't have a plan other than "warn Marcus." He was the one with the gun and the training and all that stuff.

But all of that would be useless unless I could actually *warn* him. There was no way he'd be expecting an attack from his best friend.

My eyes fell on the second bottle of brain slush. I twisted around to look at the cooler in the back seat.

I smiled my best bad-bitch smile. Oh, yeah. I was about to burn me some brains.

Chapter 35

I've never been anything remotely resembling "athletic." I'm pretty sure the very few times in my life when I actually made myself run were only after much threatening from gym teachers—back when I still went to school and suffered such fates.

But if running had ever felt like *this* I don't think I'd have ever stopped. I raced down the road like the mutant lovechild of a gazelle and a cheetah—far faster than I'd have been able to drive it, thanks to that second bottle of brains. Now I figured I had maybe ten more minutes at the pace I was going before I crashed and started to rot.

Luckily it was only about a minute later that I reached the large clearing at the end of the road. A couple of hundred yards away Marcus and Ed were busy loading gear onto two four-wheelers. *Saving the day with brains to spare!* I thought in euphoric glee.

They turned in unison at the sound of my running footsteps. Marcus's eyes widened in surprise. "Angel! What on earth are you doing here?"

Ed looked surprised as well, but his expression

quickly turned wary and for good reason. I was still running all out and had no intention of stopping until I'd knocked Ed on his ass. "Marcus!" I yelled as I charged toward them. "I know you're a zombie and you made me! Ed does too and he's—"

A loud bang slammed through the clearing, cutting off my words as I went crashing to the ground in an awkward flailing sprawl. Pain jabbed hard and deep, and I gasped raggedly as I struggled to get back to my feet. For some reason I couldn't get a deep breath. The clearing swam around me as I scrabbled upright. I needed to warn Marcus and stop Ed. I needed to breathe. Why couldn't I breathe?

I heard a second bang and something hit me hard in the chest. There was a sense of pain but it felt strangely removed. I coughed and blood bubbled out of my mouth, copper-metallic taste fading almost as soon as it hit my tongue.

Oh. That's why I can't breathe. I could only stare at the pistol in Ed's hand as I sagged first to my knees, then onto my side on the ground. Color and sensation faded with the speed of a whirlwind. I made one more try to get enough breath to yell a warning to Marcus, but it wasn't happening.

Marcus wasn't stupid. The simple fact that Ed had shot me was warning enough. He lunged for the rifle on the four-wheeler with amazing speed, especially considering he had to be wondering what the fuck was going on.

But Ed already had his gun in his hand. I could see indecision sweep across his face, but in the next instant it was gone, replaced by rabid determination. He swung his arm around as Marcus's hand closed on the rifle. Another shot slammed through the clearing, and for a split-second I thought Marcus had won and gotten his shot off first.

Then he crumpled to the ground with a hole in his forehead while Ed slowly lowered his gun.

I wanted to scream in horror, but I still couldn't make much sound—just a couple of gurgles of blood, and not too much of that, either. I couldn't feel my heart beating at all anymore. I was pretty far into being dead at this point. Those extra nine minutes worth of brains had been chewed through in seconds.

I couldn't tear my eyes away from Marcus's still form. Had I been wrong about him being a zombie? And, if he was, could a bullet to the head kill him? He wasn't moving at all.

Ed let out a shaky breath. "God damn it." Pain flashed over his face. "Damn it. It wasn't supposed to be like this!"

I wanted to scream in rage. *Oh, gee, sorry I fucked up your intentions of killing him all nice and neatly.*

He shifted his gaze to where I was lying then wiped a trembling hand over his face. "I know you're not really dead. I only slowed you down." A shudder crawled over him. "Ah, god . . . I liked you," he said, voice rough. "You seemed so normal. Why'd you have to turn out to be a *goddamn monster!*" He let out an inarticulate scream of rage that seemed to be directed more at the heavens than at me, then he sagged and swiped at his eyes with the sleeve of his jacket. "Fucking zombies," he muttered. "You motherfuckers take everything, don't you. If I love it, you fucking take it." He took a ragged breath and seemed to focus on me again. "Angel died in that wreck. I know you think you're Angel, but she died."

I shook my head, fear and anger battling it out inside me. "No," I managed to rasp out. "You're wrong. I'm Angel."

Ed's mouth trembled for a brief second. "No. You're a monster. The worst kind of monster, because you make people think you're alive. Then you go and bash their head in with a fucking anchor and—" He spun away abruptly as his words roiled within me.

Ah, shit. Boating accident, my ass.

"It wasn't supposed to be like this," Ed said in a hoarse whisper. He swiped at his face again, and I realized he was crying—which only pissed me off more. He was going to be all weepy and emo because he'd shot me *and* his best friend? Fuck him!

"I'd wondered about Marcus," Ed went on, voice still hoarse. "Marianne's dog acted a bit funny around him at first, but then he kept playing with the dog. Told myself it wasn't possible." He flicked a glance my way. "Then Kudzu indicated on you. I didn't believe it then either." Anger flashed in his eyes. "I was an idiot. All this time your bodies have been desecrated. Animated by this monstrous shit."

"I'm not a monster, you stupid fuck!" I tried to yell, but it came out as mostly rasps and gurgles, and I had no idea if any of it was understandable.

But even if it was, Ed ignored it. He was too caught up in his self-righteous pity-party. "Now I'll give you both the mercy of a true death," he said, squaring his shoulders He slowly holstered his gun, then—almost reluctantly—looked over to where Marcus lay sprawled on his back on the ground. He was silent for several seconds, then shook his head. "I'll finish you off quickly," Ed said to the possibly dead Marcus. "I owe you that much."

He turned away and began to dig through the gear on the four wheeler. He wasn't paying attention to me anymore. I figured he was going to let me crawl around and moan a bit before he gave me his "mercy."

Yeah, well, I had no desire to roll over and give up yet. Part of me felt sorry for him, but the rest of me was simply pissed off. I knew I had it in me to get back on my feet and move toward Ed. It would take a lot more than two bullets in the chest to keep me down. When he shot me, I'd collapsed from the shock as my body took a hard nosedive into being a helluva lot more dead than usual, but that had pretty well worn off by now. My chest was a mess, but it didn't hurt. I still couldn't breathe, but I didn't need to. Whatever made me a zombie was taking care of all that shit. I'd be slow, though, and pretty damn uncoordinated. I was definitely a mess. Ed would have no trouble hacking my head off.

Good thing I had an ace up my sleeve. Or rather, something much better than an ace. Two of 'em, in fact.

I shifted slightly—not enough to draw his attention, just to where I could pull one of the plastic bags out of the side pocket of my cargo pants. The contents were still pretty frozen, and swallowing the chunks of icy brains down began to hurt like shit after the first few gulps, but that faded quickly beneath the blissful feel of my chest knitting itself back together. I finished that one and let the empty bag drop, then pulled the second bag out and ripped it open.

I clambered to my feet, still shoving frozen brains into my mouth as fast as I could swallow them down. Oh, yeah, this was the good shit. I was whole again. Better than whole.

Ed saw me stand out of the corner of his eye and spun, machete in his right hand. He raked a narrowed-eyed gaze over me. I wasn't sure if he could see that I'd healed up. The front of my shirt was still covered in blood, and it wasn't as if bullets really left big gaping craters in flesh like in the movies.

"So you're still strong enough to stand." Ed said, answering my question. His hand tightened on the machete. "You fuckers don't like to stay down, do you?" His mouth twisted in a parody of a smile, but there were still tears in his eyes. "But once I take your head off and burn the skull, then it'll all be over."

"I don't think so," I said, then crammed the last piece of frozen brain into my mouth and let the plastic bag drop to the ground. Ed looked puzzled for only a couple of seconds before comprehension flashed across his face. He took a step toward Marcus, raising the machete up high in his left hand while pulling his gun out with his right.

"This has to be done," Ed said through clenched teeth. "I know you don't believe it, but you're a monster."

"Nah, not buying it," I said with a shake of my head. "I'm still Angel. I've never killed anyone. Yeah, what happened to your dad was horrible, but we all make choices. Right now *you're* the monster."

Agony swept across his face as I ruthlessly shoved down the surge of pity that rose in me. "You can't stop me," he said, doing his best to curl his lip into a proud sneer. "I'll finish him, then finish you."

"Oh yeah?" I said. Then I couldn't resist. I took a deep breath and yelled: "Zombie Super Powers, Activate!"

Then I *moved*.

Chapter 36

Oh, Ed did his best to shoot me again, but I'd just gobbled down two brains worth of brainsicle, and I was fast. Not outrun-speeding-bullet fast, but my reflexes were pegged at *Fuck Yeah!* He got two shots off, but I could tell exactly where he was aiming and see the tightening of his trigger finger. It felt almost effortless to simply step out of the paths of the bullets. In the next breath I was on him and had the gun and machete ripped out of his hands.

I took three steps back from him, then stepped on the machete blade to break it. I had a split second of worry that I was going to stomp on the blade only to have my foot bounce right off it, but my super-brainy state didn't fail me, and the metal snapped with a terrifically satisfying *crack*.

I almost tried to see if my zombie-strength would let me break the gun but figured it'd be way too embarrassing if I failed at that. Instead I flung it as far as I could into the woods, watching with satisfaction as it sailed several hundred yards. He'd be a long time trying to find it.

But then I suddenly didn't know what to do. I watched the terror crawl across Ed's face as he looked at me, his eyes wide and full of white. He saw me as a monster, no doubt about that. I could smell the fear. My senses were so high I could hear every thump of his heart. Beads of sweat popped out on his upper lip as we stared at each other. I was hungry too, but not in the stomach-clawing, wolverine-in-the-belly way I was used to. Beneath his terror I could smell that he was *prey*. In this moment I was predator. Yeah, I *could* be the monster. A really awesome monster. I could be like this all the time. Strong and fast. Fucking invincible.

I moved toward him, and he stumbled back against the four-wheeler. "No, oh God, please," he stammered, his breath coming in harsh pants.

"You smell good," I murmured. Hunger swirled through me as I listened to the rapid flutter of his pulse. I could smell his brains beneath it all—every time he exhaled, I could smell it. How awesome it would be, warm and fresh . . . .

A scrape of motion drew my attention, and I flicked my gaze to the side long enough to see Marcus's leg slowly moving. *He's alive!* Relief slammed through me, and I took a step back from Ed, forcing down the feeling that I was allowing prey to escape. *Marcus is alive! Err, sorta. He's a zombie. He's really a zombie!* Wow, that would've sucked if Ed and I had both been wrong about that.

I took a deep breath and speared Ed with as menacing a gaze as I could manage. I must have done a pretty good job of it, because he went whiter than I ever thought anyone could be. Regret twined through me, but I knew I couldn't back down. I liked him and I even felt a little sorry for him.

But he was perfectly willing to murder his best friend.

"Go. Run," I snarled. "I don't ever want to see you

again. And if you kill any more zombies, I'll hunt you down and eat you. Then I'll kill you." Heh. I cracked myself up sometimes.

He made a strange sort of gibbering noise, then spun and took off running toward the woods. He stumbled a couple of times, but scrabbled up and kept going. After a couple of minutes the sounds of him crashing through the underbrush faded away. I hoped he fell into a few patches of poison ivy along the way. Followed by a sticker bush. Then maybe a wasp's nest.

A low gurgle came from Marcus, and I abandoned my brief desire to chase Ed down. I hurried over and crouched beside him. His eyes were open, but he didn't seem to be seeing anything.

"Wow, babe, you're a mess," I muttered. I knew what he needed. Unfortunately, I'd downed all the backup brains I had on me in my big showdown with Ed the Zombie Hunter.

I did a quick and frenzied search through the cab of the truck and then through Marcus's pockets, but failed to turn up keys to the truck. Aggravating. They were probably still in Ed's pocket.

Whatever. I was still strong as shit and fast as well. And it was only about a quarter mile to the car.

I turned to the moaning Marcus. "Okay, big guy, up you go!" Grabbing his wrist, I pulled him upright. He swayed and would have fallen if not for my hold on him. Worry sliced through me. How much damage had the bullet done? If I gave him brains, would everything in his head grow back to what it had been before he was shot? Or would he be a . . . vegetable zombie?

I couldn't think about that right now. I slung him over my shoulder in a fireman's carry, got a solid grip on his wrists, wrapped my other arm around his legs, and took off running.

Marcus was a fairly solid pile of muscle, I quickly discovered. I wasn't doing as much gazelle-cheetah this time—more like rampaging water buffalo. I was pretty high on brains, but carrying Mr. Two Hundred Pounds If He's An Ounce had me fading right about the time the car came into sight. I staggered the last few steps and let him slide off my shoulders onto the ground, barely keeping his head from cracking down hard.

Hunger growled at me as I yanked open the back door of my car and popped the cooler open. I grabbed the most-thawed bag I could find, fighting back the desire to feed myself first. Ripping the bag open, I scooped out a handful and carefully dribbled it into Marcus's mouth—not too difficult since he was all slack-jawed and drooling.

But apparently even a brain-damaged zombie still knew what to do. He gulped them down, and I quickly slopped another handful into his mouth, watching the bullet hole in his head for any sign that it was closing. I continued to hand-shovel brains into his mouth while he made low grunting noises and swallowed down everything I gave him.

I thought I could see the edges of the bullet hole begin to close as I tore open the second bag. By the time I was halfway through, the hole had definitely healed over. More encouraging was the fact that his eyes were beginning to lose the vacant stare. At least I hoped so and that it wasn't merely my wishful thinking.

I was nearly through feeding him a third bag when he suddenly seized my wrist. "Angel," he said, voice hoarse. "You're okay?"

I nearly laughed in hysterical relief. He was still Marcus—and I'd been the one to save us both. Never would have thought that would happen. "Yeah. I'm cool. You still hungry?"

He struggled up to a sitting position, then leaned up

against the car. "Fuck, yes. But I can hold on if you don't have any more."

I pulled two more bags out, handed one to him with a grin. "Eat up. I kinda hit the mother lode recently."

I leaned up against the car next to him while we ate. A strange and comfortable silence descended.

"Did you kill Ed?" Marcus asked after a while. His tone was as conversational as if he'd been asking me if I'd found the car keys, but I could see aching regret in his eyes.

"No," I replied. "I . . . wanted to. But not because I wanted to keep him from killing anyone else, or for revenge. I mean, I *did*, but—"

"You wanted to kill him for his brains," he said.

I winced. "Yeah. And I think I would have if you hadn't started moving." I swallowed the hard knot in my throat. "It, um, kinda freaks me out."

He surprised me by taking my hand. "But you didn't. You have control of this."

I wasn't sure what to say to that. I didn't feel like I had control of this. Even now I could feel the urge to do whatever it took to get back to feeling so wonderfully high.

"You're not a killer," he continued. "You're not a bad person at all."

I gave him a weak smile. His hand was nice and warm in mine. He certainly wasn't dead anymore. I liked the feel of it.

"Why did you change me?" I asked, meeting his eyes. "Why *me*?"

He gave my hand a squeeze. "Well, it's not like I'd planned it ahead of time. But I always thought you got screwed by life in general. You had so much to overcome. And when I came up on that wreck and saw you," he let out a heavy breath, "I figured I'd give you a second chance."

"Oh. Um. Thanks." Again, what was I supposed to say to that? Okay, so at least it wasn't a random "I'll-turn-her-into-a-zombie-whether-she-likes-it-or-not" sort of thing. He *did* save my life.

He cleared his throat. "And in case you think it was purely a pity thing, I, uh, also think you're damn cute."

I regarded him for several seconds. "Was it a Bride-of-Frankenstein type of thing? The monster wanted a monster girlfriend?"

His eyes widened in shock, and it was all I could do to keep from bursting out laughing.

"No!" he exclaimed. "Oh, god, no. I never would have turned you for that. I swear! But you were dying, and that cocksucker had drugged you—"

"Marcus, it's cool," I said, grinning. "Look, dying was the best thing that ever happened to me."

He visibly relaxed. "Okay. Yeah. Good. I mean, not good that you had to die, but, you know."

"How long have you been one?" I asked. "I mean, Ed said the two of you had been friends since you were kids." Then I scowled. "And yet he was still ready to kill you."

He let out a soft sigh. "Yeah, Ed and I grew up together. About six years ago Ed and my uncle and I went out hunting, and we came across a family of raccoons. I was a dumbass and tried to catch one and got bit."

I frowned. "I don't get it. You became a zombie 'cause you got bit by a raccoon?"

A grim smile crossed his face. "No, I got rabies. Turns out that raccoons and bats are the big carriers of rabies in the U.S. And unless you get the shots within the first couple of days after a bite, it's pretty much one hundred percent fatal. Once symptoms start appearing, it's too late."

"Rabics. Arc you fucking serious?"

"Completely!"

I blinked. "Wow. I had no idea. That's so weird. So, who turned you?"

"My Uncle Pietro. He felt responsible even though I was the dumbshit." He gave a small smile. "One of his businesses is a funeral home down in Thibodeaux. He keeps me well-supplied with brains."

"Wow," I said again. I took a few seconds to digest everything he'd said. "There's one thing I don't understand." Marcus looked at me expectantly, and I gave him my best suspicious look. "Why the hell was I *naked* when the ambulance showed up?"

"The blood," he stated, completely seriously. "Your clothes were torn and covered in blood—both yours and the driver's." He surprised me then by giving an embarrassed wince. "I undressed you and, uh, dunked you in the bayou to get the blood off. Then took you as far away as I could so no one would connect you with the accident." He grimaced. "It was stupid coincidence that I decided to 'find' you on the same road where a murder victim would be found at about the same time."

"Oh." That actually made sense. Of course that also meant that he'd not only seen me naked but had also had his hands all over me. Oh, hell. Now I needed a cold shower.

"We, uh, should probably get out of here," I said, hoping he wouldn't notice how suddenly flushed I was. "I don't think Ed will be coming back any time soon, but there's always the chance."

Marcus nodded. "You're right. There's just one thing I want to do first."

I suppose I should have seen it coming, but I was still completely taken by surprise when he slipped a hand to the back of my neck and pulled me in for a kiss. My surprise only lasted for about half a second though, and after that I was pretty cool with the whole thing. More than cool. To hell with the cold shower.

An eternity later we finally pulled apart, though his hand remained gently entwined in my hair.

"I'm hungry," he murmured, smiling.

"Me too," I replied. Somehow I knew that neither of us were talking about brains.

Chapter 37

Together we managed to get my Honda unstuck, but before we headed back to town we returned to where the four-wheelers were parked. We drove them both a good ways into the woods, then I stayed put while Marcus veered off down a trail. He returned on foot about ten minutes later and climbed onto the back of the one I was driving.

"Pushed it into the river," he explained.

After that, we cleaned ourselves up as best we could. My shirt was inconveniently full of bullet holes and blood, but that was easily remedied since I still had all my worldly possessions in the trunk of my car. As soon as we were presentable, Marcus used my phone—since his had "somehow" lost its battery—to call the Sheriff's Office to report that he and Ed had become separated in the woods, and that Ed was still missing. I wasn't sure why he bothered to do that since I knew Ed was still alive, but Marcus merely gave me a grim smile.

"Gotta cover our asses. If Ed never shows up again it's going to look really funny that I came back from our hunting trip without him and didn't say anything. And if he does show up, then no harm no foul."

I had a feeling there was more going on, but I didn't really want to ask.

I drove Marcus home but didn't make a move to get out of the car with him. He paused with his hand on the door and gave me a slightly puzzled look.

"Would you like to come in?" he asked.

"Yeah," I replied. "But I gotta go deal with some stuff first."

"Your dad." It wasn't a question, and I was relieved to see complete understanding in his eyes. "Will you come back by when you're done?"

I smiled, relieved for a number of reasons. "You know it."

Dad was sitting on the porch when I pulled into the driveway. He had a beer in one hand and a cigarette in the other, but I didn't see any empties beside his chair. He watched me as I got out of the car and walked up to the house, a wary and almost painfully expectant look on his face.

"Didn't think you'd have the balls to come back here," he said as I climbed the steps, a sneer settling onto his face as if he knew he needed to have it. "Run out of guys who you could fuck for a place to stay?"

I could only smile. I'd lost my fear of him. I also knew I wasn't tied to him. Whether I stayed with Marcus or slept in my car, I knew I had options. "That's not gonna work anymore. I don't really care what you think of me. I know I'm not a loser." I leaned against one of the porch supports and crossed my arms over my chest. "You're the one who needs me."

He scowled. "I got enough money to get by. I don't need your know-it-all bullshit."

"Cut the crap, Dad," I said. "This isn't about money, and you know it. You have no one. Just me. Who the hell you gonna turn to if I walk away from you forever?"

Anger flashed across his face and he stood, but I didn't shift from where I was—simply continued to regard him with a calm that seemed to permeate every fiber of my being. It helped that I'd wolfed down another brainsicle on the way over so that I could be as sharp and aware as possible.

And as fast and strong as possible too, in case my charm and tact didn't carry me through. I wasn't going to let anyone smack me ever again. "The funny thing is that I still love you, Dad," I said. "I've been thinking about this a lot. Thinking about the fact that it would kill me if anything bad happened to you and I could have done something about it."

"I can take care of myself," he said, voice rising.

"Is that what you want?" I asked, keeping my own voice deliberately low. "Do you want me out of your life?"

His hands unclenched, and his face seemed to sag. "No. God. I have ... I...." He swallowed. "When your mom...."

"You had to choose between the two of us, and you chose me," I said as I met his eyes. "And I know you probably regretted that choice a million times."

Guilt flashed across his face. "It's all right," I said before he could try to deny it. "I didn't exactly make it easy on you. I made a bunch of shit choices. I was a serious fuckup of a daughter."

He slumped and shook his head. "No, you got it wrong. I coulda given you up to the state and kept your mom." He ran his hands through his thinning hair. "But I knew she wasn't right." He tapped the side of his head. "She was fun and wild," he went on, "but she couldn't handle any sort of stress. Never shoulda been a mom.

And you . . . you were my little Angelkins." His voice caught, and he took a quick sip of beer to cover it. "But after she was gone I figured out that maybe I never shoulda been a dad."

Emotion threatened to squeeze my heart right out of my chest as he lifted his watery eyes to mine. "I never regretted having them take your mom away," he said. "But," he took a shuddering breath. "Sometimes I regretted stayin' on as your dad." He looked away. "I'd think that if I'd let the state take you, then maybe you'd have ended up with folks who'd known how to rein you in and keep you straight and out of trouble." He sighed. "I couldn't. I couldn't deal with it."

I wasn't sure I'd be able to speak around the big knot in my throat. "Maybe," I managed to say. "Maybe not. But it doesn't matter now. I'm clean, I got me a good job. . . ." I trailed off, then sighed and sat heavily on the porch steps. "I can't take any credit for any of that shit, though. I got lucky. Someone helped me out when I needed it." I dug my fingers through my hair and grimaced. "I came here thinking I was gonna be all like, 'oh, you need to do rehab and stop drinking' but that would be a bunch of hypocritical shit, because I sure as hell never had the guts to go through that."

"I'll do it," he said quietly. "I'll do rehab, counseling, whatever it takes. Is that what you want from me?" He looked at me, a painful hope in his eyes.

I wasn't sure what to say to that. I mean, there was so much I wanted. This whole conversation could end up being a goddamned Hallmark Movie of the Week with us falling into each other's arms and tearfully promising that everything was going to be wonderful now because he'd stop drinking and I'd be a devoted and supportive daughter. I knew damn good and well that nothing was as easy as that. If I hadn't been zombified I probably never would have found the strength to stop doing the pills and hold down a job. I never had any desire to. Why the hell should I? I had no pride, no drive. I'd never been able to see a world beyond what I'd always known.

And expecting my dad to become a better person just for me was totally unrealistic.

"How 'bout we start by getting the beer cans out of the driveway," I said. He gave me a perplexed look, and I resisted the urge to smile. He sure as hell hadn't been expecting that.

"The beer cans? I don't understand."

"It looks like shit," I told him. "Yeah, it's funny like 'Ha ha we're such white trash' because we've always figured that everyone is gonna look down on us anyway, so why not embrace it, right?" I shook my head firmly. "Well fuck 'em all. We're only trash if we keep acting like it. Fuck those bastards."

He looked toward the driveway, then his gaze swept the rest of the yard and the house. Distaste and regret darkened his eyes. "This place is a goddamn dump."

I let out a small laugh. "Yeah, no wonder we drink and get high."

He turned back to me, a ghost of a smile on his face. "So, you'll stay?"

"I'm kinda seeing someone." I paused. Probably better if I didn't tell him just yet that it was the cop who arrested him—and me, for that matter. "But this is still my home."

"You broke up with Randy?" He eyed me with a frown.

"Yeah. That's over."

He narrowed his eyes at me. "Over for good?"

"Completely over. Dead. Buried," I said emphatically.

To my surprise he gave a nod of approval. "About

damn time. I always thought you were too good for that loser."

I burst out laughing while my dad gave me a per-plexed look

"You're absolutely right, Dad," I said with a grin. "I *am* too good for him."

Chapter 38

My dad and I raked up beer cans for the last couple of hours of daylight, then I headed back over to Marcus's house. But not before shocking the shit out of my dad by giving him a hug. Things were still far from perfect between us, but it was one hell of a start.

Marcus opened the door before I could knock, took me by the hand and pulled me inside. He kicked the door closed and in the next second his lips were on mine, and his hands were tangled in my hair. I pulled his shirt off and oh, yeah, for a zombie he had some seriously awesome abs.

"Hang on," he gasped after about half a minute of frenzied groping. Somehow I'd lost my shirt as well, and his jeans were unzipped, and I wasn't really in the frame of mind to "hang on" at all. But he grabbed me by the hand and pulled me to the kitchen, yanked the fridge open and removed a bowl of what looked like tapioca. He handed me the bowl, pushed the fridge door shut, and snatched two spoons out of a drawer.

"This isn't tapioca, is it?" I said, taking one of the spoons.

Marcus shook his head, a sly smile on his face. "I think a better name for it is 'foreplay.'"

The pudding lived up to its name. And nothing fell off that wasn't supposed to.

Diana Rowland

The Kara Gillian Novels

"Rowland's hot streak continues as she gives her fans another big helping of urban fantasy goodness! The plot twists are plentiful and the action is hard-edged. Another great entry in this compelling series." —*RT Book Review*

"Rowland's world of arcane magic and demons is fresh and original [and her] characters are well-developed and distinct.... Dark, fast-paced, and gripping." —*SciFiChick*

Secrets of the Demon
978-0-7564-0652-3

Sins of the Demon
978-0-7564-0705-6

Touch of the Demon
978-0-7564-0775-9

To Order Call: 1-800-788-6262
www.dawbooks.com

DAW 176

Gini Koch
The Alien *Novels*

TOUCHED BY AN ALIEN
978-0-7564-0600-4

ALIEN TANGO
978-0-7564-0632-5

ALIEN IN THE FAMILY
978-0-7564-0668-4

ALIEN PROLIFERATION
978-0-7564-0697-4

ALIEN DIPLOMACY
978-0-7564-0716-2

ALIEN vs. ALIEN
978-0-7564-0770-4

ALIEN IN THE HOUSE
978-0-7564-0757-5
(Available May 2013)

To Order Call: 1-800-788-6262
www.dawbooks.com